# FELONIOUS MONK

## OTHER BOOKS BY WILLIAM KOTZWINKLE

*Elephant Bangs Train* (short stories)
*Hermes 3000*
*The Fan Man*
*Nightbook*
*Swimmer in the Secret Sea*
*Doctor Rat*
*Fata Morgana*
*Herr Nightingale and the Satin Woman*
*Jack in the Box*
*Christmas at Fontaine's*
*Queen of Swords*
*Jewel of the Moon* (short stories)
*The Exile*
*The Midnight Examiner*
*The Hot Jazz Trio* (short stories)
*The Game of Thirty*
*The Bear Went over the Mountain*
*The Amphora Project*

# WILLIAM KOTZWINKLE

# FELONIOUS MONK

**BLACK STONE**
PUBLISHING

Printed in the United States of America

First edition: 2021
ISBN 978-1-0940-0925-4
Fiction / Crime

Blackstone Publishing
31 Mistletoe Rd.
Ashland, OR 97520

www.BlackstonePublishing.com

# I

Midnight kidnappings, street warfare, and murder in broad daylight are typical for Modelo. It's in the Sovereign State of Chihuahua, Mexico. I was supposed to be in the sovereign state of grace, as a monk in the monastery of San Juan Diego. I fell from grace one afternoon.

I went to Modelo to buy hay and oats for our horses. The monastery had been my home for the past five years, during which a drug lord known as the Camel came to power in Modelo.

"Hey, Brother Martini, how you doing!" called the regulars loafing about as I parked the monastery truck at the feed store.

I answered them in the passable Spanish I'd learned during my five years. Strictly speaking, I shouldn't have talked to them, but the monastery relaxes that rule in the interest of getting along in town. On the day I fell from grace, I was approached by a woman I'd never met before, but it was clear she had been waiting for me.

"Father, can you help me?"

I was only twenty-six years old and hardly worthy of being called "Father." She was about thirty, and her clothes looked homemade. She was poor and there was pain in her face.

"I'm at your service, senora."

"The layabouts are watching us," she said. "Can you walk with me away from such eyes?"

We walked toward the plaza fountain. She said quietly, as if fearing that the plaza could hear us, "The Camel is recruiting my son. This is a knife in my heart. He's only thirteen."

"What does he say about this?"

"His friends have gone over to the Camel."

When your friends go, you go. In the Sovereign State of Chihuahua, thirteen-year-old assassins are common.

"The Camel wants to give him a gun and show him how to use it." She was gazing into the water of the fountain, as at something holy. "But my boy has been going to the School for Social Improvement. He wants to become something better."

I'd spent my years in the monastery making up for a single bad moment of my own. Like her son, I wanted to become better. So I was sympathetic to her problem.

She dipped her hand in the water, her small fingers playing in the ripples. "My husband is dead. He was shot one night."

People were often shot at night around Modelo, for reasons that usually had to do with the Camel. She said, "I'm alone in this matter."

"Perhaps not," I said.

She lifted her face toward mine. I saw the struggle of thirteen years in her eyes, to raise a son in poverty yet hope that he escapes the corruption that breeds everywhere in the Sovereign State of Chihuahua. I followed her from the plaza.

She said, "The cartel devils know that if a boy is older, he may think about what will happen to him. At thirteen, he doesn't think. He grabs a gun and shoots someone."

She led me to the place where her son was to meet the recruiter. It was a bus stop, and across the street was a restaurant. Parked in front of it was an SUV with the window rolled down. The man at the wheel was a Camel assassin named Bustamante. He swaggered around Modelo each day in aviator sunglasses, gold chains gleaming on his neck.

The bus from the School for Social Improvement pulled to the curb, and the woman pointed out her son to me as he stepped down. Then she withdrew so that he wouldn't see her. He was walking toward the SUV when I intercepted him.

"Do you like horses?"

He looked at me, startled.

I continued, "Horses can tell a predator by its eyes."

I was breaking the momentum of his thought, the one he'd been turning over all day—a thought of glory and power.

"The son of a bitch waiting for you is a predator. Do you know what a horse does when he sees a predator?"

"No." He was staring at a six-foot-tall monk who had come out of nowhere, like something from a dream.

I said, "A horse is made for running. It's not lack of courage. Running is a power, do you understand?"

I heard the door of the SUV opening. I had expected that. Saving this boy would require a demonstration.

I said to him, "If, for some reason, the horse can't run, he kicks. His kick can crush the skull of a mountain lion."

From the moment I spoke to the woman, I had joined myself to folly. Now I was deep in it, about to throw five years into the flames.

The boy was staring past me, toward Bustamante. His eyes told me how close the man was. At the correct moment, I turned with the full force of my two hundred pounds, grabbing him by the throat. His aviator sunglasses flew off his face.

I heard the other door of the SUV open quickly. I had expected this too.

Using Bustamante as a shield against his partner, I looked at the boy and said, "Run like the horse. Run to the world of the spirit. This man is the turd of a coyote."

Spanish has a natural formality and eloquence built into it. I often think it was meant for moments like this. The boy stared at me, and I saw he was at that place we rarely get to, when a wild chance appears.

He ran, not with fear but with the spirit.

Bustamante's partner was swaggering confidently toward us, in preparation for solving the problem. He was a cartel specialist who built impenetrable security systems for his employer's many residences. I heard him rack a round into the chamber of his automatic. But he was not about to shoot Bustamante in the back to get at me.

Bustamante's eyes bulged as I held his throat. He couldn't breathe, and his feeble punches merely caught in my robe. I shifted him slightly so that he continued to shield me.

When the partner reached us, I drove Bustamante into him, plowing them both backward and smashing the security specialist against their SUV. He crumpled to the street, unconscious and out of the fight. I held Bustamante in the air. His face had now turned blue.

Each day after morning prayer, I opened a medicine bottle and tapped out a little pill to control my anger. You might think it wasn't working, but it was, because instead of following the urge to drive Bustamante's head through the window of his SUV, I dropped him onto his partner. As he clutched at his throat, trying to get more air, I removed the pistol from his belt. I got his partner's gun too. I was now a monk with a pistol in each hand.

I returned to the feed store and bought the hay and oats I'd come for.

# 2

Our abbot was a man who had worked half his life on the mountain slopes of northern Chihuahua, harvesting candelilla plants and then processing them over poisonous fumes of sulfuric acid to turn them into wax. With the same strong purpose, he processed a group of unruly men into a unity of spirit. When we chanted, his rich bass voice seemed to come out of the earth, and in those deep tones we heard his faith and his sacrifice. The wild life he loved, on the mountain slopes, was inside him now. We felt his longing for that life—a match to our own longing and our own sacrifice.

When I received the order to go to his office, I prepared myself for a lecture and heavy penance. A few bare bulbs lit the way to him. The stone floor was worn from the tread of generations of silent men. The stone walls breathed cold, moist air, the air of renunciation.

When I entered the abbot's office, he said, "The boy's mother got word to me about your intervention."

His big hands were covered with burn scars, and there was a scar across his forehead where a vat of sulfuric wax had once exploded in his face. "Her message was accompanied by a dozen tortillas, which will be on our table tonight."

"I regret subjecting the monastery to reprisals."

"I baptized the Camel's son. There will be no reprisals. But dealing with such a man is complicated. He hires children to kill for him, but he also gives tractors to farmers, and soccer equipment to schools. But Busta-mante never gave anyone anything but a bullet in the back of the head. So I don't reproach you for what you did. I would have enjoyed doing it myself. But Bustamante is your enemy now. However, we won't worry about that until you come back."

"Am I going somewhere?"

"Your uncle has sent for you. He's dying."

My uncle had brought me here five years ago, during my bad moment.

"You should go to him," the abbot continued. "He's been your protector."

"I'll make my travel arrangements now."

"I've made them for you. You fly to Phoenix tomorrow morning."

# 3

In the air, with a bright layer of clouds below me, I prayed for my uncle and for the young man I had killed in a barroom five years before.

At Sky Harbor International in Phoenix, I rented a Chevy Impala. I could have had a Chevy Spark for ten bucks less, but guys my size don't fit well in small cars. The Impala moved me along easily through the high desert country of Arizona, but when I pushed down hard for more power, I felt a lazy transmission. And on fast turns, the suspension didn't accommodate the g-forces very well. I'd grown up in a car mechanic's family. I knew all about cars, had worked on them, raced them, and put them behind me, but I couldn't resist testing the Impala. Conclusion: same old General Motors, two steps behind. But the speaker system, while not up to the acoustics of an old Mexican monastery, did the job. I was listening to a CD the abbot had given me on my departure: the Benedictine monks of Fontgombault in France. "These are the best," he'd said. "You'll need them out in the world."

He was right. The world was calling me with a strength that seemed supernatural. I'd gotten used to narrow stone corridors, frankincense and solemn bells, and the support of men who had chosen renunciation. Their support had been largely silent, but the strength of their commitment somehow found me, and I felt what might be called grace.

Now a barren desert called me with its distances, with its tumbleweed crossing the road in front of me and telling me to just keep rolling. The mountain peaks said I could lose myself in them just as easily as in a monastery.

Landscapes without human habitations appeal to the spirit. They, too, instruct in silence, but they don't demand abstinence.

I was vulnerable outside the monastery. What faith I had was built on ritual. When you wake each day to solemn morning bells and walk with other monks in silence to a chapel laden with the smell of frankincense, even the statues seem to speak. Tiers of red votive candles offered to the dead are a form of eloquence.

A coyote crossed the road in front of me. Every particle of its being was in readiness. A coyote doesn't require ceremony to stay focused on what matters.

Benedictine monks chanted from the four speakers surrounding me. *"The man of God, Benedict, was full of the spirit; may he intercede for all those of the monastic profession . . ."*

I'd escaped having to go to Catholic high school, because the football team wasn't good enough and I wanted to bang heads with the best. A wrestling scholarship took me to the state university, and during the summers, to keep in fighting form, I worked as a bouncer. And then I killed someone and wound up in a monastery. I didn't rediscover my religion. I found peace of mind. And now, after just twenty-four hours, I felt it slipping away from me.

I got off the interstate, onto an old two-lane highway. It had once been important; now it was almost abandoned. I followed it north for two hours, and only a few cars appeared from the other direction. Occasionally, I saw a ranch house reached by a dirt road that wound through low hills. I saw a solitude that rivaled or surpassed the monastery's. Whoever lived out here was going it alone. Maybe there were ranch hands. Maybe there was family. I saw no one.

Finally, the old highway connected with a more traveled road. The low hills gave way to dramatic outcroppings of rock. The rocks turned red and massive, and suddenly I was seeing formations that were surreal—huge red shapes reminiscent of Eastern temples and Egyptian tombs, spires of red rock shaped by wind and rain over millions of years. I was approaching

Paloma. And Paloma knew that it was blessed by these ancient red shapes. Shops, restaurants, and motels began to line the road. Solitude was no longer the theme of the landscape.

I felt uneasy. Now I was going to have to cope with the real temptations of the world, but I told myself I was being unnecessarily cautious. I wasn't entering Sodom and Gomorrah, only a tourist town in the desert.

Dominating the skyline was a mountain that looked like an enormous red eagle's head. This majestic image was diminished by a nearby five-star hotel whose illuminated sign indicated it was hosting the 25th Annual National UFO Convention.

This was the town my uncle had chosen for his retirement. I assumed that it was not for things like the UFO conference. His address was in my GPS, and I followed directions into the center of town, then turned onto Thunderbird Road. Modest bungalows lined both sides. I kept preparing to stop, expecting one of them to be his.

But the GPS took me higher, and the houses got bigger. They were no longer bungalows. They were expensive dwellings of smoothly rounded adobe in the pueblo style, with beautiful red-tiled roofs. Round, polished beams protruded from the adobe walls. Other wooden beams framed elaborate entranceways. These had to be the homes of well-to-do retirees or working professionals with plenty of extra money for celebrating stylish desert living. They weren't priests, which is what my uncle had been. How had he gotten the money to live here?

Thunderbird Road took me to the base of Storm Mountain. It was another red rock temple, and my uncle's house, as upscale as any I'd seen, was directly across from it. The old priest had done very well for himself.

My cousins had gotten to Uncle Vittorio's house ahead of me, all of them watching each other to make sure nobody swiped anything, for the blood of the Mafia was in all our veins.

# 4

My cousin Angelina, who cheated at cards in our childhood, put her arms around me, giving me the feeling I always had with her—that she was picking my pocket.

Her husband, Frank, shook my hand. "The air is thin here," he said. "You feel it?"

"I've been living in the mountains; I'm used to it."

"I go for a walk, I'm gasping. It's a mile high here."

"It's forty-five hundred feet," corrected Angelina, and gave him a look that said he should shut up about his problems, there was a dying man in the house. To me she said, "The end is very near. But he wants for nothing."

She had adopted a somber tone for the occasion.

Her sister, Rose, came over to me. "I'm glad you could make it," she said, a suspicious look in her eyes. She'd always had that look, as if expecting to be cheated. It probably came from playing cards with Angelina. "I wish we saw you more often," she added. "We used to have fun."

When I was five, she locked me in a cellarway and stared through the latticework at me in silent curiosity, as if I were an animal in the zoo. And predicted—correctly, as it turned out—in her taunting little girl's voice, "You're going to jail."

"It's not possible to see Uncle Vittorio at the moment," said Angelina, her voice changing to nurse-like efficiency.

I assumed there was some medical procedure going on, and I took a seat by the huge living room window that looked out at the mountain of red rock across the road. Its craggy face was so close, I felt that it was leaning over us, and the sensation gave birth to the idea that it was aware of our presence beneath its eternal gaze.

My cousin Dominic, a concrete contractor, sat down beside me. Like his ready-mix truck, Dominic was huge. His voice rumbled as if amplified. "How've you been?"

"Fine."

"Still inside?" He made it sound like prison, which had always played its part in our family as uncles and other male relatives disappeared for months or years on end, *for health reasons*. "What do you do? Bake bread, grow basil, stuff like that?"

"I take care of horses and do some stonework."

"You remember during summer vacations you and me carried buckets of wet mix up a ladder for my old man? Two buckets at a time. You were a strong kid."

He touched my shoulder with his fist. "You still look in good shape. You work out in your cell?"

"Push-ups and prayer."

A laugh rumbled in his guts. "That's good." When I was orphaned as a kid, he gave me half his toys.

His gaze traveled to the wall, and a huge crucifix made of barbed wire. "Mexican. They sell stuff like that in this town." His gaze lingered on the cross. "It's weird, but I like it. The barbed wire says something."

Little kids I'd never met were playing in the house. Dominic told them to knock it off or go outside. They went outside. He shook his head. "Vittorio blessed them yesterday. They don't know what it means. They're Catholics, but it means nothing." He pronounced it "Cat-licks." I had pronounced it that way myself until I went to college and had my ears opened.

Dominic looked at the kids running around in the yard. "They want to go to the Grand Canyon and ride a donkey."

"Mules," said his wife.

"Okay, mules."

She held out her hand to me. "Nice to see you, Tommy."

I stood up, kissed her cheek. "You, too, Bianca."

"How do you like Brazil?"

"Mexico."

"That's right, Mexico. It's three-quarters Cat-lick, right?"

Dominic picked up a free local paper and snapped it open in front of me. It showed an ad for the services of an Indian medicine man.

"He look like an Indian to you? He's got the feathers and beads, but he's white as Wonder Bread."

He thumbed through more pages showing ads for channelers, psychics, and healers. "Paloma is a crazy town. Look at this . . ." It was an ad for Jeep rides into the canyons. "The Jeeps are pink. I ride in a Jeep, it ain't goin' to be pink."

Dominic had always hung out around training gyms. He knew a couple of boxing managers, and just before I had my trouble, he'd tried to get me started in that profession. *You hit like a fucking piledriver, cousin.* But I hit somebody too hard in a bar and killed him. At the time, I was in my junior year of college and competing in Division One NCAA wrestling, headed for the Olympics.

Dominic closed the paper and tapped the cigarette pack in his shirt. "I'm goin' outside to send a smoke signal to the medicine man."

He left me alone with Angelina, Rose, and Bianca. After a while, I realized they didn't want me to see Vittorio. Despite my vow of poverty, they weren't taking any chances on a last-minute change to his will.

I got up and headed toward the bedroom. Angelina cut me off. "You can't go in yet, Tommy."

"Cut the crap, Angelina."

"He's very sick."

"I know that. That's why I'm here."

"He's resting. I'll call you when he wakes up."

I moved past her. She stepped back in front of me. "I won't have you busting in there."

"I don't want anything from him," I said. "You've got nothing to worry about."

She tossed her hair cinematically. "What are you suggesting?"

"He sent a message that he wanted to see me. I came to say goodbye to him. Nothing else. I'm a monk in the order of Benedict. I don't own anything, and I don't want to."

She studied me carefully, like she used to when we played cards, reading what I had in my hand by looking in my eyes.

Her gaze softened as much as Angelina's gaze could soften, which wasn't much. But she'd taken my measure and knew that my life as a monk wasn't going to change. I'd killed a man and had exiled myself into a monastery for penance, for self-punishment, for whatever. I was staying there and I didn't want Vittorio's house and money.

She did, and she was going to get it.

She stepped aside, and I entered my uncle's bedroom.

He lay in bed, small and wrinkled, resembling already the preserved body of a saint I'd seen in a basilica in Italy. A rosary was threaded through his fingers, and a missal lay open on his chest.

"The vultures are circling," he said, gesturing weakly toward the closed door.

"They mean well," I said.

"Now they love me. A sudden love. It came on them unexpectedly about five days ago."

I tried to stick up for them, but he said, "You're not surprised, don't try to kid me."

He spoke with the same gravelly voice as his father, the old mafia don who once ran the Martini family. I'd been afraid of Grandfather Primo ever since being conducted as a kid into his basement by Angelina, who showed me how the floor was slanted toward a drain in the center. "For the blood. I don't mean chickens."

Grandfather Primo had never said much to me. I remember his gray suit, his gray hair, his gray eyes, which had been filled with poison so strong they could paralyze you.

Vittorio's eyes had only a drop of poison in them. He said, "I have something to tell you. About your father. And the garage."

My father and his brothers had owned Martini Towing. "They told you your father died of a heart attack. What actually happened was, one of their jacks slipped and crushed him. They lied about it so their workmen's compensation rates wouldn't go up."

"How do you know this?"

"I'm the priest in the family. They always told me everything."

He turned his head on his pillow, picked up his crucifix, and pressed it into my hand. "Primo took you from your mother then. She wasn't Italian. She was outside the fold. I should have intervened in her behalf. I didn't. After losing you, she started to drink. You know the rest."

I knew that she drank herself to death while still a young woman, but I had few memories of her or my father.

"I ask your forgiveness." Vittorio closed his hands around mine, clasping the crucifix within both our hands. "Had I looked after you better, you might not have gotten into trouble."

"I made my own trouble, Vittorio."

"Yes, you thought you were a tough guy. Like your uncles. Like your grandfather Primo."

He began to cough, tears coming to his eyes. He got his breath again. "I feel the strength of your holy order. You bring sanctity into my house. It comes off you like mist from the mountain."

He pointed to the craggy face of the mountain looming over us. His skinny arm fell back to the bed. He continued to look at the mountain in silence for a long while. "You carry the order with you, but you have no vocation. Trust me on that."

He died that night.

# 5

We drove in a mourners' caravan out of Paloma, toward an old copper mining town ten miles away, where Vittorio had asked to be buried. The copper was long gone, but its imprint remained in the huge symmetrical patterns traced by obsolete mining machinery in the sandy yellow ground.

"Like crop circles," said Dominic. "I just read about them. Flying saucer freaks meet there, waiting to get beamed up."

He had chosen to ride to the church with me rather than with his wife because, as he said to me now, "We got things to talk about, Tommy."

I knew he would be coming after me. He continued, "Cage fighting is perfect for you. Light gloves, anything goes."

"Thanks, but I'm not interested."

"You got a fighter's heart, Tommy. And I got connections. I can get you in on a very good level."

"I don't fight anymore, Dominic."

"You had some bad luck. But fuck it, life goes on. You're burying yourself in that goddamn monastery."

"And today we're burying Vittorio. Let's leave it at that."

Dominic wasn't one to stop when he was rolling. "Okay, you killed a guy. But in our family, that's no shame."

His voice became flat, even. "You know what I mean? With you it was an accident. Primo offed dozens of guys, and it was no accident."

He took out a cigarette, tapped it on the dash. "It's what we are. It's fucking evolution."

He lit his cigarette, lowered the window, looked out at the old copper field that spread for miles. "That's some crop circle."

"Who's running Primo's crew now?"

"Phil Branca. He's dialed back the violence. That's the new way. Real estate, insurance, prepaid telephone cards, small brokerage houses. Everybody's gone under the radar. Miami, Chicago, Jersey—it's a different world."

"That doesn't sound like the Phil Branca I remember."

"He doesn't want the heat anymore. The big busts taught everybody a lesson. There are plenty of made guys in the five New York families right now, but the rule is, you lay low. You keep the action quiet. It's the only way to survive these days."

"And the political clout?"

"Gone. Phil still has his hooks into a few local judges and a couple of bent cops, but nobody talks to senators or congressmen anymore."

We reflected in silence on the state of the changing world. When we were kids, we had felt Primo's power at a distance, which may have magnified it, but we knew that people lived in fear of him. I'd seen a picture of Zeus in a history book and thought, *that's my grandfather.*

Dominic looked back at me. "I saw all of your matches when you were at State. You gave them two national championships and you would've given them a third, but you had to leave town."

"Give it a rest, okay?"

"I saw the rage in you. That's what it takes in cage fighting. And you've still got the rage. It's in your voice."

"I take medicine now. To curb my rage."

"No shit? I didn't know they had stuff for that."

"Eufexor."

"Well, as your primary care provider, I recommend you flush it. Rage is good. You need rage." He blew smoke out the window. "It's part of evolution."

"Dominic, what is this? You've been reading Charles Darwin?"

"I read the fucking newspaper. You can get shot in your car by some bottom-feeder who thinks you looked at him the wrong way. We live in a time of the short fuse. You've got to be ready."

He held out his hand. "Lemme see your rage remedy."

I removed the little pill bottle from my pocket. He took it from me and threw it out the window.

"Goddamn it, Dominic . . ."

"Rage, baby, rage. It's good for you." He puffed on his cigarette. "I don't want to manage you for the money. Okay? I got enough money. Bianca wants more money, but that's another story. All the women in this family think they should be wearing crowns."

Smoke jetted from his nostrils and swirled down around a large, newly purchased turquoise belt buckle, all but buried by his protruding gut. "I just want to bring you back to life. See you doing what you do best, which is breaking arms. You remember when you popped the elbow of that guy from Penn State? I could hear it from the tenth row."

"I'm into prayer and meditation, Dominic. That's what I do these days."

"I'm fine with prayer, don't get me wrong. But you carry it too far."

We swung off the highway into the little copper mining town. As if to greet visitors, two decaying railroad cars were parked on an abandoned stretch of track. There were no red rocks and no upscale houses. It was very different from Paloma. The three blocks of Main Street looked as if they hadn't changed in a hundred years, which lent them a certain old-West charm, but there were no tourists. No one was even on the street.

Vittorio's body had been carried to a small mission church at the edge of town. Its white walls were made whiter by the bright Arizona sun. There were three small windows and a small bell tower. The charm of this relic from earlier days was lost on Dominic. "Why did Vittorio want to go out from a dump like this?"

"The priest here is old-school. He has permission from the Vatican to say mass in Latin. Vittorio was old-school too."

"So am I." He parked in the lot beside the sun-faded walls of the church and opened the car door. "I don't go to church to listen to some kid play his guitar."

We climbed out, Dominic still giving me his views on the degeneration of Cat-lick ceremony. "At the end of mass, you turn and shake hands with the person next to you? I don't shake hands unless I'm making a deal."

The sidewalk was blazing. The other family cars were pulling into the lot. Car doors opened, and Angelina fell into step beside me.

She was more relaxed now, knowing I hadn't forced a pen into Vittorio's hand as he drew his last breath. We would bury him, and I'd go back to the monastery in Mexico. I was uncomfortable out here in the world. Twenty-four hours with my relatives in the tourist town of Paloma had shown me how much I'd gained from living the ordered life of a monk. I felt that life still functioning in me, and the simplicity of this old Spanish church reinforced the feeling. I belonged in a monastic setting.

Dominic and I walked to the door of the little church, the rest of the family behind us, the kids bringing up the rear, expressing boredom in every limb.

The tiny altar was loaded with flowers, huge bouquets surrounding Vittorio's casket. More giant bouquets were arranged in the side aisles, stretching all the way to the front doors—tribute from various mob families. A connected priest was going to get a show of hands. The biggest bouquets were from the bosses in Phoenix and Vegas: Aldo Santini and Carmine Cremona.

It was hot inside the church, a couple of overhead fans only redistributing the heat. The place was overflowing with mourners. When everyone was seated, the service began. Dominic shifted on his kneeling bench many times, making it creak under his bulk.

His suit coat was open, and I saw a shoulder holster and the butt of an automatic.

Vittorio was seen out of this world in Latin. At the cemetery, Angelina and her sister shed a few tears, and the kids kept an eye out for rattlers, which they were hoping to see. The cemetery was small, surrounded by an old iron fence, and beyond it was the desert. The copper miners and their families were buried here. It was high, lonesome country, and I figured that was why Vittorio had chosen it: to rest in a barren landscape and be forgotten. Dirt was thrown into the grave, and we left.

Dominic insisted that he and I walk around the old mining town. Half the stores were closed, and not much was happening in the others. The most interesting items in town were a couple of vintage pickup trucks that drove by. They weren't rusted out. They had never run on salty roads. The desert gives you a break that way.

We walked to the park and sat in the shade of a small outdoor bandstand. I said to him, "I see you're packing."

"It's Vittorio's. I found it at the house." He stretched his legs out, hooked his thumb in his belt beside the big turquoise buckle. "I'm in the Wild West. I want to be prepared."

"What are you expecting?"

"This ain't no fancy tourist town like Paloma. It's a meth lab town. Bad shit could go down anywhere around us."

"You know this how?"

"I look at a house, the front yard, the windows, I get a feeling. If somebody is cooking up meth inside, it telegraphs. You have to know the signs. Comes from long experience."

"I thought you were in the concrete business."

"Take it from me, meth is the only thing that makes money in this town. And where there are meth labs, there are crazies. So . . ." He patted his jacket. "Arizona is a stand-and-defend state. I'm comfortable with that."

I gazed across the empty park. Nothing was stirring in any direction. It looked like the most peaceful place on the planet. The narrow streets had been made for mule teams, and there had been no significant alterations in a hundred years. If there were crazies, I didn't see them.

Dominic was puffing another cigarette. "The bosses didn't come in person. You can't expect that. But you might get a friendly call, just an acknowledgment of your existence."

"Do you know them?"

"I know Carmine from Vegas. And that's why you wouldn't have to crawl over a bunch of amateurs to get on the bill in a big casino match. Tommy Martini, the Sicilian Sizzler."

"It sounds like an Italian steakhouse."

"Whatever, we'll come up with something snappy."

"It's not going to happen. I'm through with the ring."

"Okay, I'm done." He flipped his cigarette into the dry grass, where it smoldered and died without setting the town on fire. "But the offer stands. These are your best years. Prime fighting time." I saw the love in his eyes when he looked my way. He was two years older. He had watched over me when we were kids, and he was still doing it. Now he asked, "Mind me asking you what you do about women?"

"I took a vow of celibacy."

"So when you look at her . . ." He nodded to a young woman coming into view on the park path, clad for the desert heat in a thin dress that the sun shone through.

"I'm not blind."

"Like I say, these are your best years."

Dominic followed the young woman's progress closely. "That ain't scrap metal."

"It certainly isn't."

"But the monk isn't having any. You gave yourself this penance? It's not official or anything?"

"I put a young guy in the ground, Dominic, so let's say I'm doing it for him."

"He started it. So he got what he was asking for."

"He wasn't asking to die."

"He wanted to test the local hero. He failed the test."

# 6

Our family was gathered around the conference table in the lawyer's office. I could see Storm Mountain through the window, its red face rising above the tree line.

The lawyer wore a cream white shirt with a bolo tie held by a turquoise slider. His cowboy boots looked custom-made. His haircut was perfect. He opened a manila folder and said, "It was Father Vittorio's wish that things be handled promptly."

"He always thought of others," said Angelina. Rose and Bianca nodded their agreement.

Frank and Dominic sat beside me. The lawyer slid a sealed envelope toward me. "Your uncle told me to give this to you."

I didn't open it, but I could feel a flat, round object inside. I said, "A religious medal." I wanted Angelina to be sure nothing was going on behind her back.

She gave me a warm smile. This morning, she'd told me I'd always been a brother to her.

"And now the will," said the lawyer. "It's a very simple document. Father Vittorio was a simple man."

The lawyer adjusted his bolo tie, ran a hand over his perfect haircut, and began. "As you might expect, your uncle left small amounts of money to several Catholic charities. Chief among them is the Little Sisters of the Poor. Father Vittorio had a special affection for them."

"They've got a convent near us in Coalville," said Angelina, approving the bequest. "They do very good work." She turned to Rose. "You know where it is? Over on Clifton Street?"

Rose nodded devoutly.

"He also left a modest sum of money to the Apache nation." The lawyer gestured toward the window. "All this land around here is sacred to them. Father Vittorio had many friends among Native Americans."

"He was so compassionate," said Rose. She had brought out her handkerchief.

"There's also a bequest to a monastery in Mexico. The rest of his money, along with his home, has been left to his nephew, Tommy. He expressed this wish to me many times over the years, and he finalized it in his will."

The lawyer nodded toward me. "Everything in the home goes to Tommy, with the exception of certain items that are earmarked for Angelina, Bianca, and Rose." The lawyer closed the folder. "As I said, a very simple will."

Angelina looked like wrestlers I've seen, caught in a choke hold that cuts off oxygen and makes speech impossible. Rose said, "He's a monk. He ain't allowed to own nothing."

"How he chooses to use his bequest is entirely up to him." The lawyer knew that the moment was tense. He had, however, seen such moments before. He was secure in his cowboy-kitsch office.

Angelina broke the choke hold. "I'm going to fight this."

"Of course, that option is open to you," said the lawyer.

"You're goddamned right it is."

The lawyer gave us all his professional smile. "Tommy, if you wouldn't mind staying . . ." Which was his polite way of telling the rest of them there was nothing more to be said. Then he beat a retreat into an adjacent office.

Angelina hissed in my ear, "*Finocchio.*" Italian for queer. The poison of Primo was burning in her eyes. She and Rose flounced out of the office together, hatching plans for battle.

Bianca looked at me and said, "Go to confession, Tommy." She snatched up her purse and seemed ready to brain me with it. "You twisted an old man's mind." And she followed the other women, her newly purchased Southwestern sandals slapping on the tiled hallway.

Frank came up behind me. Like Dominic, he was a big man, a construction contractor used to working with his hands. I wondered if he wanted to put them around my throat. He spoke softly, but in our family, quiet speech does not necessarily convey gentleness. In that same voice, Grandfather Primo had ordered men killed. Frank said, "We got another day here before our flight leaves. I'll go get our shit out of the house now."

"Frank, that's crazy. Stay in the house."

"Tommy, Angelina will cut your fucking throat while you're sleeping in your bed tonight, and Rose will slice off your tackle." His voice remained soft. He didn't want his kids watching an ugly scene starring their mother.

He smiled the Primo smile, which never reached the eyes. "Angelina has been on me about taking her to an inn here called the Manzano. Four bedrooms, a mountain view—the perfect vacation spot. We'll hang out there for a day and then head home."

He took both my arms at the biceps, his eyes still not joining the smile on his thin lips. "Manzano—almost sounds Italian, right?"

I turned toward Dominic. His feeling for me was still shining in his eyes. I was still the boy he'd protected, and nothing was going to change that. He said, "Now you can worry about roofs and drains. Welcome to the real world, cousin."

They left the office. As they stepped into the reception room, Bianca started in on Frank. "Why dincha get in the lawyer's face?"

"Take it easy."

"You sat there like a *polpetta*." Italian for meatball.

The lawyer wisely waited until they'd all left the building, and then came back into the conference room. "I've seen it before. Nine times out of ten, resentment dies down and no action is taken."

"You don't know my family."

"I noticed one of them was armed."

"That's not the half of it."

"Nevertheless, your cousin Angelina is whistling in the dark." He tapped his finger on the will lying on the conference table. "This was signed by the testator in the presence and hearing of two witnesses."

"Angelina will say he wasn't in his right mind."

"In Arizona, the testator can show signs of mental illness and yet still have the testamentary capacity to sign a will."

"I don't care about the will. I just don't want her thinking I influenced him."

"You were in a monastery in Mexico. A charge of undue influence would be very hard to prove."

"She doesn't have to prove anything. She and her sister can have it all."

"Vittorio had great respect for you and wanted you to have everything, with the exclusion of the charitable bequests."

"I don't want any of it."

"His religion did not forbid him from making sound investments. As I understand it, his brothers began sending him money when he was ordained many years ago. And he, quite wisely, bought stock in IBM, Coca-Cola, and a little company called Apple. They're worth just over a million dollars."

"Holy God."

"In this instance, an apt expression."

"I still don't want the money. Or the house."

"Or the SUV?" He took a set of BMW key fobs out of his pocket and slid them over to me. "Father Vittorio anticipated your reaction. In the envelope I gave you is a letter from him. He offers some guidance."

"It doesn't matter. I can't accept his gift."

"Well, he set up a bank account in your name. The bank is Wells Fargo here in town. The money is already there. He slid a bank folder across the desk to me. "I wouldn't be serving your uncle if I didn't tell you to think things over carefully. Paloma is a good place to do that. Spend a few weeks here before you decide anything."

I opened Vittorio's envelope and took out a gold medal. Saint Benedict's figure was on it, holding a cross in his right hand and in his left a book—his rules for monastery living. I took out Vittorio's letter. The handwriting was clear, almost like calligraphy. He had been a parish priest for a lifetime, and he'd had to write many letters for his flock.

*Dear Tommy,*

*Christ has forgiven you for killing that guy in the bar. You can't add to His forgiveness by spending your life on your knees. Or chanting with monks. That music is powerful, and in the end all you'll have in your soul is a song. Keep your eyes open and a sign will confirm what I'm saying.*

*Sell the house if you want, but keep the money. You're meant to live in this world. Trust me. If you don't, I'll fucking haunt you.*

*Vittorio*

# 7

Vittorio's cell phone rang. I was carrying it now, with the painful sense that it was like a fishhook through my lips. It would pull me into a world whose air I couldn't breathe. It was Dominic.

"We're staying in your house tonight, like you suggested."

"Good, perfect."

"Angelina decided the bed-and-breakfast was too expensive. What it really is, she's performing a thorough search of Vittorio's house—excuse me, your house. She's looking for an earlier will. Every fucking drawer is open. But don't worry, Frank will sit on her if she tries to carry off the furniture."

"Tell her to take whatever she wants."

"I tell her that, she'll take the pipes out of the wall. Anyway, we're leaving for Phoenix tomorrow. Our flight's at noon. She won't have time to order a moving van."

"Have a good trip back."

"Think over what I said about fighting in Vegas." And he switched off.

I would find somewhere else to sleep tonight and think things over, as the lawyer had suggested.

Frank had named a fancy inn, and there were plenty of those around Paloma. But I was used to monastery life. I chose the dumpiest motel I could find. The desk clerk was a misanthrope who wanted recognition on that basis. Any question addressed to him about anything would be answered with grudging resentment. In the monastery, I'd met men further gone on that path than he would ever be, and after a second or two of my staring at him, he got the sense we were kindred spirits. It even seemed to lift him slightly, and he almost uttered a human word as he slid my keycard to me.

I went to my room, reread Vittorio's letter, and stared at the wall. Both paintings on the wall were the same. Identical desert landscapes.

Motels like this buy their furnishings from secondhand warehouses, complete with burn marks and other damage from previous ownership. The bedside tables are like lead, as is everything else, to prevent the occupant from walking away with them.

I lay on the floor and pressed the nightstand up and down a few hundred times. It was better than a barbell because it offered no easy handhold. I followed this by a hundred squats with it on my shoulders.

Then I did a hundred push-ups.

Then I did some more staring at the wall. The monastery walls had been blackened with the smoke of candles burned over centuries. Faith had burned there too, and it remained in the air, left behind by men long gone. If you've ever lived under the influence of such shadows, you know how real they are. I wanted to return to them. I would visit the lawyer in the morning and have him draw up documents that turned the property over to Angelina, Rose, and Bianca.

I left the motel room and found an Indian restaurant nearby, where I ate staring into a candle. The faint smell of melting wax took me back to the monastery, to the empty spaces around the altar, to silent men struggling with their devils. That was my real life. With any luck, in two days I'd be back there again.

I looked at my watch. Time for my rage medicine. I felt in my pocket, then remembered Dominic throwing it out the window.

The doctor who gave it to me had strongly advised against skipping a dose, which could cause a boomerang reaction.

The drug was metabolizing out of me. The flame in the candle on my table was matched by one flaming in my gut. It was probably what Angelina felt right now. It's in our family. It had made Grandfather Primo a leader over other vicious men.

I was back where I used to be, raging inside at nothing at all, just raging. It was my state of mind on the night I killed that guy in a bar, ending my college career and my future as an Olympic athlete.

My rage had faded in the monastery, thanks to Eufexor and a quiet daily regimen. Athletes understand regimen. We get hooked on it because the rewards are big. Before, during, and after every game, superstitious ritual is obeyed to ensure victory. So monastery life wasn't much of a stretch for me. My problem was being apart from it. I was getting jumpy.

I distracted myself by looking around the restaurant. The single women of Paloma were well represented at the surrounding tables. I caught references to vortices, healing, and Eastern forms of meditation.

On every table was a laminated brochure offering a device to turn tap water into something called "structured water." Such water, I learned, contains important information that the body will assimilate. Apparently, my blood cells are stuck together in an unfortunate way. Buying this device, for sale at the restaurant, would loosen up my blood cells. I risked the tap water.

When my food came, I ate as I did at the monastery, head down. But the restaurant wasn't a monastery, and my concentration faltered. I caught a few glances from the women. Somebody my size usually rates a cautionary look. Mentally scratching their heads, I suppose. Who's this new guy in town?

I wouldn't have been able to answer them, because I no longer knew myself.

When I got up to leave, one of the women was also getting up. She smiled and said, "I saw you reading about structured water."

Her voice became suddenly intimate. "Cellular hydration is so important." The tone of her voice suggested it was right up there after orgasm. "I recommend it to all my patients."

She opened her purse and handed me a business card. It had the drawing of a bird on it, the wings framing the name *Regina Silver Hawk* and her profession: *Practicing Intuitive.*

"Beautiful star-shaped molecules—that's what your water should be."

I went back to my motel and drank a can of Coca-Cola, enjoying its beautiful sugar-shaped molecules. Now that I was a shareholder, I felt loyalty to the brand.

A woman's scream came around midnight. I thought it might be a TV program, but when her next scream was accompanied by something hitting the wall, I knew it was live-action. The thinness of the wall permitted me to hear what passed for conversation.

*"Hugster, please stop!"*

Then I heard Hugster, whose voice sounded as if it had been run through witness protection software—a deep baritone vibrating my wall. *"I'm just startin' with you, bitch . . ."*

I stepped out of my room. The parking lot had gradually filled. A battered ice machine hulked in the shadows.

I stood for a moment in front of Hugster's door, hoping the argument would resolve. But the woman continued pleading, so I knocked, loud enough to be heard over the thumping from inside.

It stopped abruptly, followed by Hugster observing angrily, "*What the fuck. . . ?*"

The door flew open. From the looks of it, Hugster was a powerlifter, stacking with steroids. Huge neck, massive chest, monster biceps.

I didn't want to hurt him, just calm him down. His bulk filled the doorway, but I could see the woman on her knees beside the bed. What must have been a carefully sculpted hairdo was now ruined. Her nightgown was ripped, and her face was swollen.

She looked at me with desperate eyes, unsure what new level of anger I might generate in her Hugster. I tried appealing to his better nature.

"I need my sleep, okay? And you're cracking the plaster."

He stared at me in drunken disbelief. I was interrupting an intimate moment between him and his date. "Crack this, motherfucker . . ."

Powerlifters push their punches, as if they were still lifting weights, huge trapezoid muscles supporting the arm as it drives slowly forward. To his surprise, I wasn't where I should have been, and he swung at empty air. His missed punch brought him forward and down; losing elevation, he exposed the top of his head. I hit him with a palm strike, which drove his head down into my quickly rising knee.

His head snapped back, and he was looking up to the motel lights. His eyes reflected them beautifully in two tiny points, as if he'd been suddenly enlightened. Perfect for Paloma.

He shook his head to clear the blow. He should have quit, but it was a matter of a strong man's pride. He came at me again, and my rage, unchecked by Eufexor, bubbled up to my brain. When that happens, it appears to me as if I'm teaching somebody an important lesson that they badly need, to show them what it means to lose big-time.

Then memory flooded me—a sensation of something giving way in a young man's body, something vital inside him collapsing, my fist driving into the core of his life and ending it. I settled for a short body hook near Hugster's tenth rib.

He folded like a puppet whose strings have been cut. Sitting in the doorway, he said matter-of-factly, "You broke my leg."

"No, I punched you in the liver."

He looked at me dully and remained seated in the doorway, leaning against the motel wall. A shot to the liver stops a man's focus and drive instantly, because the liver is a big organ and a good shot there impedes blood circulation. That and the booze had slowed him way down.

He put his head back, closed his eyes, and sighed deeply, like a buffalo in mud. Then he went to sleep.

His girlfriend was pulling clothes on over her nightgown. She slipped into her shoes, grabbed her suitcase, and charged through the doorway. Looking down at him, she said, "He seemed so nice online. He said let's go to Paloma, let's climb the red rocks."

"Better luck next time."

"I liked the cute name he had for himself online. Hugster. I thought he'd be like a big teddy bear."

"He's big."

"So are you." She gave me a look that wasn't quite sober.

"I'm a monk."

"No shit? Just my luck." She looked toward the office. "I'm going to get another room."

"You're okay for money?"

"I'm not a total loser. But thanks." She rose on tiptoes and kissed me on the cheek. Then she walked to the office and, in a few minutes, came back out with another keycard. First, she stopped at the ice machine and carried a bucket of it to her new room. She'd be needing it on her swollen cheeks.

The depressed desk clerk stepped out of his office and walked over to me. "You've done this before."

"Many times."

"Can we get him back into the room? He creates a bad impression."

We dragged Hugster in and dumped him on the bed. When we stepped back outside, the desk clerk said, "Care for a drink?"

"Got any structured water?"

We walked back to the motel office, and he took a couple of beers from a miniature bar. As we clicked cans, he asked, "How will he be tomorrow?"

"We'll find out."

He nodded and stopped worrying about tomorrow. He had a night of other demons ahead of him.

We drank in silence. The pump of an old soda machine turned on, expanding the gas in its creaking coils. Through the window, we could see the two empty lanes of the main drag. Occasional headlights went by, but Paloma isn't a late-night town, except for UFO spotters watching for the mothership.

The desk clerk said, in a voice that sounded as if it were coming from a casket, "Structured water is bullshit."

"I gathered that."

"They show pictures of star-shaped water molecules."

"I saw those at the restaurant next door."

"If you had water molecules like that in your body, you'd be dead." His voice sounded as if he were dead. He continued, "Or you'd have to be living in a deep freeze."

The coils of the old refrigerator beside us gave a particularly loud creak, as if in agreement. I asked, "So what are those pictures of?"

"Ice crystals. Probably snowflakes." He paused, sipped his beer. "Snowflakes are built around a spot of dirt. Another reason why you don't want them in your body. I used to be in the sciences."

He didn't elaborate on his previous career, so we finished our beers and I went back to my room. The duplicate landscapes greeted me.

I had no bruises from the battle, no sore muscles. And I hadn't killed anyone. In fact, I had enjoyed my little skirmish with Hugster. Our brief bout had blown away some of the fog I'd been in since leaving the monastery.

Vittorio had said there would be a sign. He was right. I wasn't going to give the house to Angelina, Rose, and Bianca.

# 8

I was sitting outside my room on a metal folding chair the next morning when the shuttle to Phoenix came for the young woman. She gave me a wave and climbed aboard. A while later, Hugster came out of his room and walked over to me.

Daylight showed his bulk in sharper detail. A lot of dead-lift shrugs with huge weights had gone into creating his giant traps. But he had some evidence of mush in those muscles—fluid retention, probably caused by overuse of creatine, whose molecules attract water. It had slowed him down when he came at me last night, but he had morning energy now.

I got up from my chair and folded it, for possible use against his head.

He said, "We got into it last night, right?"

"We did."

He was calm now, but his eyes were still those of a troglodyte peering out from his cave. Deca, Androxon, Sustanon—all the steroids produced that look. It was slightly veiled today owing to his hangover. But it was there.

"I still had plenty left in me."

"They counted you out, Hugster."

He consulted his strong man's pride and decided his reputation was intact. "Yeah, what the fuck . . ." He brought a suitcase from the room and tossed it in his car. He backed out and drove away.

I hung around until it was time to vacate the room. By then the desk clerk from the night before was back on the job. "Staying on?"

"No, I'll push off."

"You always have a home here," he said in his undertaker's voice.

"Thanks, I appreciate it." I gave him back the keycard and took a couple of tourist brochures from a rack in the lobby. I had to kill some time until my family left the house I now owned.

I walked to one of Paloma's many shops and entered under the sound of door chimes, into the fragrance of incense and scented candles. From shelves on both sides of the store, statues of sexy fairies and dragons looked out, their colorful bodies a blend of old mythology and current cartoon spirituality.

Highly polished stones of every hue filled other shelves. Mystical self-help books lined one wall.

The two women minding the store gave me smiles that were open and knowing, as if we were all attending the same spiritual seminar.

Incense vapors curled around me, and meditation music played softly in the background. At the monastery, the smell of frankincense was part of daily worship. I was there again, until the women's voices brought me back:

"The vortex energy was incredible at Eagle Rock this morning."

"I felt it too. I just went perfectly still and let it spin my chakras."

I'd read about Paloma's claim of being a center of swirling magnetic energies called vortices, which created magical conditions that brought people here from around the country and the world. I had lived with men in cowled robes, whose dark devotion pulled them ever deeper into the life of the solitary, which is unsparing in its demands. I had failed to meet its test, but it left me sympathetic to these women. The religion of their grandmothers was dead, but religious feelings remained in them, and I understood their yearning.

Leaving them to their gentle spinning, I stepped back out into the street. The desert sun was beating down on the pavement, and my shadow was sharply etched, suggesting another me whose identity was less defined. I preferred it, just couldn't get to it.

Vittorio's mountain dominated the skyline. I visited a few more stores, including one that sold wrought iron crucifixes. I studied the welds, the twists, the edges. I felt the same way: heated and then twisted into a shape supposed to resemble something spiritual.

One of Grandfather Primo's last acts on earth was to keep me out of jail. The word came down from him, and the right parties were paid off. Manslaughter charges went away, and the deadly fight I'd been in was never even reported in the newspapers. But when it came time for the Olympics, I was in a monastery in Mexico. Primo had suggested I go there "to make it look good. You're sorry for what happened, it makes the civil suit go away." He settled money on the young man's family, told me to come back in a few months. I had stayed five years, not only out of remorse, but also because I loved the stone walls, the candles, the chanting. The power of such places must be experienced to be understood. They are places of enchantment. They work on something ancient in us. If we linger, then we're lost, though some would say we've found our way.

Now I turned toward Vittorio's mountain. The long shadows told me my family's flight had taken off. I started walking up Thunderbird Road. Once again the modest bungalows gave way to large houses protected by red adobe walls. They might resemble Hopi pueblos, but it was only a whimsical likeness. These houses were expensive to build and loaded with amenities. As I reached the top of Thunderbird Road and looked at Vittorio's house, I wondered how, with his priestly vow of poverty, he could have purchased it. And how could I, with my monk's vow of poverty, be moving into it?

But I did. I triggered the remote that opened the garage door. Vittorio's BMW was there, a black SUV with a crucifix on the license plate. Why, I wondered, had he bought himself such a big vehicle? I entered the house through the garage.

In the living room, hints of my cousins' perfumes and colognes lingered in the air. The Mexican crucifix was gone. I assumed that other things had walked. But the furniture was still there.

I looked out through the cathedral-style window, feeling the retired priest in his mountain lair. I opened his desk and found prayer books and Catholic bookmarks, letters from fellow priests, and the phone number of a Las Vegas bookie. There were old postcards from Primo, written in a peasant's crude hand, each concluding with a request that Vittorio pray for him.

In Vittorio's nightstand, I found his pistol. Dominic had unloaded it and put it back where he found it. With it was a box of ammunition and a license to carry a concealed weapon.

It was a Beretta subcompact. I smiled, knowing that Vittorio would have liked owning an Italian-made gun. It was small in the hand and perfect for concealed carry. The finish was smooth as glass. I pushed the eject button on the side and removed the magazine. You don't grow up in a family like mine without knowing how to load an automatic. I opened the box of American Eagle cartridges and remembered something I'd once heard Primo say as he loaded his own automatic: *Bullets are teeth. They want to bite flesh.*

I pushed one into the clip, felt the spring resisting, and pressed. The cartridge clicked into place with a satisfying sound. I added twelve more, the resistance of the spring increasing with each round I pressed into the clip. When the clip was fully loaded, I slipped it back into the grip. Another satisfying click.

The monk and his gun.

# 9

I had tended trees in the monastery, so I knew something about those I now owned: apple, apricot, and cherry, growing in my backyard. The leaves looked healthy. Vittorio had done a good job.

As I was admiring them, I heard a car pull up in front of the house. From the concealment of my trees, I saw the two guys getting out of the car. The shoes, the silk suits and slick hair—every inch of them said *enforcer*.

They weren't like Hugster at the motel. I had dealt with his kind hundreds of times while working as a bouncer. He was an amateur. These guys were pros. But the visit could still be a cordial one. They might be representing Aldo Santini or Carmine Cremona.

Even so, I stayed in the backyard until they went to the front door. Then I entered through the back door and got Vittorio's loaded Beretta. The doorbell rang. They wanted in. Friendly or unfriendly, this is standard practice for mob guys. Once inside your house, they have an advantage. Grandfather Primo had taught me that. Get into a man's home and you've got him on the defensive. He's protecting his junk, his attention divided across everything he owns, all of it screaming *save me*.

They'd be coming around to the rear of the house when they got no answer in front. I tucked the Beretta under my belt in back and entered the yard again. I'd grown up around guys like this. Born without a conscience, and beating the crap out of people their whole lives. So it paid to be cautious.

They came around the corner of the house with the deadly earnestness of hired guns. But that's not unusual for soldiers working on their image.

I was screened by the wall of a metal toolshed. They walked past me, and I stepped out behind them. "Boys, how can I help you?"

They turned. I was the nephew they'd heard about, the monk. Probably bigger than they expected. But not a problem. Somebody who lived in a monastery and spent his days in prayer and good works was somebody you kicked in the kidneys a few times and that ended the matter.

"You're Tommy," said goon number one, putting out his hand. "I'm sorry for your loss."

His grip was soft, hardly there at all, as he added, "I'm Fortunato."

His voice matched his handshake—an approach I understood. He was saying to anyone he met, I hardly need to lift a finger to fuck you over. "Me and Clemente came to pay our respects."

"Sorry about Vittorio," Clemente said, and held out his hand. Same limp touch. Nicely manicured nails. He did his punching with gloves on, when he had you tied to a chair. Both of them were in the middleweight range. No martial arts training noticeable in their stance. A baseball bat across the kneecaps was what they were good at.

"I appreciate you coming by." Then I added, out of courtesy to their boss, "I've been out of the loop for a while, so pardon me if I don't know the family you represent."

They hesitated, and now I knew. They weren't connected.

They were from outside, and I was going toward the only explanation that made sense. It was extreme, but it fit the picture: Angelina had flipped her lid. She couldn't reach out to someone in our family; that would be a disgrace. But she knew the wannabes who were always sucking around, ready to do a favor to get themselves noticed.

How far they were ready to take it today, I didn't know. Angelina wouldn't have ordered a hit, but having me worked over suited her temperament. Even if I didn't cave to her demands, she would have the satisfaction of knowing I'd had my ass kicked. Our family would accept this. If I couldn't protect myself, then tough luck for me.

"We did business with your uncle," said Clemente. "He sold us some churches. You know about that? He tell you anything about him being a middleman?"

Clemente saw my puzzled look and continued. "Okay, he didn't tell you. No reason why he should. But we worked with him. We represent some people in Rome. They want to save old churches once they're decommissioned."

"Desacralized," I said.

Clemente nodded. "There you go. You *do* know about it. Probably more than we do. I mean about the faith getting hammered."

Fortunato chimed in. "It's a fucking shame. The old churches get turned into nightclubs, banks, libraries, whatever. So our employers buy them. To protect them."

To which Clemente added, "You get some actress turning a tabernacle into her jewelry box."

Even in Mexico, where the faith was strong, I'd seen churches boarded up, then torn down. Clemente saw I was on the same page with him now. "Tommy, there's a guy using a confessional as his entertainment center. Is that a kick in the balls, or what?"

He put one finger in the collar of his shirt and stretched it a little. "We'd like to give you a little background on what Vittorio was doing. How 'bout we go inside and talk about it?"

I pointed at the picnic table and chairs under the fruit trees. "We can sit in the shade."

"Sure, whatever you like."

We all took a seat. "The thing is this," said Clemente, "you got a bishop losing his beautiful church, he's worried about where he'll be sent next. He's worried about being shipped to a slum, so he's distracted. And he's no businessman." Clemente opened the button on his jacket and leaned forward. "He don't know what the fuck he's doing. He gets taken advantage of. You see where I'm going with this?"

I had no idea—only that when guys like Fortunato and Clemente are going anywhere, somebody's getting screwed.

Clemente continued, "So that's where our employer steps in. He's buying *for the right reason*." Clemente blessed himself to show his sincerity.

"To preserve and protect the sacred shit that's in the church," added Fortunato. "So the stained glass windows don't wind up in a rapper's bathroom."

They paused so I could take in the sincerity of their mission to safeguard church property. When I said nothing, Clemente continued. "And Vittorio, see, he'd been around forever. He knew bishops all over the place. He made it a point to find out when a church was going under and brought it to our employer's attention. He even helped negotiate the deal." Clemente smoothed the lapel of his jacket. "We did a lot of business with Vittorio."

"Business," I said.

"Big business," said Clemente. "A church in the right location is worth plenty. Just before Vittorio passed away, God rest his soul, he facilitated a pair of church sales. A parish up in Seattle, another one in Santa Fe. He had hooks in both those places. Our employer gave two million and change for them."

"That's big business."

"Right, and Vittorio didn't work for nothing. He took a taste. We're fine with that. And these deals were strictly cash because bishops don't want people poking into their financial arrangements. Even your local priest doesn't want somebody counting the Sunday collection, because he does a certain amount of skimming. You didn't know that? Happens all the time. Me, I don't begrudge any priest a little on the side."

We pondered this together for a few moments, and then they got down to the real reason for their visit.

"So our employer gives Vittorio two million to complete the sale. Only Vittorio dies. The sale doesn't happen. There's two million outstanding. That's why we're here, Tommy. For two million outstanding."

I fixed him with my gaze. "Vittorio left me the house and some stocks. That's it. I don't know anything about two million outstanding."

Fortunato smiled at me, but his eyes said something very different. "It's not a satisfactory answer, kid."

"I can't help that."

"It's a debt, Tommy. It's got to be paid. We been instructed to take this house as down payment."

A really good beating, one that would leave me with missing teeth and blood in my bowel movements, was their next move. It saves time and makes the point. They didn't have the patience for long discussion. And why should they? They knew what worked.

In preparation for this, Fortunato eased his chair back. Clemente was reaching for something in his pants pocket. "Tommy, I understand it's a shock, but we can work it out."

The shock was going to be theirs. I shoved the table into their laps, spilling them off their chairs into some large prickly pear cactus plants. The prickly pear has given many millions of years to its defense. Supplementing its large spines are tiny clusters of much smaller spines. They're the most fiendish part because they look as innocent as peach fuzz, but they go into you by the hundreds, carpeting you with pain.

Fortunato and Clemente shot their hands out to break their fall. The little flowers from hell met their palms. The plant's main armament of three-inch bayonets went through their silk suits.

The last three seconds had put me into kill mode. My calming medication was totally out of my system, and my crazy raging self was now reporting for action. I wedged the hard edge of the table into their bellies. Fortunato puked up his most recent meal.

Clemente managed to squirm out from under the table, but I met him with a kick to the head that made the bones in his neck click—a nice audible adjustment to the top of his spinal column. He reached for his gun and stopped. Hundreds of little daggers in his palm and fingers were telling him that grabbing anything would only add to his pain.

I spun him around and held him facedown over the prickly pear. With guys like this, it doesn't pay to bounce them gently out the door. You've got to let them know you're twice the animal they are—more vicious and more deranged. "How'd you like a few in the eyeballs?"

I held him there, inches above the little daggers, until he got the message. Then I flipped him around and jammed him down. His back arched with pain and he just lay there, staring at the sky, unable to figure out which way to move.

I lifted the table off Fortunato and threw it aside like an empty match flap. It bounced off the trunk of an apricot tree and came apart.

Maybe the raging thing inside me comes from prehistoric ancestors, hunters who shoved spears into mastodons. Or maybe it's just infantile, brainless anger. Whatever it is and wherever it comes from, I could have snapped the backs of both these soldiers without a second thought.

Fortunato realized this. With a stripe of puke across his nice shirt, he lifted his hands. They were pincushions. "Take it easy," he managed to groan.

He knew the stage I had reached, knew what it was just to keep going with the baseball bat, the lead pipe, and turn somebody into pulp. He knew that I was right there, right at that edge, and that I didn't care whether he lived or died. "We . . . made a mistake."

I pulled the Beretta from behind my back, bent over, and put it against his head. "If you get out of here alive, it'll be the luckiest day of your life."

"Calm down, for Christ's fucking sake. It ain't worth it." Puke trickled from the corner of his mouth. "You've got neighbors."

"And you've got one minute to disappear. If you come back, the neighbors won't matter. Because listen to me . . ." I lifted both of them off the ground. With the adrenaline that was pumping through me, they came up with no effort, floating like balloons in the air. I shook them. ". . . because monastery or jail, it's all the same to me."

I set them down, yanked an arm on each of them up between their shoulder blades. And marched them toward their car. I opened the car door and shoved them both inside. "You'll have to go the hospital for those hands. Tell them you fell. They're used to it. It happens around here."

Fortunato worked the ignition with the tips of his fingers. He drove the same way, just the tips touching the wheel.

I was energized. I felt like going eleven more rounds. The signs just kept on coming. It was as if Vittorio had arranged them.

# 10

I opened Vittorio's desk again and read his correspondence with an entity known as *Promessa Solenne*—Sacred Promise. The letterhead showed offices in Rome, Chicago, and Phoenix. The letters showed that Vittorio had worked as their middleman. Church property had been paid for, amounts unspecified. Reading between the lines, I could tell that the deals had been sealed by a handshake. With cash.

Italian connections, handshakes and cash—it could have been run by Grandfather Primo himself. Sign nothing, and deal only in hard currency.

What else did I expect? Vittorio was Primo's son. He did business the old way. And the Vatican itself liked to deal in the old way. Omertà was the rule in Rome. Getting a look at the books of any church in Italy or America wasn't going to happen. The faithful put their money in an envelope every Sunday, and how much was nobody's business but God's and Bishop O'Malley's.

A little more reading between the lines showed that Vittorio was taking a taste out of every deal he brokered between Sacred Promise and the bishops. I was beginning to see how he had been able to afford this house. But had he ripped off Sacred Promise for two million bucks?

I found a letter from a grateful bishop, thanking Vittorio for his help in the painful matter of selling his church to Sacred Promise. It was followed by another letter, from the same bishop, dated much later.

*You told me Sacred Promise would preserve the architectural integrity of my church and see that it was used for a decent community purpose. Instead, they immediately sold the stained glass windows and anything that wasn't nailed down. After which they sold that glorious spiritual landmark to a nightclub developer. My church is now a disco bar. The DJ spins his records from God's altar, and there are fights every night. A month ago, somebody was murdered in the parking lot.*

Then the bishop's tone changed to something more practical.

*I have since learned Sacred Promise lowballed me on the price, then flipped the property for twice what they gave me. They doubled their money, thanks to you snowing me in regards to their intentions.*

His tone switched back to that of a brokenhearted pastor.

*Just so you know, Vittorio, my flock camped on the doorstep of our church, trying to save it. We held mass in the street outside, praying for a miracle. Now the street belongs to drug dealers. Inside, it resembles Dante's inferno. It's all on you, Father. May God forgive you.*

I found Vittorio's business records for flights to Sicily and Rome, but the people he saw were identified as Mr. X, Mr. Y, Mr. Z—that was all. The same was true of his meetings with the princes of the Church: Cardinal X, Archbishop Y. Omertà in action.

As a teenager, I had been to the Vatican with Vittorio. He said he wanted me to see "the life." Even through my teenage haze, I had seen how Father Vittorio got respect from those above him in the church hierarchy. Except for the black cassocks and crosses, I might have been listening to corporate CEOs. These priests lived in luxurious apartments and villas, and their tastes ran to the ornate.

On that trip, I also met a civilian. He had laughed with us, tousled my hair, called me "Young Monster." I later learned he was a Mafia financial lord who handled the Vatican's investments. He died in prison, poisoned shortly after he got there, to keep him from talking about what he knew concerning the investments of Holy Mother Church.

Now Vittorio was gone, but he'd left some dirty business for me to sort out. And under a loose floorboard in the laundry room, I found an AK-47 with a fifty-round mag.

So he'd been expecting company.

I called Dominic. He answered with a growl, but hearing my voice, he got cheerful. "Cousin, what's up?"

"A pair of *paisanos* visited me. They work for an outfit called Sacred Promise. It buys up church real estate and flips it. Vittorio was their middleman. The faithful get snowed in the process, and that was Vittorio's contribution. He did the snowing. The *paisanos* say he held back two million dollars for himself."

"That old devil." There was admiration in Dominic's voice.

"I need to know if Sacred Promise is protected by anybody. The two soldiers came here acting like they could squash me without repercussions. Either they don't know about our family, or they don't care."

"Names?"

"Fortunato and Clemente. That's all I know."

He pondered in silence for a few moments. "Why didn't Vittorio tip you off to where the two mill is stashed? You're the heir."

"There's a whole hell of a lot we don't know about our dear Uncle Vittorio."

"Maybe he expected you to figure it out."

"I hope I can."

"All right. Hang tight, and I'll get back to you."

"How's business?"

"I'm pouring lots of concrete."

"I thought housing starts were slow."

"I'm pouring for the city. We put the mayor in office, and he hasn't forgotten it."

"Who's 'we'?"

"Just me and some friends. Matter of fact, I'll be talking to one of them about your *paisanos*."

"Thanks for your help, Dominic."

"What I can do, I'll do." It was the same rough style he always had, but his affection had come through the line. I felt it right down to my shoes. He would always be there for me.

I spent the day prowling the house. Nothing else turned up. At seven o'clock, the door chimes sounded. Through the side window, I saw a voluptuous redhead who had been at Vittorio's funeral service. I gazed at her for a moment through the glass. A more perfect argument against the monastic life couldn't be made. At the funeral, I'd been able to follow my vow of celibacy and look away. There was no looking away now. Even through the glass, I felt her fire.

I opened the door. Her wavy red hair was sculpted loosely around her face. Her curves were accented by cowgirl-style shirt and jeans, and she had the milk-white skin of a natural redhead.

"I hope we're not barging in. We were friends of Vittorio's."

With her was a suntanned little brunette, who held out her hand. "We loved your uncle. He was as real as a bowl of grits. I'm Cheyenne." She had a twanging western accent, but her long, plain-black dress made her look as if she belonged in a convent—an image helped by a bad hairdo chopped off straight across her brow and chopped once again just below her ears, resembling a nun's stiff headdress.

The redhead introduced herself as Sally. Her western accent was softer than Cheyenne's. Everything about her was softer. After a bit of choreography inside the front door, I pointed them to the living room. The minute they stepped into it, they turned toward the high window framing the mountain. Cheyenne said, "You don't turn your back on that sucker."

Sally said, "We used to go with your uncle to Apache ceremonies around here. There's one tomorrow at sunrise, and we thought maybe you'd like to go."

Cheyenne added, "Prayers for the dead are part of it, white men included. I bet Vittorio will be tuned in." She smiled, and I noticed how deep was the blue of her eyes.

Sunrise ceremonies had been a regular part of my life for the past five years. *And if Sally is going*, said the little devil jamming open the door to the monk's cell in my soul, *you'll want to be there.*

Sally said, in her gentler version of Cheyenne's twang, "We know this is a tough time for you."

There was no enticement in her face, no come-on—nothing to feed my devil except for the fire of her hair, and her unmistakable voluptuousness. "We'll be your support group," she added with a kindness unconnected to her sexual allure. I had the feeling Sally was not looking for a man. So either she had one or she and Cheyenne were a couple. Then Cheyenne cleared up that last point.

"My husband will come along so you won't be overwhelmed by female energy."

But I already had been. I asked if they wanted a drink.

"Got any beer in a boot?" Cheyenne asked.

"Best I can do is a bottle."

"Just kidding. We've got a seminar to get to. We'll come by for you at five tomorrow morning."

At the door, Sally gave me more of her kindly smile. Vittorio's yellow porch light spilled over her, tinting the soft red waves of her hair.

After polite goodbyes, I closed the door and returned to the living room. Sitting in Vittorio's house, it was hard to refute his view of me. Priests are trained to spot mistaken vocations, because those who suffer from illusions of spirituality are disruptive to those with a real calling. But shedding monastic life was painful. I'd once seen a seagull drop a clam from fifty feet in the air to crack it open on the rocks below. I felt my own shell cracking and my soul exposed. If I had secreted my shell out of vain hopes and fears, losing it still wasn't easy. I had loved my small cell and the quiet reflection I'd performed within it. I put the CD of the Benedictines into Vittorio's player. When the perfectly blended voices of the monks broke over me, I had to stifle the cry in my heart.

"You set me up, but for what?" I asked the shadow of Vittorio's soul still lingering in this house he'd given me. For the first time, I felt the full weight of his priestly power. There's no other word for it when you feel an invisible hand working to arrange its version of your identity.

# 10

I heard a pack rat burrowing through the bushes. The sound was small and furtive, and it told me I hadn't seen the last of Clemente and Fortunato. Those rats would be coming back.

It was the hour before dawn, and I was standing in front of the house. The pack rat found his hole, and there weren't any other sounds until a half-ton truck rounded the corner. Its headlights swung toward me, and Cheyenne lowered the passenger window. The driver, a man, was in shadow. I got into the cramped back seat beside Sally.

Cheyenne's husband, introduced as Dez, short for Desmond, was at the wheel. He was a lanky, soft-spoken cowboy who, I learned, gave Jeep tours for tourists, taking them as far into the canyons as their money could pay for. Now he drove us along Thunderbird Road. The houses were dark, and the streets equally so. The town of Paloma isn't interested in lighting itself up like Phoenix.

The truck's headlights picked up what appeared to be a group of wild pigs trotting determinedly across the road. "Javelinas," said Cheyenne. "They look cute, but they crowded a gal I know off the edge of a cliff."

We turned onto Magic Canyon Road. There were a few expensive houses along the way, and then a wrought iron security gate. "A couple of movie stars own in there," said Sally. "As the Chamber of Commerce says, God made the Grand Canyon, but he lives in Paloma."

We crossed a dry riverbed and wound along beside it for several miles.

There were no houses now. We were in wild desert country. And then, as if to refute this, a sentry gatehouse appeared ahead of us.

"Magic Resort is the most exclusive resort in America," said Cheyenne, "and they built it right smack on sacred Apache ground."

"How did they get away with that?"

"I don't know, but it must piss off old Geronimo."

I could feel Sally's heat in the darkness, the red from her hair lighting me up. My vow of celibacy felt like a spent force. I caught Dez checking us out in his rearview mirror. As his eyes met mine, he seemed to be sympathizing with the dilemma of a fellow male sitting next to a blaze of female fire.

A security guard leaned out of the gatehouse. Dez said, "We're here for the ceremony."

"You know the way?"

"We do."

We passed another uniformed security guard watching over small streets that wound through the resort. Large pueblo-style houses stood on terraces cut out of the mountain.

I could see other cars parking ahead of us, their headlights shining into mesquite and juniper trees. Girls in tribal costume climbed out of a pickup. Their skirts and blouses danced with long colored fringe.

"Follow the fringe," said Cheyenne.

We followed them through the darkness, toward a bonfire. The tribe had been allotted a small clearing at the far edge of the resort property. A chain-link fence snaked its way through the nearby trees—a reminder that the land was now owned and guarded by new tenants. A shadowy figure turned our way, and I saw the high cheekbones of an Apache male under the brim of a cowboy hat. The dark canyon and this gathering were his, not mine. I didn't feel comfortable as a spectator. I was here on ground not sacred to me. Magic Resort hired guys like me to work security, to protect *their* sacred ground.

"Fancy meeting you here," said a woman coming up alongside me. "Regina Silver Hawk," she whispered, as if sharing a secret. It was the practicing intuitive from the restaurant. I returned her greeting and she squeezed my hand. Continuing in a whisper, she said, "The spirits are very strong here." She gave my hand another squeeze and moved on.

"You don't waste much time," said Sally.

I tried to clarify my position regarding Regina Silver Hawk. "I was at the Indian restaurant, and she told me about structured water."

"I'll bet she did."

The bonfire was dry desert wood, crackling loudly. The faces of the elders were another product of the desert, leathery and lined. I saw more high cheekbones and straight, thin lips.

The desert doesn't hold its heat, and the temperature had fallen dramatically during the night. Many of the women were wrapped in blankets. The young girls were braving the cold to show off their costumes. Sally, in tight blue jeans and a fringed leather jacket, looked every inch the well-rounded cowboy sweetheart. She took a place close to the fire, and I stepped in beside her.

Poles were being twisted into the ground to mark off the sacred space of the ceremony. One pole held a large crucifix of twisted mesquite wood. Sally saw me looking at it. "You've got a place at the table."

Men carrying drums crossed in front of us and sat on a bench facing the fire. They were all Apache elders in cowboy hats.

We waited as the circle filled out. People shifted from foot to foot, keeping circulation going against the cold. Finally, one of the older women called out, "We're freezing here, Luther. Let's get started."

The medicine man stepped into the firelight, apologized for letting people get cold, and gave a blessing in Apache. He continued in English, thanking everyone for coming, and reminding them that in these canyons the Apache savior was born long ago.

He gestured toward the unseen cliffs above us. "They are the red stone people. They stand for millions of years. We come here to listen to them. You can cure a lot of stuff out here. But you have to walk in sobriety so you can feel the spirits blessing you."

All I could feel were the spirits of the two goons I had shoved into the cactus. They were still in bed at this hour, dreaming of revenge.

"Look at those little sparks from the fire. That's the way of the spark, to fly up and dance. That's our dance too. We fly up and dance."

Primo would have wasted the goons and danced on their dead bodies.

I had stopped before the job was done. It was the difference between my grandfather and me.

I watched the sparks and wondered why Vittorio had come to these ceremonies. He wasn't like this medicine man, filled with concern for his people. Vittorio was an operator in a turned-around collar.

The practicing intuitive piped up with a question for the medicine man. "Would you talk a little bit about the vortexes in the canyon?"

He looked at her in silence for a moment, then said, "We know nothing about a vortex. That was invented by your people."

The older woman called out again, "That's enough, Luther. We're freezing."

"Okay, I'm done. We'll get to the prayers and drum songs. But first, I asked one of our Tribal Council members to add a few words. Bob, why don't you come forward?"

A middle-aged man moved into the firelight, pushed back the brim of his hat, and stared into the fire for a few moments.

Then he looked up. "I thought a lot about what I was going to say here this morning. And I couldn't come up with anything." And he stepped back into the darkness, leaving me to marvel at his honesty. If a politician had said that, it would have been the end of his career.

The drums sprang to life. The rhythm was simple. The elders chanted, their sharp cries punctuating each crescendo. It was the chanting of warriors, and I realized I had no business taking Eufexor to quiet my warrior's heart— not with Clemente and Fortunato coming after me. I wouldn't be renewing my prescription.

Women around the bonfire were swaying, long black braids swinging beside huge earrings decorated with feathers. I noticed a good-looking young white man moving to the beat in a peculiar way, jerky and uncoordinated, as if he were being pulled on strings by someone sitting above on a canyon ledge.

Cheyenne said, "Beautiful and cracked. He's loaded with alien implants. That's what gives him that mechanical look."

Dez said to me, "Cheyenne and Sally read energy. A man's gotta watch his thoughts around them."

"Can't cain't can't be done, hon," said Cheyenne.

The chanting lasted until the first light of dawn broke the spell. The fire was put out, the drums were packed up, and we all went to long folding tables, where coffee and doughnuts were served.

"Lord," said Sally, "the only thing'll ever beat the Apaches are these doughnuts. They go right to my backside."

Luther, the medicine man, came over to us. His quiet formality had its roots in warrior diplomacy. He was from a race that had been stunned in battle, but below the surface something was in readiness. I had reason to feel the same way.

"I'm glad you could make it," he said to Cheyenne.

"We appreciate you letting us share your fire."

"I been coming here since I was a boy."

"How do you feel about the resort?"

He looked through the trees, toward the luxury dwellings. "It's our sorrow."

Cheyenne opened her fanny pack. "Got this for you." She handed him a plastic bag.

He extracted a handful of black roots and examined them respectfully. "Thank you."

"Only reason I found them was you showed me how to look."

He put the bag in his jacket. "I'll say so long, then." Before he walked away, his gaze swept over me—the hard and serious gaze of a medicine man. "You're riding a big horse," he said. "Make sure it doesn't throw you."

The sun was rising, and I felt the way I always feel at dawn: that in a senseless fight, I had stolen the sunrise from another man's life.

"You're in a black hole, hon," said Cheyenne.

I looked at Dez. "She *does* read minds."

"I warned you."

Sally asked if I missed the monastery.

"Sure he does," said Cheyenne, glancing at Sally, and I saw something like a plan in their eyes concerning me.

The tables were being folded up, and Dez and I helped the Apache men load them into pickup trucks headed back to the reservation. Dez said, "What Cheyenne does is over my head. But I've seen her help people."

He shifted gears and added, "I don't know what your plans are, partner, but Sally's not looking for an alpha dog, which is sure what you are."

"So what is she looking for?"

"Damned if I know. But she's a wanderer. Has a sweet little trailer she drags around the country with her."

The four of us climbed into the truck and followed other vehicles out past the gatehouse to the main road. Sally pointed to a small buck grazing in the desert brush.

"Deer antler is good medicine for a man," said Cheyenne.

"Get me some, why don't you?" Dez asked.

"Not while you're toting those pretty tourist gals around in your Jeep. We could lose you for days."

As we climbed out of the canyon, Sally started humming to herself, and when I looked at her my little devil said, don't fight it, brother; it's good for you.

I looked away. The habit of ignoring female beauty was still with me.

When we pulled up at Vittorio's house, Cheyenne opened her fanny pack. "You've got some Mexican microbes using you as their dinner plate. Take two of these tonight and two more tomorrow morning." She handed me a box of worm pills for puppies.

I waited until they drove off before tossing the puppy pills. I don't want anybody screwing around with my Mexican worms.

**11**

I was jogging around Eagle Rock when Dominic's call came.

"You were visited by Fortunato Fabiocchi and Clemente Presto. They're muscle guys working for the guy running Sacred Promise, one Nico Bottazzi."

"Is he connected?"

"Not to the Mafia."

"To somebody else?"

"His brother is a bishop in the Vatican. So that gives Nico clout in his chosen field, which is screwing the church in real estate deals. We're talking hundreds of millions. He drops his brother's name, and people think he speaks for Rome."

"What's your source for this?"

"My union buddies. Specifically, Plasterers and Cement Masons International."

"What do you guys have to do with Rome?"

"We built the churches, cousin. And now we're rebuilding them, into whatever the fuck you want. Or I should say into whatever Nico wants. He made a fortune doing it in Italy, and now he's doing it here. He moves around, but right now he's working out of Phoenix."

"And what does his brother do for the Vatican?"

"Wait a second. If I can read my own handwriting . . . I traced it in cement with my finger . . . Bishop Bottazzi runs the Pontifical Council for Culture. Visual arts, music, shit like that. He's probably the son of a bitch who likes folk singing during the mass."

"So Bishop Bottazzi is a big wheel."

"His Mercedes has license plates that say *Città del Vaticano*. He can drive on the sidewalk if he wants to. Give him a ticket, and you spend time in purgatory."

I was sitting on a red boulder, watching some parents trying to inspire their bored teenagers to admire the scenery, but the kids would rather be doing what I was doing, talking on a tiny device with their friends. "I'm going to have to pay a call on Nico."

"You're pissed, right?"

"I am since you threw my anger medicine away."

"I'm basically satisfied with the way things are going. You're out of the monastery less than a week and you're beating the crap out of people."

"They started it."

"Whatever. The point is, you've always had a taste for the action."

"That's not what this is about."

"Actually, you're right. I'll tell you what it's about——"

A man was being pushed along in a wheelchair in front of me, the wheels crunching the stone. He wasn't looking at the mountain. He wasn't looking at anything. He was wondering what had happened to his life. His wife was pushing the wheelchair, talking to him as if he might be listening, but he wasn't.

"What it's about, Tommy, is the code of the vendetta. It's our family tradition. Somebody fucks with you, and the code kicks in. Never allow the slightest insult to go unavenged."

When I went into the monastery, I knew I belonged there, not for religious purposes but to quell this genetically bestowed blessing. "Can you arrange the sit-down?"

"I can."

"How soon?"

"I can set it up fast. But Nico comes out of a very decadent culture."

"What are you, a sociologist?"

"Romans have seen everything, cousin. Two thousand years of corruption is in their blood. It gives them a very different outlook on life."

# 12

I wore Vittorio's Beretta all the time now, in a shoulder holster under my jacket. I wore it to a building that rented office space to an acupuncturist, a chiropractor, and a massage therapist. Clemente and Fortunato could show up anywhere. Primo had offed an enemy in a pet shop *because he sang like a canary*.

I stood outside the building with Dez. He said, "Cheyenne rents the back room for her meetings. She'll be glad you came. You made quite an impression on her at that Apache fire."

"I just stood there shivering my ass off."

"She said you paid close attention."

"To the Indian maidens, maybe. That's about it."

"I'm the same way. I go 'cause Cheyenne drags me. But hey, those Indian gals know how to sew beads on a dress and take it dancing."

He looked down the street. We were waiting for Sally, which was my reason for being here. My little devil had suggested I check her out again, that it couldn't hurt, that it would clarify my position regarding celibacy.

Dez was looking at the bulge under my thin nylon jacket. "Loaded for bear?"

"It gives me a comfortable feeling."

"I like a Colt revolver. All cowboys carry Colts, right?"

"The gun that won the West."

"That was the Peacemaker."

"And yours?"

"A Colt Python with a three-inch barrel. You can't hardly find one these days. It's a good size for Cheyenne."

A Jeep was heading our way. Sally parked and stepped out in her colorful cowboy boots. She was in her jeans and her fringed leather jacket. It hung open on a tight white T-shirt. When we went inside, she started chatting to me in a friendly way, and it would have been awkward not to sit beside her. The fire of her red hair was about eleven inches from my face. Her perfume was in my nose. And when she removed her leather jacket, arching her back and sliding it onto the chair, her white T-shirt filled with the outline of her bra. In the monastery, I had often prayed before a statue of the Virgin Mary, my eyes lowered to her marble toes. *Take your pick*, said my devil.

"Cheyenne's a great visionary," Sally murmured, her breath tickling my ear.

Cheyenne started the meeting by stating that those here for the first time might be in for an unpleasant dose of reality. She hadn't said three more sentences before an unpleasant dose of reality did hit me, though not the one she intended. If I hadn't been around Primo for most of my childhood, I might not have seen so quickly what she was. Primo had been good at finding people like Cheyenne. *They're everywhere, Tommy, and they're useful.*

She brought a troubled young woman to the front of the room and told her that an entity from another planet had implanted its code in her. Then, using Sally as an assistant, she went through the motions of removing the implanted code, which she referred to as noncorporal energy.

*Good hustlers believe in themselves, Tommy, right into their bones.*

I had seen an exorcism performed at a rural village in Mexico. The air in the room dropped twenty degrees, and I watched a human being rescued from torment. I have no idea what actually went on that day, but I knew what was going on with Cheyenne. She had found an urban myth perfectly suited to her theatrical ability.

The bliss in the woman's eyes as she returned to her seat was familiar to me, because the atmosphere in the Mexican monastery swarms with medieval beliefs. Cheyenne was producing that medieval atmosphere in a colorless back room in a mundane office building, which was quite an achievement. She spiced up her act with lurid details of alien sexuality, medical jargon, and snatches of country-and-western songs. When we were standing outside afterward, she said to me, "That was the simple version. The real truth is much deeper."

I was looking into her dark-blue eyes, and now I saw that the blue was flecked with bits of iridescent green that gave the impression of continuous change, like a mood ring. As Sally said, she was a visionary. But her real vision was of herself. Alien beings were just her prop.

Above us hung the huge desert night sky, in which you could easily imagine UFOs skimming along. If your imagination runs along these lines, it will thrive in Paloma. The stars seem closer—are certainly brighter—and the Milky Way streams overhead. Hurtling out of it come the aliens, heading our way, to impregnate women with their vile DNA.

The potential victims of this violation dispersed to their cars. Cheyenne said, "I need some Jack Daniel's," and we rode to a bar in uptown Paloma. When we took our seats, Sally was close enough for me to smell her perfume again, but she was ignoring me. Instead, she was hanging on Cheyenne's assessment of the meeting.

Observing the conversation, I remembered how Primo used people like Cheyenne in city government, in state and federal agencies, on the police force, in unions, even in funeral parlors—wherever the skill set of the born hustler flourished. He drew no distinction between a bureaucrat helping him get a dicey construction job approved, and a grifter explaining how he lost his wallet, can you give him bus fare home.

And Sally had swallowed Cheyenne's hustle, so if I was going to make any time with her, I'd have to keep my opinion about Cheyenne to myself. Dez had swallowed it, too, but at that moment he'd had enough of aliens for one evening.

"Martini and me are going out to the balcony."

We made our way to a balcony facing the red rock mountains. On the street below us, a horse-drawn tourist carriage rolled by.

Dez said, "I miss horses."

"You can't have one here?"

"The price of hay in desert country is out of sight. I'd be broke in a month."

He paused to gaze at the carriage rolling by. Then he seemed to fall back into the theme of the meeting. "I've been a person without virtue for much of my life." He said this in the odd biblical style rural people sometimes fall into. "I hung out with a rough crowd in Wyoming. Herded cattle all day and got drunk every night. Cheyenne made me see what a slime dog I was. She says there's UFO critters called alien grays. Says they latched on to me when I was a kid, and never let go."

"And what do you think?"

"Hell, I don't know. I sure don't feel like so much of a slime dog anymore." He tipped his glass and drank deeply, a line of foam remaining on his lip until he wiped it off with the back of his hand. "I can come home feeling all slimed up, and Cheyenne works on me and I feel better. And that's good enough. I don't need to get fancy about it."

A shooting star crossed the heavens. Dust and rock falling into the earth's atmosphere and burning up. Nobody at the helm.

Dez said, "Sally and Cheyenne are on a mission. I just want to develop virtue."

I had tried it myself in a Catholic monastery. I'd been out only a week, and virtue was eluding me.

"About once a month I get slimed," Dez continued, studying the foam on his glass of beer. "Cheyenne says because of my old habits, I'm still vulnerable to slime. It's like being an alcoholic, I guess."

He raised his glass. "At least I'm no longer a drunk. Moderation in all things, right?"

He sipped in moderation, and I did the same. When I was a bouncer, I watched other people getting loaded, studied the slow progression to belligerence. I can pretty much see the fights a man has had. They're written in his eyes, voice, and manner. Dez was the kind who just goes quiet. And then watch out. He was the wiry type who hits fast and accurately.

"So," he asked, "the laid-back town of Paloma treating you all right so far?"

"No complaints."

"Plenty of women around. Guess you noticed."

"It's hard to miss."

"Yessir, there are some real beauties in these parts." A distant look came into his eyes, and it wasn't UFOs he was seeing. "The point is, Sally's not the only one."

"I haven't given up yet."

"I'll tell you what I think, I think she's right next door to a nun."

"She doesn't dress like one. Those jeans couldn't get any tighter."

"Another of life's mysteries, old buddy."

We clinked glasses, and on that note, we rejoined Sally and Cheyenne. Cheyenne scrutinized us. "What do men talk about when they're alone?"

Dez slipped into the chair beside her. "Mystery women and horses."

"Stick to the horses, Dez; the other part's too deep for you."

I'd sat where I could watch the door. Every time it opened, I imagined Clemente and Fortunato coming through. It's not a healthy way to live. Primo never went anywhere without muscle around him, and he still had chronic indigestion.

Three women walked into the bar, and with them was an imitation of Christ, with long blond hair and a beard to match. Sally frowned at his entrance, and Cheyenne murmured, "We've got us a spiritual circus here in Paloma. Guess you're getting the picture."

"The field seems crowded."

"Yeah, we're thick on the ground. A stranger comes into town, and before the hour is out, ladies are following him around."

"I must have flubbed my entrance."

"What do you mean? Sally and I are hanging on your every word." Her eyes shone. She had an endless supply of glimmer. But I'd heard a hundred monks chanting in rainbows of light coming through a rose window. Their devotion, inside which I had found a place, was still sounding in my soul, their voices slow to fade. Cheyenne's song-and-dance about entities from another planet couldn't compete with that, and when she looked at me she knew it.

But I caught that other look in her eyes then, the one that said she had plans regarding me. I felt someone walking on my grave. And it wasn't Clemente and Fortunato.

# 13

My next attempt to hang out with Sally cost me twenty-five bucks. But she picked me up in her Jeep. "Why do you always wear a gun?" she asked as I got in. "I thought you were a monk."

"I'm concerned about religious intolerance."

She drove us to Paloma's five-star hotel. The National UFO Convention had ended. When we entered the conference center, we were given a program from the Universal Psychical Research Foundation.

The program explained that the medium had been discovered in a remote mountainous region of China and that he incarnated Judge Bao Gong, who lived a thousand years ago and was known for his great acumen in rooting out evil. For two hundred bucks, we could have a private consultation with him. The place was packed, including a contingent of Chinese from Phoenix.

To my surprise, the medium was a teenager. He sat down behind a long table, with rice paper, ink pad, and a woodblock in front of him.

He was joined by a translator who sat beside him. The medium let his gaze travel slowly over the audience. In a soft, youthful voice, he greeted us in Chinese. Then he lowered his eyes. His body jumped as if zapped by a Taser.

The voice that came next was not that of a teenager, but the gruff guttural tones of an older man supremely confident of his authority. He pointed to a Chinese woman in the audience.

She came forward, bowed, and asked her question in Chinese. The judge snapped out an answer in Chinese, and the woman covered her face with her hands, muffling a sob. The judge inked his woodblock and brought it down onto a sheet of rice paper with a resounding thump. The seal of Judge Bao.

He handed the sheet of paper to the woman. She took it dully, and when she turned toward us, tears were rolling down her cheeks.

The translator said, "The matter was deeply personal. I don't feel right in translating the exchange you've just seen."

That we were in the dark about what happened didn't matter. The judge had shattered the woman before our eyes. A few moments later, I heard her leaving.

Two Chinese men dragged a young man into the room. He was growling savagely, shaking his head back and forth, with spittle flying from his lips.

When he saw the judge, he let out a howl. The judge pointed a finger. A single word came out of him like a gunshot. The young man went limp. The judge brought his woodblock down. Case closed.

The young man appeared dazed for a moment but then began conversing normally with his astonished escorts. They no longer had to restrain him. If it was an exorcism, it was the fastest anyone had ever seen.

Cheyenne asked about "dark forces intruding into our dimension." The judge went silent for a long time as he stared at her. The skin of his forehead seemed to move independently, like a cloth being wrinkled by an invisible hand that drew it downward into a severe frown.

Finally, he gestured upward, the loose black sleeve falling down his arm as he spoke. His translator repeated the words in English. "The dark force is not up there. Not in the sky."

The judge gestured again, pointing to the floor. "It's not down there, either, in the earth."

The judge pointed at Cheyenne and smashed his woodblock down on the rice paper. "The Demon Country is in *you*."

After the meeting ended, we stood around outside. Cheyenne said, "He was covered in alien drains, every kind you can imagine. That's what happens to mediums—they get trashed. Comes of opening yourself up that way. The gift of mediumship is no gift worth having."

Dez asked, "What did he mean saying the Demon Country is in you?"

"He saw how much negativity I have to transmute every day."

Whatever he was, Judge Bao was no fool. Cheyenne was on the hustle, and he had called her on it. I looked at her, and the look she gave me back was like a cat's—gleaming with plans for the mice of the world.

Sally had lingered around inside, wanting to talk to the translator. When she joined us, she said, "That Chinese woman? The judge told her that her husband had taken a second wife."

Cheyenne looked at Dez. "You try that, cowboy, and I won't need a medium."

"Try what?"

"A second wife."

"Jesus, Cheyenne, one of you is more than enough."

"It better be."

Sally drove me back to Vittorio's house and parked with the engine still running. By this time, I knew that my life as a monk was over. I wanted this woman.

Staring straight out through the windshield, she said, "I'm all in with Cheyenne. That's my life. I don't want to string you along."

"I didn't think you were."

"You just got out of a monastery. You'd fall for anything that jiggles when it walks."

She reached her hand out to me and rested her fingers lightly on my wrist. "I hope you get into the work Cheyenne is doing. Then you and I can be real good friends." She leaned over and kissed me on the cheek. "You have great energy."

I watched her drive away, and male pride being what it is, I felt I was making progress.

As I went through my front door, I heard a noise at the back door. I took out the Beretta and moved silently through the house. The town of Paloma has a very low crime rate. Break-ins are rare. I didn't think I was dealing with a garden-variety burglar. It felt like something very different. Then I heard the back door closing.

I ran toward it but couldn't get it open. The intruder had wedged something against it from the outside. I pushed hard, moving a porch chair that was blocking the door. By the time I circled the backyard, he was already running up a hiking trail on the face of Storm Mountain.

I ran after him, and as I reached the trailhead, a bullet whined past me. I dived off the trail, driving cactus spines into my chest. He fired twice more, and as I rolled away from the shots, I landed in more cactus. They went through my shirt, into my back.

When I resumed the chase, my back and chest felt as if they had just been tattooed with a red-hot needle, and he was far ahead of me again. He was trying to lose himself in darkness, but the mountain had been a mistake. He had to stick to the narrow trail or he'd be in the cactus too.

I put the Beretta away. I didn't want to kill him. I wanted to know who sent him. But guys my size don't travel fast, and I didn't get close to him again until we were high up on the mountainside. And by that time, he needed his flashlight to navigate the twisting trail. Each time he switched it on, I knew where he was. And my two hundred pounds sliding on loose rock told him where *I* was.

Another bullet sailed past me, forcing me down into the cactus for further tattooing. I waited until I saw his flashlight moving again, then moved forward. Without a flashlight of my own, I had no idea which way the trail was going to twist. All I knew was that it angled steeply upward and I had to move slowly, feeling my way along the curving face of the mountain. He wasn't using his flashlight now, and I had no idea of the distance between us. I found out. He hadn't moved at all. As I felt my way around the curving trail, he was waiting, aiming at me with both hands. But his arms tilted suddenly upward. The gun fired wildly, I heard his cry, and he fell out of sight.

I worked my way slowly to where he'd been standing, and saw what had happened: heavy rain had weakened the trail, and the frail desert rock beneath it had given way. The flashlight was still shining below, illuminating the base of the cliff. The beam didn't move.

I backed up until I found what I needed: mesquite tree roots that the rain had exposed in the cliff face. They formed a crude ladder down. Clutching them, I worked my way to him.

He lay spread-eagle on a bed of swords. The sharp spines of an agave had gone through his chest and neck. He was hemorrhaging from the mouth, blowing bubbles from his lips like a fish out of water. His body was twitching, his lungs trying to draw in air, but his windpipe was blocked. It was too late to ask him who sent him. He had a sword through his vocal cords.

He bled out or suffocated. It didn't take long.

I saw he was only a kid, and from his hair and complexion I thought he was probably Mexican. And all I could think was, I should have let him go, let him run, go free. What was so important in my house that I needed this? Here was another young man dead at my feet. It felt like a family curse, that when you come from violence it follows you, arranging circumstances that call for blood.

I lifted out his wallet and checked his driver's license.

GOBIERNO DEL DISTRITO FEDERAL

LICENSIA PARA CONDUCIR

Mexican but an obvious fake. The bar code looked as if it had been cut out and pasted in. But the photograph matched, as a brief check of his dead face showed. Name, Roberto Vargas. Common enough, telling me nothing.

His gun had landed a few feet away from him. I took it and trod carefully until I found the path again. Without the gun, he was a hiker who had missed his step.

# 14

When I got back to my house, I could hardly walk. My legs felt stitched together, and I couldn't sit down. Someone had to pull all these needles out of me, and I didn't want to go to the emergency room, not with a dead body about to be found not far from my house. I called Sally. She didn't ask any questions, just said she'd be right over.

While waiting for her, I went to the rear of the house and found that the back door lock had been expertly picked. So young Roberto Vargas had been trained, but this didn't explain what he'd been looking for or who had sent him. I shuffled through the house, cactus needles pulling on my skin. I checked around. Valuables were where they belonged. He hadn't had time to pinch anything. He died for nothing.

When Sally's car pulled up, I stowed the young man's gun and wallet under Vittorio's loose floorboard and shuffled to the door. I let Sally in and led the way into the living room, where I took off my shirt and trousers.

"Oh my Lord . . ." She came closer, looking me up and down. "You've got to go to the emergency room."

"No. No doctors."

"If we don't do this right, you'll get an infection." She was already calling Cheyenne. "I'm at Martini's. He had a run-in with a cactus."

After finishing the call, she went at me with a pair of tweezers, not once asking how I'd gotten into a cactus patch. In her world, bad things could always be traced back to the baleful influence of unseen entities. One of them must have tripped me.

"The big needles are easy. It's these little ones. They disappear under the skin and fester up."

When I was chasing Roberto Vargas, adrenaline and endorphins had allowed me to crawl over the cactus without feeling it. I felt it now.

When Cheyenne arrived, she looked me over quickly. "We got us a damn porcupine." She handed me a thermos. "Drink this."

It was a foul brew, but I got it down and she went to work on me with her own tweezers. Like Sally, she didn't ask how I had done this to myself. Her comment was, "Needles are vestigial leaves. You have to admit, the cactus family is pretty smart."

My respect for the cactus family was immeasurably greater at this moment.

They worked diligently, sometimes standing, sometimes kneeling as they slowly circled me with their tweezers. I stared at Storm Mountain, trying to maintain my dignity while they joked about my predicament. But they were patient, took no breaks, and after two hours they were still running their fingers over me, searching for hidden needles. Finally, Cheyenne said, "I think he's clear." She opened a jar of green goo. "It's mostly comfrey. But, of course, it also has a few secret ingredients to make you my slave."

She spread it over my chest and legs. "We'll let that sink in. How about a beer?"

She and Sally sat on the couch drinking beer and I remained standing. Cheyenne said, "The cactus god has initiated you."

The god had also initiated Roberto Vargas and was the last thing he had seen on this earth. I chanted quietly, *Media Vita in Morte Sumus*, in the midst of life, we are in death.

And here was Sally, robustly alive and finally paying some attention to me. Every inch of my flesh felt swollen and inflamed, but so what? Sally was in tender-sympathy mode. And then I found myself remembering a time in college when I ruptured myself in the weight room. Hernia repair is a simple operation. After stitching me up, the surgeon told me to go home and rest for a week until my stitches healed. My girlfriend drove me back to my apartment and we had sex, during which all my stitches popped, and she had to drive me back to the hospital to get sewn up again.

When Sally finished her beer, I didn't try to detain her. I went to bed alone, wondering whether I'd lost my edge.

# 15

The next morning, to induce sobriety, I raked small stones in the back-yard. As the ground evened out, the teeth of the rake created uniform lines that suggested harmonious existence might just be possible. The twelve o'clock news suggested otherwise. A body had been found on Storm Mountain—"that of a man whose identity has not yet been released."

And it wasn't going to be released, because I had his ID under my floor-board. If he had a family, they were never going to see him again. But they would know the business he was in and that it entailed risks. The question was whether he'd been working for Sacred Promise. If so, I could expect more visitors.

Like the cactus, all I could do was wait.

I finished raking the garden, then ran through some karate forms. It was the first time I had done them since coming to Paloma. It made me feel close to the desert predators who must fight to live—coyotes, badgers, rattlesnakes. Their form is always perfect. Better than mine, better than any man's.

I was in the middle of a form when I heard Cheyenne's truck pull up. Its door opened and closed, and she didn't bother going to my front door—just came around the side of the house. She moved lightly, and her footsteps barely made a sound on the gravel walkway. She stopped when she saw me and watched in silence as I moved through the second half of the form. Then she came toward me, her eyes running over me from head to foot. "You're clear of intrusive entities. Except for me, of course."

"You're not intruding."

She nodded toward Storm Mountain. "They found a body at the bottom of a cliff this morning."

"Yes, I heard. Must have lost his footing."

"It happens," she said.

"To someone you know, as I remember."

"That's right. The pigs pushed her off. You figure the pigs pushed him off?"

"It might have been the pigs. Or he might've been out of his mind on crystal meth."

"We had us a drug dealer in Wyoming. Lived right next door. And he had a big nasty dog with foam dripping from his jaws when he barked. Totally possessed by evil. There was a fence between his yard and ours, and he was always trying to get over it because he was intent on murder. One day he managed to get two paws over the top of the fence. His eyes were blazing with hate. I got our shotgun and blew him away. I saw the demon fly right out of him. Maybe there was a demon on Storm Mountain last night."

She wanted me to know she suspected my ass full of cactus had something to do with the dead man on Storm Mountain. But all she said was, "I just came by to check your wounds. Take off your shirt."

I took it off, and she ran her hands over my chest and back. Then she opened her fanny pack and took out the jar of green lotion. "You need some more of this. You've probably got some little ones still in you, and they can fester into little volcanoes. This will draw them out."

Her gentle touch contrasted with her tough-talking schoolmarm style. When she finished with my chest, she ordered me to take off my pants and applied the salve up and down my legs. "Let that soak in for a bit."

So we sat at the table in the backyard, with me in my underwear. She said, "You're big as a longhorn steer. What the hell did your mama feed you?"

"Meatballs."

"You should try buffalo burgers. Makes you brave in battle."

"I'm steering clear of battles."

"So what's all this punching and kicking I saw you doing?"

"It's just a hobby."

"It looked pretty damn serious to me." She straightened the hem of her long schoolmarm skirt. It hung just above the tips of some plain flat shoes. "I'm in rotten shape myself. No time for exercise."

"Busy hunting aliens?"

"Give me time, I'll make you a believer." The look of the three-card monte player was always in those dark-blue eyes. Her daily exercise was performing the fast shuffle. But unlike the Chinese medium, she wasn't filling the hotel conference room and charging believers twenty-five bucks a head. Maybe a small audience was all she needed. Or more likely, when she was better known in Paloma she would charge all that the traffic could bear.

"And while I've got you in your underwear, I'd like to ask you to slow down your romance with Sally."

"No problem there. She's made it pretty clear she's not interested in me."

"She's interested, all right, but she's in a fragile state. Her ex-husband was a real bastard, and she's not over him yet. I see deep unhealed wounds in her."

Sally was part of Cheyenne's medicine show—a big and beautiful woman helps draw the crowd into the tent. And to keep her in the tent, Cheyenne didn't want her focused on me.

She continued, "I don't want to stand in the way of true love, 'cause I think you and Sally are the perfect match, but timing is important in matters of the heart. Working with me helps her wounds heal, and if she starts falling for you, the demons will move in on her again."

I had no trouble acquiescing, because Sally would make up her own mind whether it was going to be me or demonology. "I'll keep my distance."

"Saying which, the gallant gentleman put on his pants." Cheyenne stood up, gave a yank at her skirt to straighten it, and walked back to her truck.

As I was putting the rake away, Dominic called and said I had a sit-down with Nico Bottazzi. He gave me a date and address and hung up. Our family never used long goodbyes.

# 16

The weapon Roberto Vargas had chosen or been given for his task was the Public Defender Ultra-Lite by Taurus, a perfect gun for your night table, accurate at twenty-one feet or less. It hadn't been up to the job of picking me off the mountainside. Vargas hadn't anticipated using it that way. Which told me they had sent the wrong guy. He had panicked, and instead of jumping over my fence into a labyrinth of backyards where he could easily have hidden himself, he headed for the mountain. That choice made me think he was a country kid, going toward what he knew.

Why would Sacred Promise send a hayseed to do a hit?

He hadn't scoped out my routines, had chosen his time badly, and had gotten himself caught. The only thing he did right was pick my lock. Nothing was forced. He knew how to manipulate the pins. And that made me think his normal profession was burglary. But burglars don't usually carry firearms, because it increases jail time if they're caught.

The pieces surrounding Roberto Vargas weren't fitting snugly together. The only thing that fit snugly was .45-caliber ammunition into his Ultra-Lite. I was loading it when the phone rang. When I answered, the woman on the other end identified herself as Beatrice. "We met briefly at your uncle's funeral. I hate to bother you at a time like this . . ."

She paused, and I could hear the sob stuck in her throat. "Sorry about that. It's just—golly, I don't even know how to say it. But I'd so like to talk to you about him."

I assumed there would be parishioners whom Vittorio had touched, who would be missing him and who wanted to sift the ashes of memory one last time. I had already reconciled myself to seeing them as part of my debt to Vittorio for all he'd given me. She named an hour around sunset and arrived in a Mini Cooper convertible.

I watched from the window as she removed the scarf from her head, along with her sunglasses. Her carefully made-up face was that of a middle-aged woman who had not said goodbye to the art of enchantment. I remembered her now, for she had come up to me after Vittorio's mass. She was petite, in a skirt shorter than the one she had worn at the funeral. It was a muted shade of red that matched the mountains. The skirt, blouse, hair, and nails gave the impression of exacting decisions on what was to be worn when and for whom.

"I remembered correctly," she said, looking up at me in the doorway. "You *are* about twice as big as I am."

"I've had chairs collapse under me, but fortunately, the furniture here is well made." I led her through the entranceway into the living room.

"You're the one who's well made, Tom. You don't mind if I call you Tom, do you? And you'll call me Trixie—it's much easier than Beatrice, and Trixie is what Vittorio always called me."

She sat down on the sofa facing me, knees primly together. Her ankles were a little swollen, or was it her shoes pinching her? They were on the flashy side, red sandals with four-inch heels. If they were too small for her, they preserved the look she was after, of the perfect little doll.

"Heavens, it's awful to be here without him." She looked back at me. "I'm sorry, I think I just insulted you."

"I feel the way you do. He should still be here."

I was sitting adjacent to her on the angled couches. The high living-room window was bringing us the twilight on Storm Mountain. She leaned forward. Her eyes were gray and large, but the corners were pulled a little tighter than nature had intended. "Vittorio and I were very close."

"That makes it tough, I know."

"We shared ever so much together." She had the remnant of a southern accent, lengthening her "O's," with a soft cadence, slightly breathy. "I mean, we appreciated the same things."

She gestured toward the high window, bracelets tinkling together. "He loved that mountain, and I used to say to him, 'Vittorio, it listens to every word.' Even the unspoken ones."

She ran her tongue over her upper lip, just the tip, as if tasting her lipstick. "Unspoken words speak louder, don't you think?"

I didn't know what to think. She reminded me of a bobcat I'd seen that morning. Walking through the backyard with a proprietary air, it suddenly stopped, sat down, and proceeded to wash its paws, perfectly comfortable so close to the house. And when it looked up, taking me in at the window, it registered cold indifference. And went on washing its paws in preparation for some soundless stalking.

Trixie's words came out slowly as she played with the memory of her Vittorio. "We'd often just sit here as the shadows slid across the mountain. And we let the darkness in. Not turning on the lights, I mean. It was so soothing to feel that darkness come in."

She crossed her legs, which were still good. She kept herself fit, but she was no athlete. There was something soft and idle about her that came out in her slow southern style.

"And we'd sit here and let that darkness wrap us up, until we were like a pair of old Navajos."

"You're not old."

"Only a young man would think that. Men my age know exactly how old I am, and that's too old." She looked at the ancient mountain as if feeling some kind of kinship with agelessness.

"Can I get you some tea? A beer? Anything?"

"Let's just sit here, Tom, and let the shadows come over us."

I and the shadows obliged, and the wrinkles on the face of Storm Mountain gradually lost definition, and Trixie's face underwent the same transformation. The coldness of her eyes was slowly veiled, the harsh lines of time on her brow softened. This hour was part of her plan. She was prettier now.

"I loved him, I guess that's no secret," she said and sighed. "Such an interesting man. So unusual. So worldly and at the same time, like a child. That's hard to resist."

By this time, I'd realized we weren't having a conversation. Trixie listened only to her own voice. She listened to you the way a bobcat listens, for opportunity. What wasn't opportune was ignored, like road traffic. Road traffic means nothing to the bobcat. They never get hit crossing the road. They figured that out long ago.

"The childlike part of him, which made him so lovable, was also a blind spot for him."

She put a hand to her hair, gently tracing a wave that tucked around her ear. "In spite of everything we had between us, he didn't seem to know what it would be like for me when he was gone. He lived in a sort of eternity. I suppose that's what the church does to you if you spend your whole life in it. I swear, sometimes when we sat here just like you and I are sitting now, he'd go so quiet and still, you'd think he was a statue. With that silver hair of his, it was like the statue of an angel."

Her hand went from her own hair to the corner of her eye. If a tear was falling, the shadows hid it, but the gesture sufficed. It was the semblance of crying. "I'm sorry, Tom. It's still very early since he left."

"I understand, Trixie." Though I didn't understand anything yet.

"We were *so* close. More than just friends. This is difficult . . ."

I waited. She let the shadows wrap her in a little more before she resumed. "He was a man with a man's need. I filled that need, if you know what I mean."

"You were intimate."

"Thank you, Tom, for putting it delicately. And wisely."

She pulled the hem of her skirt down primly again, as if to indicate that she did not offer intimacy freely. "We had a very special arrangement. Because of his position. You understand."

"Yes, I do."

"The arrangement included certain financial aspects. I don't know what else to call them."

She broke off. Again we sat in silence, until she said, "Even though he was retired, a priest can't really call his time his own. People were always after him for advice. I had to fit myself to his uncertain way of life. Can I put it that way? When he called, I'd come. But to do that, I had to be free. He said, I'll take care of business; you take care of me. So I gave up my job and devoted myself to him. Much of the time I just sat around waiting."

"What were the financial aspects?"

"He paid my expenses. Rent, food, car—everything. And I assumed— quite naturally, I think—that he would make sure I was to be taken care of when he passed. But you see, Tom, I forgot about the little boy, the irresponsible child who only thought about the moment. Our moments." Her voice seemed to choke up, and again her hand went to her eye. "Those . . . precious . . . moments . . ."

I recalled a line of porcelain figurines by that name, with teardrop eyes— cute little things like Trixie. I wondered whether she owned any.

"So here I am without a job. I used to sell real estate. I was quite good at it. The market is bad right now, and there's certainly no room for another realtor around here. We've got a town full of them. By the way, you aren't interested in selling this house, are you?"

I felt we needed some light. I turned on the one recessed in the adobe shelf that ran around the living room. A gentle light shone upward on the walls.

"Such a lovely house," she said. "Vittorio had very good taste for a man who'd lived in parish rectories for a good part of his life."

She looked back at me. "I have our precious moments, Tom. But that's all I have."

She touched a hand to her throat, then traced a line along her collarbone, as if remembering a necklace that had once been there.

"So, Tom, I'm going to risk my pride here."

Her fingers drifted down to her chest as if locating the exact place of her pride. She left her hand there, her little fingers spread wide as if in supplication, and then bowed her head and closed her eyes.

"If you can find a way to continue the arrangement I had with Vittorio, I'd be ever so grateful."

She kept silent for a bit, then opened her eyes and looked at me. "Of course, I wouldn't expect the arrangement to be as generous as when Vittorio was still alive. I'm not so silly as that. But as I said, he was part angel. I miss him terribly, and men my age are looking for younger women. They want rebirth. I'm just looking for grocery money."

"Trixie, you're a piece of work."

"I beg your pardon?"

"You never knew Vittorio."

As I switched on more lights, she pleaded, "Tom, please don't." As if too much light would injure her bloom.

She remained sitting where she was. I could see the machinery work-ing behind her eyes. She'd played this game before. I was five times her size, but she would be harder to handle than Mafia soldiers if I didn't get her out before she started crying rape or some other injured-woman accusation designed to make me want to bargain.

"Hit the road, Trixie."

I got up, walked to the door, and when I opened it I slammed it against the wall so hard it bounced back at me. I've escorted pissed-off women out of barrooms; startling sound effects go deeper with them than words. I think it must awaken archaic memory of nonverbal times in the cave. If you get in a shouting match with them, they'll tear you apart. They're much better at it. As the door hit the wall, Trixie came off the sofa as if it had exploded underneath her.

"Tom, don't do this." But she was walking toward me on her too-tight sandals. She really was cute as hell.

I slammed the door off the wall a second time, and it kept her moving. These were the crucial seconds. I couldn't let her get another game started. I'd been an idiot to let this one get going. No threat must be uttered, just sound effects. I kept banging the door repeatedly against the wall, like an army drumbeat.

She marched on past me, another game forming undoubtedly, but a man's home is his castle. What crazy people do in your yard is their busi-ness, not yours. Of course, Trixie was far from crazy.

"I'll get you for this," she hissed at me just before I slammed the door behind her.

I waited for the Mini's little power plant to fire up, and only when I heard those twin turbos carrying it away from me did I walk to the kitchen and pour myself a shot from Vittorio's plentiful liquor cabinet.

I raised my glass to him. "Vittorio, she made one mistake. Anybody who really knew you would never describe you as an angel."

# 17

So now I knew two women in the charming little town of Paloma, home of the vortex. I went to Cheyenne's next meeting, not to hear about unidentified flying objects but to see the clearly identified Sally, whose fringed cowboy shirt was worn loosely over a tight-fitting black T-shirt. Under my jacket, I was wearing Vittorio's Beretta. Tucked into my belt was Roberto Vargas's .45-caliber Public Defender. Unable to choose between them, I'd taken both, and I liked the feeling.

"Man is destined to be controlled by forces he doesn't understand." Cheyenne had moved up the success ladder and was holding her meeting in a new place—a carpeted circular room in a meditation center that had belonged to a venerated swami with an architectural flair. It was a beautiful building. Some walls were entirely of glass, looking out to the mountain. Highly polished structural beams formed a cathedral ceiling from which, according to Sally, had once dangled a giant brass mobile in the shape of a sacred Hindu syllable.

Small meditation chambers, each with a little barred window for the swami to check on his devotees' meditation, lined the curving wall.

A state-of-the-art kitchen, for which he had imported a five-star chef from Bombay, completed the swami's design. Wealthy followers had indulged him in this dream for several years.

Part one of his teaching had been that enlightened beings always had a large skull, housing a large brain where higher spiritual cognition could be given full play. Apparently, he'd had such a skull himself.

Part two of his teaching was that he could help you make up for having an average-size skull. When it was discovered that his wife in India had a very small skull (because she was only eight years old), pointed questions were asked. He left in a huff, taking with him his chef, whatever cash he could get his hands on, and the huge brass mobile.

To pay off the mortgage, his followers opened a gift shop on one floor and turned the rest of the building into a corporate retreat center. A pet groomer now washed poodles in what had been the swami's huge walk-in shower and bath, and local psychics like Cheyenne could rent his luxurious private theater. The seats were very comfortable.

Cheyenne was stalking around in her pilgrim skirt and unfortunate haircut, delivering her usual mix of science fragments and mystical buzzwords, loosely blended to explain the evolution of alien grays, how they'd managed to get here in the first place, what their grand scheme was, and which celebrities were possessed by them. "You can tell just by looking at them. There's something reptilian around the eyes."

She named several movie stars possessed by aliens, and this set off a flurry of questions she didn't try to answer. She just shuffled her deck and spread the cards again. "The real problem isn't movie stars. It's high government officials possessed by aliens."

This led to a man in the audience introducing himself as an aerospace engineer and telling his own story about UFOs and the government.

"I was living in Vegas. Every morning, a government security detail flew a half-dozen of us to Area Fifty-One, where we did reverse engineering on an alien spaceship. It was powered by an energy source none of us had ever encountered before. We called it element one fifteen. And when I started working with it, I wondered why we were still using rocket fuel at NASA."

Cheyenne beamed with pleasure. A reputable scientist had just backed her up, providing an unexpected addition to her medicine show. When the meeting was over, she and Sally remained to chat with him.

I was hoping for some time alone with Sally, but Dez joined me at the back of the room. "They'll be going to their regular bar when they're done here. How about you and me go somewhere else for a drink?"

We drove to a place that had pool tables. Dez asked, "How are you with a pool cue?"

"Usually I'm taking it away from somebody."

We drank at the bar, and Dez looked at the TV screen for a while, but he didn't react strongly to a Diamondback home run. He seemed to be thinking about something else. Finally, he turned back to me. "How'd you like the meeting?"

"It was much like the last one."

"Too weird for you, I reckon."

"I can take a lot of weirdness." I saw a future murky with crackpot ideas I'd have to wade through to get to Sally, and still I was hanging around, which proves the simplicity of men's souls when it comes to pretty women.

Dez looked back at the ball game, but he didn't seem to be watching. I felt he was working up his courage. So I drank my beer and waited.

Finally, he got to it. "I see myself as a lamp that can't clean itself. I leave the house in the morning, and in no time I've got slime on me. It makes me susceptible to . . . to things."

"What kind of things?"

He nodded toward the ballplayers on the TV screen. "You know about secrets of the locker room?"

"I've been in lots of locker rooms."

"And what guys say to each other stays there. It's sacred. Like if one of them was using steroids."

"I've known plenty of those."

"And you didn't tell on them."

"Nobody asked me to."

"Hell, what's the point of tiptoeing around. I have darkness on me that I can't ask Cheyenne to remove."

"Because?"

"Can't you guess?"

"A woman."

"Just about the sexiest I'll ever meet. And she drives a Jeep."

"Which makes her even sexier."

"It makes her nearby." He sipped his beer thoughtfully. "At the end of the day, no more tourists, and we're out there sitting in our Jeeps as the sun splashes all over the sky. And for reasons still to be determined, she has a hankering for this dumb cowboy."

He stared into his glass of beer. "She showed me some photos of sunsets on her iPhone. In there was a nude photo of her. Knocked the wind right out of me. I mean, gals are raised different nowadays. They make porno films with their boyfriends and post them on the web. No thought of how someday their kids might see them. It's all about *now*."

"There's a lot to be said for now."

"Amen and alleluia." He emptied his glass. "What do you think of my situation?"

"I just got out of a monastery. I'm in no position to comment."

"Maybe I should join a monastery."

"I don't recommend it."

"Cheyenne's old-fashioned. Not like the young lady I'm talking about. Cheyenne's a churchgoing woman. 'Cept *she's* the church. Guess I belong to it."

"I thought you were happy belonging to it."

"I do like that clean feeling."

We both turned back to the Diamondback game. Dez was really watching it now, getting away from his dilemma. He asked, "You ever hear of Sandy Koufax?"

"He pitched for the Dodgers. Blazing fastball."

"I met a senior citizen out here who'd batted against him in college. Koufax knocked the bat right out of his hand."

We discussed current pitching velocity and assorted other topics men engage in while watching baseball in a barroom. But I knew we'd return to the lady in the Jeep. And so we did.

"Jeeps are just temporary for her. What she really likes is horses. Says she's got a job lined up at a dude ranch in Texas. Place called the Lazy Nine. Used to be a big cattle spread, but now it's just for your weekend cowboys. Says she told the boss about me and there's a job for me there, too. Doing what I'm good at."

"I see your problem."

"When I'm around horses, I feel clean inside."

"I worked with horses at the monastery."

"So you know. When it comes to spirit, a horse has got a lot to give. You can ride a horse to death. It won't quit until its heart gives out. There's nobility in a horse. And this gal, she's in line with all that. Physically and spiritually, she's rugged. She's all about the outdoors. You should see her hands. You'd know what I mean."

"And Cheyenne?"

"Cheyenne says the only thing dumber than a horse is the man who takes care of one."

He paused, watched a few more pitches on the TV. Without looking back at me, he said, "If Cheyenne has a fault, it's her feeling about animals."

"She shot the drug dealer's dog."

"Didn't think twice about it."

A ball sailed over the right-field fence, crowd noises poured from the TV speaker, and Dez pushed his glass away.

"She don't understand horses." He said this as if trying to convince himself of something final, some incontrovertible fact that was to determine his future. "I don't mind that she bosses me around. But I mind about the horses."

He picked up his glass and drained it. "If I disappear, she'll come looking for me."

"Are you going to disappear?"

"I just might."

"With the horse lady."

"Sounds like a plan."

"But is it a good one?"

"I don't want to go back to my old soiled life with my slimeball buddies. But I want the life that suits me."

"And it's not with Cheyenne."

"I thought it was. But this gal forced me to remember who I am. Deep down, even when I'm covered with alien entities."

"Since you're contemplating leaving Cheyenne's teaching, I hope you won't mind me saying that Cheyenne's teaching is, at best, a fairy tale. Harmless but still a fairy tale."

"What about the cures?"

"The illness she deals with is psychosomatic. She cures it by suggestion. She's not the first. The Catholic Church got there ahead of her."

"We're havin' a fateful talk here."

I wasn't quite sure what he meant, but he was certainly serious. His hard face, with its deep tan and deeper lines, was set against an opponent, and it wasn't me.

"She'll come looking for me, but I'm gonna be far off and riding a chest-nut Appaloosa. Tall and rangy, just like the gal who'll be riding with me."

He'd made his decision. He was already riding with her, off into a cowboy sunset. I knew enough not to argue or even comment. But the crowd on the TV gave a cheer, right on cue.

"So do me one favor, partner. Tell Cheyenne you always knew, you being a monk and all, that I was a slimeball."

"I think she'll come to that conclusion on her own."

"She don't let go easily. And I don't want her wearing herself out on my account. She's got her work, and that's what she should do. Not come chasing after me."

"When are you going to do this?"

"The moment is upon us." He'd reverted to his biblical style. He got up from his chair. "Let's ride."

I drove him to the room his lady friend was renting in a snazzy home on Dry Creek Road. I commented on this and Dez said, "She has no trou-ble making friends. Woman looks like that, you want to rent her your spare room."

"What do I tell Cheyenne?"

"That we had us a beer and then you dropped me off outside the bar where she and Sally were jawing with the man from NASA."

"And where will you be?"

"In the wind." He held out his hand, gripped mine firmly, and walked toward the house.

# 18

Dominic arranged the promised sit-down with Nico Bottazzi. "You've got a week to prepare. He'll be a better negotiator than you are. You want me to be there? Just say the word."

"I can handle the negotiation."

"Right, milking cows at the monastery has prepared you."

"I didn't milk cows. I took care of the horses."

"Thundering hoofbeats."

"Something like that."

"You're Primo's grandson. Don't let this Roman prick fuck you over." And he hung up.

In preparation, I took my two pistols to the firing range every day. A week's worth of shooting measurably improved my aim. And on the day before the sit-down, I read through all of Vittorio's correspondence again. That's what I was doing when a black Cadillac pulled up in front of the house. I reached for my Beretta, but it was Dominic who stepped from the car. Out of habit, he shielded himself with the door as he looked around for trouble.

I greeted him from the driveway. "What are you doing here? Why aren't you pouring concrete?"

"I couldn't let you see Nico alone. I've got too much invested in you."

"You don't have anything invested in me."

"Hope, Tommy, is an investment." He grabbed my biceps in his huge mitts. "We carried buckets of mud together." His love came through his hands, and I was glad he was there.

We went into the house and sat down in the living room. He looked out the window. "That's some fuckin' mountain. Like it's gonna walk into the room."

"A guy died up there a week ago."

"Anybody you know?"

"He broke into my house and I chased him up the mountain."

"He died from overexertion?"

"He slipped and fell off a cliff. It's been ruled accidental."

"So nothing can come back to bite you. Primo would've been proud of you. You think Primo went to heaven?"

"If he did, his influence reached further than I thought."

I got some cheese and beer for us. Dominic nibbled cheese and gazed around the living room, with its high ceiling and cathedral window. "Vittorio got himself a nice place here."

"A very expensive place."

"And Primo lived in a dump. You ever wonder about that?"

"It was cover."

"So what was up with Vittorio?"

"His cover was being a priest. But he saw how bishops lived in Rome. He wanted his own little palace."

"And now you've got it and the shit that comes with it."

I showed him the intruder's ID and weapon. He studied the face on the driver's license. "Kids like this come cheap. Nico should have hired someone better, a real cat burglar you never would've seen. Instead, the cheap prick went to the bargain basement."

I thought of the kid I'd saved in the Sovereign State of Chihuahua. With any luck, he was going to school and keeping his nose clean. But Roberto Vargas was dead. I couldn't clear my slate, it seemed.

Dominic handed me back the driver's license. "When I was a kid, Vittorio used to pull quarters out of my ears. He ever do that with you?"

"All the time. And he could cut a deck of cards so he always knew where the aces were."

"He liked tricks."

"And he played one on Nico. Too bad he didn't tell me how it worked."

"He wants you to figure it out."

"Why the hell would he want to do that?"

"To build your character. It's what I'm trying to do. Roadwork, sparring, a few easy early matches, and then we head for Vegas and the big time."

"How does that build character?"

"Okay, so it doesn't build character. But it's the life you were meant to lead."

"Let's get Nico out of the way first."

"Fair enough. How about we get some supper? All I had on the plane was a pretzel and half a glass of water."

# 19

At the heart of Paloma is a facsimile of a walled Mexican village. A collection of craft boutiques and art galleries form its interior. We entered through a vine-covered wall and were greeted by a splashing fountain surrounded by stone flowerbeds and giant sycamores. Tourists were looking in shop windows and posing for photographs. It was a busy evening.

Dominic put his foot on the fountain's edge and gazed into it. "Two of Nico Bottazzi's competitors in Rome recently died untimely deaths. One had an automobile accident, and the other just disappeared."

He fished out a penny and tossed it in the fountain. "Turns out real estate isn't Nico's only business. He also does cleanup for industrial jobs. He works with contractors, comes to the construction site, keeps it neat, carts everything to his own landfill." Dominic looked at me. "Who do you think is in that landfill?"

"His competitors."

"What do you say we forget the sit-down? You sell up here and come back home with me for some training. Nico's not going to chase you there, that's our territory. And we let the whole thing fade."

"He sent two goons after me, and then the Mexican kid."

"So fucking what? You put his goons in the emergency room, and the kid is dead. You evened the score. That should be enough for you."

"I didn't want the kid dead."

"Doesn't matter, it's done." Dominic tossed another penny in the fountain and gazed at it on the bottom, where it shimmered along with other penny wishes. "Why do you want a pissing match with Nico? You're a professional athlete. You could make serious dough doing something you like. Something you could be great at. I've seen you fight, Tommy. And I've seen the other guys. You're better than they are."

"I haven't fought for five years."

"We train you up, get you in the weight room. That's where you belong, not in this tourist trap."

"Is this what you came for?"

"I came for mountain walks. How's that?"

"You don't walk."

"Not if I can help it." He threw another penny in the fountain. "As your blood relative, I'm counseling you to forget about Nico. He's nobody. Fuck him."

"I'm pissed off, Dominic. And I'm curious."

"Those are not sufficient reasons to argue with a man like Nico Bottazzi."

"Then why did you arrange the sit-down?"

"We ran up and down ladders together, remember? So maybe I was pissed off too."

He tossed a last penny in the fountain. "Okay, we go see the prick. What kind of deal are you offering him?"

"If I can find the missing two million, I'll split it with him."

"That's good, that's fair."

And I was reflecting on how my vow of poverty seemed to be breaking down along with my vow of celibacy. We went out through another archway, following a cobblestone path. More vines and flowers decorated the wall. "Authentic all the way," said Dominic. "Makes me want to serenade a mule."

In a tiny courtyard, we found a restaurant that featured Mexican food, and we sat down in high-backed, uncushioned wooden chairs. "They get these from the Inquisition?" asked Dominic.

"They don't want you sitting too long."

We ordered a couple of margaritas, and I recommended the chimichanga.

"Which is what?"

"A deep-fried burrito. You can fill it with chicken, shrimp, or beef."

"You figure the beef is local?"

"They've got a steer grazing out back."

"All right, I'll try one." He fingered a Mexican tapestry hanging on the wall beside him. "You could make nice drapes out of this."

"Are you redecorating?"

"I like this south-of-the-border shit." He released the tapestry as his margarita came. "*Salud.*"

"*Salud.*" We touched glasses and he said, "Things we should know going in. Nico is a big-time gambler. He thinks nothing of dropping three hundred grand in a night."

"Duly noted."

"Also, he thinks he's movie star material."

"We'll offer him a part in our next picture."

Our burritos came, and Dominic ate approvingly. "Not bad."

"And it's made without lard."

"I knew something was missing."

By the time we left the restaurant, the courtyards were lit by old-style Spanish lanterns. "Romantic," said Dominic. "You been laid yet?"

"I'm working on it."

"That's it, enjoy the courtship."

"Thank you, Dr. Phil."

We stopped in front of a sculpture gallery. The sculptor was visible through the window, working in clay, a mountain lion taking shape under his fingers. "You want that in concrete," said Dominic. "Then you'd have something."

A printout in the window told us the sculptor was a former rodeo rider. I thought about Dez, in the wind.

Dominic said, "Primo told me he'd kill me if I went into the life. So I listened and went into the concrete business. Sure, we rig bids and stiff the city, but it's small shit. You know Primo had whorehouses?"

"He acquainted me with them when I turned sixteen."

"I could never look him in the eye. He froze my fucking blood."

We walked out to the parking lot, and Dominic unlocked his rented Cadillac. He paused, looking back at the replica of a walled Mexican village. "The walls are what it's about, am I right?"

"Right."

"For that protected feeling." He looked across the top of the Cadillac toward me. "Father Vittorio is our wall in heaven. Or wherever."

We got in and drove.

# 20

Nico Bottazzi's office in Phoenix was in a business park with landscaped gardens. Palm trees lined the cozy streets of the park, providing shade for the computer wizards on their way to work at Custom Database Design. Also strolling through the shade were the lawyers of Clark and Hardwick, prepared to help citizens of Phoenix with trusts, estates, and real estate in all its branches.

Dominic eyed the building. "They're gonna have exterior waterproofing problems."

We entered the lobby and waited for the elevator. It announced its arrival with a synthesized chime, and the doors slid noiselessly open.

We stood out from the other men in the elevator. We were bigger. And armed. Listening to the polite exchanges of the lawyers and tech wizards, I had a feeling of uneasiness. We were like a pair of bulls in a rodeo chute. Lots of muscle and limited vision.

The elevator opened smoothly on the twelfth floor, and we stepped out into the reception area of Sacred Promise. A picture of the pope looked back at us from the wall.

Beneath the photo, a receptionist greeted us, her bleached white smile friendly enough but her attire intimidating in its perfection. Every bit of fabric was obedient to the laws of spiffiness. Her luxuriant dark hair had been ironed into submission, and her eye makeup either had been tattooed on or had taken hours, because it was worthy of Michelangelo. Compared to her, Dominic and I were prehominids who dined on termites.

"Mr. Bottazzi will be with you shortly. Would you like anything? Coffee, tea, water?" Her accent was Italian.

"A coffee would be good," said Dominic.

She pointed to a gleaming espresso maker and a row of small cups. Of course she would not be serving us.

Dominic gave a prehominid grunt and made himself an espresso, and I sat down. Architecture magazines were fanned out neatly on the adjacent table. From the wall, the pope's gentle eyes counseled love and tenderness toward the man who'd sent his goons after me.

Nico kept us waiting. "Standard practice," said Dominic under his breath. "Who gives a shit? We can look at her."

Which we did.

We were buzzing with caffeine by the time Nico's office door opened and the man himself walked out.

He might be a bishop's brother, but everything about him said Eurotrash—the affected stubble on swarthy chin and cheeks, the tight jeans and rib-hugging shirt. He was about forty. His cologne reached us before his greeting.

"Sorry to keep you waiting. I was talking to Rome and you can't hang up on the Holy See. It's hard enough to get those guys on the line. When somebody asked the pope how many people work in the Vatican, he said 'about half.' He wasn't kidding."

With this little pleasantry, he ushered us into his office as if sending his goons after me was a bit of bother now behind us.

His office window had a high-tech blind that polarized the city panorama below us. On the wall was a large photo of an old mission-style church, its pristine white towers set off by massive carved mesquite doors. I assumed that Nico was going to sell it piece by piece or turn it into a discotheque.

He saw where I was looking, and said, "Beautiful, isn't it?"

Vittorio had once taken me to the Via dei Fori Imperiali, lined with statues of Roman conquest going back two thousand years. *That son of a bitch Mussolini knocked down six churches to build this street, Tommy.*

This was before Vittorio started knocking down churches himself.

"Congregations are disappearing," said Nico, "but the houses of worship remain. I want to see them preserved, and so does my brother, the bishop."

He gestured toward another large photo on the wall. Bishop Bottazzi's hand was held up in a blessing, two fingers rising from a limp wrist. He reminded me of Primo's *consigliere*, Johnny "Squint" Ambrosio, the genius behind the family's always-dangerous negotiations. When Johnny Squint looked at you, you felt him peeling the skin off you with his gaze. I couldn't hear Bishop Bottazzi's voice, but I imagined that it would sound like Johnny Squint's.

"He's with the Pontifical Council for Culture," said Dominic.

Nico appeared surprised, even pleased. He was smiling. Same smile as the bishop: a very slight alteration in the shape of the lips as if caused by a tart substance, the substance being the other person's existence. "You've done your homework."

"It's good to be prepared." Dominic opened his jacket, revealing Vittorio's shoulder holster and Beretta. I wore the Public Defender the Mexican kid had been carrying.

Still smiling, Nico held up his hands in mock surrender. "I'll go quietly." Then he gestured toward a couch and chairs. "Or perhaps we can sit."

We sat. Nico, radiating affluence and confidence, asked, "Which of you is Tommy?"

"It don't matter which of us is who," said Dominic. "Think of us as a united front."

Nico's smile, like his receptionist's makeup, seemed tattooed on. "I'm assuming that your visit, which I'm greatly enjoying, is about Father Vittorio."

I said, "It's about you sending your goons after me."

"If you're talking about Clemente and Fortunato, I think they're the ones who should be complaining."

"And the housebreaker."

"What housebreaker?"

"The one who wound up dead on a mountain near my house."

"I have no idea what you're talking about, but it sounds like you lead a very interesting life." He crossed his legs, dangling one loafer. No socks.

"Why would I send someone to kill you? We're going to build a meaning-ful relationship."

Nico's display of composure probably wouldn't have troubled me if I'd been taking my anger medicine. But this posturing prick had ordered me killed and now he was talking about a meaningful relationship. I started to stand, preparatory to shoving his head through the wall.

Dominic reached across to me, squeezed my forearm, and pulled me back down. "Take it easy."

Nico's voice remained calm. "Your uncle scammed me for two million dollars. And that means his family pays."

Dominic said, "You don't know the family you're dealing with."

"Primo's long dead," said Nico, which meant he'd done *his* homework. "Your family is up to its ass in indictments."

His smile was as old as the Roman catacombs—a smile of ancient corruption, of poisonings and betrayal, of every crime under the burning sun of the Caesars.

He said, "A dying organization like Primo's will make deals and share information with law enforcement. Everyone in it will be seen as made of straw. And that's what you're threatening me with? Get real. There's no muscle left in your family to resolve problems."

"We don't need Primo's muscle," said Dominic. "We can handle the situation ourselves."

"You're a cement contractor. You want to stay in business? I've shut down bigger operations than yours."

Nico was no longer the suave businessman with connections to the Holy See. He was the waste management boss with bodies buried in his landfill. He turned his lazy gaze my way. "You owe me. We can do it on installments."

"All you've given me is a story. Show me where Vittorio owes you two million."

"We're at a dangerous impasse, my friend."

"I came here with an offer."

"I haven't heard it." Nico ran a hand over his carefully layered haircut, and I remembered Dominic saying he thought of himself as movie mate-rial. "But make it fast. I've got other appointments."

His executive attitude was the final red flag. "You know what? Fuck you."

I was on my feet as a door swung open and Clemente and Fortunato entered, pieces in hand. I didn't reach for mine, because I knew they weren't going to pop me. This was a corporate building, not a landfill. But Dominic and I weren't going to do any popping either. We'd have to kill everybody in the room, followed by the receptionist and maybe a few computer wizards and lawyers along the way.

"Trouble?" asked Clemente.

"None at all," said Nico. "Show these shitheads out."

# 21

"Johnny Squint you're not."

"You toss my anger medicine, I lose my temper."

We were sitting in an Italian café on Camelback Road. "He's a bella figura," said Dominic. "You don't know that expression? What the hell kind of Italian are you?"

We were eating a sweet meringue pastry topped with whipped cream and fresh strawberries. Dominic forked the meringue delicately, taking small, catlike bites. "He's always got to look good. That's the way Romans are."

"How does this help us?"

"I'll give you a demonstration, free of charge."

Dominic held up his plate with the pastry on it. "You go into a bakeshop in Rome and the guy who's wrapping this has to put it inside colored paper closed with matching twine. Meanwhile, there are six people behind you in line. He doesn't care. He's making you a bella figura." Dominic set his plate back down. "With Nico, appearances are everything. This is weakness."

"I lost my cool, Dominic. *That's* weakness."

"Don't kid yourself, he wasn't going to negotiate right off the bat. He should've, it was a bad decision not to expect some anger from you. But negotiating with the likes of us would be bad for appearances."

"But who does he think is looking at him?"

"He has to look good to himself, that's all. First, you had to kiss his ring."

"You're telling me he doesn't care about his two million?"

"He cares. But Vittorio burned him and this greatly pisses him off. So first he has to insult you, intimidate you, and make you feel like shit. He gets back at Vittorio through you. This restores his self-respect. And then he negotiates. Only you didn't follow the script Mr. Hollywood had in mind."

"I couldn't find anything in Vittorio's correspondence that clarifies things between him and Nico."

Dominic continued taking catlike bites of his pastry. "I figure it like this: Vittorio knew he was dying. He invents a couple of churches up in Oregon or wherever. Or maybe they exist, it doesn't matter. Nico trusts him and gives him two million to buy the churches. But Vittorio knows he'll be dead soon and out of Nico's reach. So he leaves you a two-million-dollar legacy, with a challenge attached. You've got to figure out how to handle Nico."

I was tracing figures with my fork in the meringue, testing my self-discipline. How long could I last before devouring it? I looked back up at Dominic. "Maybe Nico figured me for a chump and invented the two million so he could shake me down."

"Sure, it's possible, he's a crook just like Vittorio. Either way, our next move is simple. I put out a hit on Nico. Case closed."

"I don't want that, Dominic."

"You worried about your soul? I plant him in the ground and you have a mass said for him."

"I already put two guys in the ground."

"By accident. This won't be an accident."

"That makes it better?"

"It makes it final. You put someone in the ground, he's never going to fuck with you again. It brings a wonderful feeling of relief."

"You sound like you've done it before."

"Never mind what I've done. We thought we could deal with this prick, but we were wrong . . . Should we get another one of these?" He tapped his fork on his plate.

"I'll pass."

"But I'm not going to pass on Nico. I'll reach out and get somebody in the family to do the job."

"Is our family really under indictment?"

"They've pulled some of our big earners in. But I can get a spear carrier to do Nico."

"I'll handle Nico."

"How, cousin? Tell me how. First you beat the crap out of his muscle and then you come to his office and tell him fuck you. Him, a bella figura, the lord of creation. He can't let that stand. He'll be coming after you with heavier artillery."

Dominic worked on his new offering of meringue. "I'm heading up to Vegas to talk to some fight guys. Come along, and we'll figure Nico out on the way. There's a museum we can stop off at."

"I didn't know you were interested in museums."

"It's a whorehouse museum."

I was gazing at blown-up black-and-white photos of Sophia Loren hanging on the café wall. In the space of a few hours, I'd encountered enlarged images of the pope, a sleazy Roman bishop, and the goddess of Roman love. "Nico said he didn't put the housebreaker on me."

"Yeah, I wondered about that. Maybe you've got somebody else to worry about."

# 22

I didn't go to Vegas or the whorehouse museum. I went to the tiny mission church from which Vittorio was buried. The attached rectory matched it in size—a couple of rooms of adobe brick, including an office where the priest welcomed me. He was a tough customer, as rugged as any of the retired miners in his small flock. His gray hair was short, and his hands were big with thick, strong fingers. It was hard to imagine those fingers typing, but there was a computer on his desk. Its screen saver showed tropical fish moving back and forth. He sat on the edge of his desk and waited for me to signal what kind of conversation this was going to be.

I said, "I have no illusions about Vittorio."

"That's a start."

"Did you know him well?"

"I was his confessor. And I buried him."

"Did you know he was working with an outfit called Sacred Promise?"

"Yes, he was the holy face of a dirty business. Congregations felt they could trust him. They were mistaken."

Father Zaleski was trained to forgive the failings of others. Forgiving Vittorio hadn't been easy for him.

I said, "A pair of tough guys from Sacred Promise tried to rough me up."

"And?"

"I roughed them up."

For the first time, Father Zaleski smiled. He had no problem waiving the turn-the-other-cheek rule. "Did they state the nature of their business?"

"They said Vittorio owed them two million dollars on the sale of a church he'd negotiated for them."

"I had no idea he was into it for that kind of money."

"I can't find the two million accounted for anywhere in his papers."

"Does that surprise you?" Father Zaleski walked the few paces to the only window in his office. It was narrow and oblong and didn't admit much light. "I think my church is too small for anyone to be interested in buying it."

"I don't know, it could become a quaint little gift shop."

"Nobody comes to this town."

"I was joking."

"I know you were. But I worry. The pews are usually filled on Sunday, but my parishioners are poor and I can hardly pay the light bill." He turned away from the window and looked at the cross on his wall. "Vittorio told me that you lived in a monastery in Mexico."

"I left when I heard he was dying."

"You're not going back?"

"Vittorio was against it. He said I had no vocation."

"You can't take someone else's word for that."

"I want to figure out this Sacred Promise business."

"And find the two million."

"I'll give Saint Veronica's a share of it, I promise."

"A sacred promise?" His smile was that of a man who knew much of life.

He sat down at his computer, disappearing the fish and bringing up a photograph. "Our Lady of Guadalupe, for sale in Phoenix. It was built two hundred years ago by Indian craftsmen. It's one of the few remaining churches from that era. It should be a landmark, but it's too late for that now. It's on the chopping block. Vittorio was working on selling it when he got sick."

I recognized the white walls, the bell tower, and the massive wooden door. "I saw it on the office wall of the developer in Phoenix who represents

Sacred Promise. I don't know who's behind him. Higher-ups in Rome, I suppose."

"Do you know who Brother Marcos was?"

"It doesn't ring a bell."

"Five hundred years ago, he accompanied Coronado on his quest to find the seven cities of gold. After much riding, Brother Marcos saw the cities from a distance. Sparkling like gold in the sunshine. Coronado got really excited. But when he and his soldiers rode closer, they saw that the seven cities of gold were made of adobe. Worthless, of course."

He looked at me, expecting me to understand. When I didn't, he pointed at his computer screen and the white walls of Our Lady of Guadalupe. "Worthless adobe. Turned to gold."

He scribbled down a name and phone number and handed it to me. "She'll bring you up to speed on recent developments. But I doubt if she can help you find your missing money."

# 23

She was waiting on the steps of Our Lady of Guadalupe, a baseball cap on her head, a blond ponytail threaded out through the hole in back. This sporty touch was balanced by the more subdued style of her linen slacks and a large shoulder bag that carried the daily necessities of a commercial property realtor.

She held out her hand and left it in mine for just a moment longer than I'd expected. The habit of a good saleswoman?

"I'm Wendy Wexford. You've got to be Tommy Martini."

"How can you tell?"

"Vittorio said he had a nephew who should be in the NFL. I'm sorry for your loss. Your uncle was an unusual man."

"I'm starting to find that out."

"You didn't know him well?"

"I was away."

"You make it sound like prison."

"A Catholic monastery. The food was better."

She smiled. "I actually sold a small jail. The buyer turned it into a chic little bed-and-breakfast. The bars are still on the windows. It's doing very well."

"I'd probably be comfortable there."

"I'm incorrigibly nosy. Can I ask why you became a monk?"

"I was repenting my sins."

She held my eyes for a moment, then turned toward the ornately carved wooden door of the church. "Shall we?"

"After you."

I followed the swing of her ponytail. It was all I saw as I entered the house of God, but after a few moments I was in the embrace of Our Lady of Guadalupe, and Wendy and I were just two more visitors, diminished by the beauty around us. The wooden statues were by master woodcarvers who had come down from their pueblos to depict a man from Galilee whose message had traveled from his distant desert to theirs.

A handful of people were kneeling in prayer. The smell of frankincense and burning candles added to the atmosphere of sanctity. At such moments, my broken faith is set aside and something older grips me. I'd spent five years trying to understand what it was and was still no closer.

"I love it here," she whispered, sending sweetly scented words my way, along with a hint of her perfume.

The church wasn't large, having been built when Phoenix was a western outpost. There were two narrow rows of pews on either side of us, their leather kneelers worn smooth. The altar and the walls surrounding it were covered with carvings of saints and angels. Once started, the old craftsmen couldn't stop, and their handiwork animated the altar in a way I hadn't seen in much grander churches in Rome.

And Nico would sell every bit of this to the highest bidder, to put in their game rooms, their wet bars, their waiting rooms.

All the people kneeling at the front of the church seemed to be Mexican, heads bowed, lips moving silently in prayer. "They come every day," whispered Wendy. "But they know it's over."

We left the church and moved to the courtyard beside it. The walls were made of the same white adobe and had the same look of the old Southwest. But rising beyond the walls on all sides were banks, business offices, fast-food joints, and shopping malls.

"The ground it's built on and the air above it represent a potential fortune for developers." Wendy opened her bag and took out a candy bar. "Lunch. Care to join me?"

We shared the candy bar. She ate it with the neatness women bring to such endeavors, pinky ring extended.

"I lined up several good offers from buyers who assured us that their intended use was not in conflict with the values of the church. Then suddenly I got a call from Vittorio saying a deal had been reached with Sacred Promise."

"Do you know the details?"

"In this jurisdiction, religious institutions are exempt from disclosure agreements. So it's impossible to know what Sacred Promise and the priest here have worked out. But I can tell you this—Sacred Promise short-circuited established real estate procedures. It's not illegal, but it's certainly unethical."

"You were aced out."

She tilted her baseball cap back on her head. "I'll manage. But the whole thing has me baffled. Because not only had I gotten some good offers, I learned that the parishioners had a petition under way to have the church made into a national landmark. These are not wealthy people, they're working-class, but they found the time to set things in motion. I thought, fine, I don't need the commission, and this old place should be saved."

As if spying for Nico, a lizard appeared on the white courtyard wall and hung there, watching us. I asked, "Have you ever met the guy who runs Sacred Promise?"

"Nico Bottazzi. I know him well enough to pass the time of day, that's about it. But I've heard about his connections to the Vatican. He has no special track record in America. There's no reason he should have been chosen over the buyers I had lined up. And certainly not when the landmark petition was starting to build momentum. Our Lady could've been saved."

I stopped thinking about Our Lady for a moment. I was wondering how Wendy Wexford kept her figure eating candy bars for lunch. And I was wondering about my chances for a date with her. Before I could act on the idea, she said, "You should talk to Father Don. He's in charge here. And I've got to run to my next appointment."

She hurried out on high-heeled sandals, through the courtyard gates of Our Lady of Guadalupe. I was sorry to see her go, but the old ghosts were speaking to me. Devoted hands had built these walls from bricks of sand, clay, and water, then sculpted the decorative shapes along the top edges—curling waves of white that ran across the years like ripples on a pond, touching the shore of my soul. The old ghosts wanted me to do something about Our Lady of Guadalupe.

I went back inside the church and saw a priest coming through a doorway beside the altar. He walked to the only contemporary item in the church—a microphone. He knelt not to pray but to check something in the wiring. I got up and went toward him. Bent at his task, he didn't see me until he stood up. He gave an involuntary step backward as if expecting a blow.

"Sorry, Father, I didn't mean to startle you."

He stared at me, and his look seemed to include me in a category of people he never wanted to meet. I probably looked like another muscle guy from the mob.

"Hey, I'm not going to feed you to the lions. I know you're losing your church."

"I don't need your condolences." Father Don was middle-aged and obviously not much of a mixer. But even shy priests learn to put on a welcoming face. There was no welcome in his. He wanted to get away from me. "If you'll excuse me, I'm busy."

"Vittorio Martini was my uncle."

This stopped his retreat, but he looked toward the altar door as if assuring himself he could escape if he had to. I said, "I know what Vittorio was. I've known it since I was a kid."

"What do you think he was?"

"At heart, a crook."

The front door of the church opened, and two women came in. They dipped their fingers in the basin of holy water and made the sign of the cross.

He looked at them, then said to me, "In back."

I followed him through a carved wooden door frame into the sacristy.

It was a small white-walled room. His vestments hung there. A crucifix on a staff leaned against a wall. Altar linens lay on a table. It also had something I hadn't seen since Mexico—a sink with a special drain that went straight into the ground, so baptismal water wouldn't go into the sewer system. The long-gone builders had applied their spiritual touch even to the drain.

Father Don ran his finger over the altar linens, tracing an embroidered cross, as if seeking guidance.

Finally, he said, "Yes, I'm losing my church. So are those two women you saw just now. But what's done is done."

I'd seen men that Primo had bought. They'd looked satisfied. There was no trace of satisfaction in this priest's face. There was a different look, the look of men that Primo had broken.

I was no Johnny Squint. I didn't know how to veil questions, to disarm and misdirect in order to get an answer. I just said, "Why are you accepting an offer for your church when there's a petition to save it?"

"The petition is hopeless."

"That's not what I heard. I heard it can still be declared a landmark."

"People hear all sorts of things." He was looking back down at the altar linen, still tracing the embroidered cross with his finger.

"Did you take money from Vittorio to seal the deal?"

His head came up fast, his eyes flashing angrily. "Not a penny."

If he hadn't taken Vittorio's bribe, why was he swimming in guilt? "Is Nico Bottazzi forcing your hand in some other way?"

His stricken look gave me my answer. But he said, "I have nothing more to say."

"You've said it already. Nico has his hooks in you."

"I can't drive you from this church. But your presence is making me very uncomfortable."

He was still tracing the altar linen with his finger, and I saw plaster dust under his nails. "You've been patching the building."

"It needs constant work."

"What does it matter? It's going to Nico."

"Until it's desacralized, it's still the house of God."

"Nico is no friend of mine."

"If he's not a friend, what's your relationship?"

"He tried to have me beaten to a pulp, how's that?"

I won't say his face relaxed. But he was finally looking at me as if we might have something in common. I said, "I'm in a battle with Nico. I might as well fight your fight while I'm at it."

"I've already lost."

"He hasn't threatened to kill you. That wouldn't work. Am I right? You're not afraid of dying."

"He's killed my soul. That's worse."

How was I going to get it out of him? I thought of Johnny Squint and the soft style he used, almost like a purr. I tried to match it, saying, "I just came from five years in a Mexican monastery. You know what it's like down there. Killings every day, children turned into animals. Some of the men in the monastery had very heavy crimes on their soul. There's forgiveness, Father, whatever you've done. You can't let Nico be your judge."

He was looking at me, pain and confusion playing over his face. I said, "I got into trouble a few years ago and I was going under. A violent man pulled me out." I held his gaze, the table of sacred linens still separating us. "That's all I'm offering, the help of a violent man."

He moved away from the table, reached for the staff with the crucifix on top of it. He turned it slowly in his hand, looking at the small crucified figure. In a weary voice, he said, "As Christ is my witness, I've never abused a child."

# 24

Making sure there was a vacant stool between my target and me, I sat down at the bar. A few mismatched pictures hung cockeyed on the walls, grimy with the residue of dust, smoke, and other fumes. There was no noticeable theme to the pictures, just a jumble showing oil rigs, racing cars, horses, and military transport. A vintage *Budweiser King of Beers* lamp hung over the bar, a brass chain dangling from it in a loop. The television was turned off.

The target was late twenties, stocky, in work clothes. He was doodling in the wet ring his glass made on the bar. He was the type who needed conversation. Without a sporting event to talk about, it's hard for one man to begin a conversation with another. I waited. I had all night.

Finally, he turned to me. "Mind my asking, what do you think of these traffic cameras they got around town now?"

"I hadn't noticed."

"Well, they notice *you*. Two hundred and forty-eight bucks for running a red light. They get a picture of your vehicle and your license plate."

He'd found safe ground, a manly form of bellyaching. No guy will object to another guy complaining about a traffic violation. I said, "I guess we just can't win."

"You can pay it or you can go to defensive driving school. But the school charges you. So they got you either way."

"I take it they got you?"

"I've had enough school in my life, so I paid. What're you drinking?"

"Whatever's on tap."

He waved the bartender over. "Two more here."

I said thanks and he waved my thanks away. The bartender set the refills down, and the target said to me, "The name's Brad, by the way."

"Tom." I raised my glass and he raised his. He said, "It would've been worse if I had a commercial license. Employers get pissed about traffic tickets. I work for myself."

I already knew that, but I asked, "What do you do?"

"Maintenance. Whatever needs fixing. How about you?"

"I'm a bouncer."

"No shit? Where?"

"Unemployed at the moment. I just got into Phoenix."

"Well, there are plenty of bars, and lots of people who need bouncing." He looked at the bartender. "Am I right?"

"Not here," said the bartender. "It's not that kind of place."

"Yeah, we come in here for a beer after work, that's about it."

"That's about it," acknowledged the bartender.

"Maybe somebody gets fucked up sometimes, but quietly."

The bartender had no comment on this. Fucked-up drunks, quiet or otherwise, were not a topic of interest for him. He did some wiping with his bar rag.

Brad said, "A bouncer. That's heavy." He rummaged around, needing to keep it going. "I'll tell you something that happened to me here. You want to hear this? It's weird."

"Weird is okay."

"That's what I say. I mean, you never know."

"No, you don't."

"You see that pole over there, end of the bar? It's a support beam. My professional opinion, they put it in as an afterthought when the ceiling started to sag."

I looked toward the pole, which had the same pattern of grime as the walls. "Something else about it?"

He smiled the knowing smile of one carrying special knowledge. The smile also conveyed his sudden conviction that I was worthy of receiving this knowledge. He said, "I'm sitting there one night by the pole, a woman walks in. Sits down next to me. We start to talk. Pretty soon, we're into the mysteries of life."

He waited for me to return this brightly spinning ball. I asked, "What kind of mysteries?"

"Shit that can't be explained."

I nodded my head, indicating I understood there is shit that can't be explained.

He said, "But here's the thing, after we talked for a half hour, she just got up and left. And I felt locked in my seat, like I wasn't *supposed* to move. I turned to the guy next to me and asked him what he thought of her. He says to me, you've been talking to that pole for the last half hour."

Here he gave me a conspiratorial look, indicating the guy next to him had failed a metaphysical test. "I don't go around talking to poles."

"I got that about you right away."

"Thanks for that, man." He lifted his glass like a sacramental chalice. "The mysteries of life." He drank. I saw that he was a real skunk.

He looked past me toward the pole. "I never saw her again." He had now established that the pole was a thing of potential, a secret meeting place for spiritual travelers. "That's why I come in here. I figure if I ever see her again, it'll be here. But I have the feeling I never will. It was a one-time thing."

He had told the story many times. It had its entry and exit. We were out of it now. He'd be on to the next thing. He was a skunk who needed to star in little made-up dramas about himself. Nico had seen this and knew he had the perfect false witness.

"My girlfriend has a problem with sugar."

"I'm sorry to hear that."

"The doctors are like, *no sugar*. I give her ice cream. It straightens her right out." He put his tongue into his cheek, pushing it out as he nodded, a sign to me that he understood something the medical profession could not. "Every so often, she goes off the deep end and winds up at St. Luke's Behavioral Center. Last time she was there, she danced on the tables. Told them she was a dancer."

"I take it she isn't."

"She dances, same as everyone. The impression she gave at St. Luke's was that she did it for a living. I brought her some ice cream, she ate it, got off the table, and I took her home."

Here his special powers had shown themselves again, and I was given a look of collegiality, as between two professionals. "You'd think the doctors could figure it out, but no. So I keep her balanced. It's no big deal."

He drank a little more, smacking his lips with satisfaction over his diagnostic powers. "I have my methods and they have theirs."

I went silent again. He asked, "How about you, Tom?"

"I just throw people into the street."

"You ever think of some other line of work?"

"Not really."

"I've had some offers."

This was a new entry point. It was why he asked me about my line of work, so he could spin another bright ball into the air.

I asked, "What kind of offers?"

"In Nevada. They're doing special work there I can't discuss in detail, but it's about building some towers."

He gave me a searching look, as if weighing whether I could be trusted. Apparently, I could. "I'm hesitating. You know what I mean? I might get into something that I couldn't get out of. Secret clearances, shit like that."

No high-security project would ever hire this guy, but he could still enjoy the daydream. His secret-clearance fantasy was going to make my move on him easier. I helped him along. I said, "So the money's good but you're having second thoughts."

"I found out that prisons are being built in the same area. It's all part of a larger operation, the full extent of which has yet to be determined. I just don't happen to believe in the incarceration of my fellow man." He paused significantly. "I don't think I should say any more about it. But hey, you trust our government?"

"I hear you, Brad. We're on the same page."

"We've got to be, man. I just do maintenance work, but I try to make it quality. I only work one way, that's how I am. I'm all about finessing a job, the details, the fine points. Then I find out it's government work and I think, maybe not."

He was warming to this new fantasy. "Not just a city contract. But way fucking out in the desert, nobody around for a hundred miles, and I'm thinking, you get into this, my friend, and you'll be marked."

He drained his glass. He'd reached some kind of quota for the evening regarding his imagined life. He was ready for a dramatic exit.

He shoved some change toward the bartender and slipped off the stool. Turning to me, he said, "Been nice talking with you."

"Yeah," I said, "same here."

I let him get out of the bar and then followed him up the street. He was taking it slow, enjoying his little nightly stroll after a few beers. I came up behind him and said, "We've been watching you, Brad."

He spun around, shocked to see me again. But he pulled himself together and snapped out, "What's that supposed to mean?"

"We're investigating Nico Bottazzi. That's what it means."

"I don't know anybody by that name."

"It'd be a lot better for you, Brad, if you'd cut the bullshit. You just might come out of this in one piece."

"I need to see some ID."

"You think *we* carry ID?"

"Then how do I know who you are?"

"Because I knew where you were tonight. Because I know you work for Nico Bottazzi. Because I know it isn't just maintenance you do for him. Because I know you received a large payment from him. And I know why you received it. But you fucked up. The priest at Our Lady is one of ours."

"One of *yours*?"

"We don't give a shit about the money you received from Bottazzi. You can keep it. If you cooperate. If you don't, we won't be serving you a subpoena. We'll just eliminate you. We have to do that sometimes."

His eyes darted left and right. "Are you . . . ?" He was afraid to frame the question.

"A smart guy like you should be able to figure out what I am, Brad."

His face showed surprise for a moment but then gave way to acceptance that the CIA was everywhere, even in the Catholic Church.

I continued. "If I was with regular law enforcement, you'd be looking at blackmail and racketeering charges."

"Hey, I'm just a maintenance guy."

"Not quite, Brad. You branched out. You went to a priest you'd never met before, and told him he'd molested you at the age of twelve and if he didn't cooperate, you were going to the police."

"No, no, I just talked to him."

"And now you're going to talk to him again."

"I've got nothing more to say to him."

"Sorry, you've got something very important to say to him."

"Yeah, what?"

"That you made a mistake. That he never molested you, that you never saw him before, that you made the whole thing up."

"Sure, fine. I'm down with that. I mean, as it happens, I didn't like the impression I was supposed to convey. Because when I was a kid I never would've let a priest touch me."

"Right, Brad, your heart is pure."

"We all experiment a little at that age, with friends. But that's the extent of the matter."

I put my hand on his shoulder. I have a very big hand. I applied a little pressure. "But before you see the priest, you're going to do something else for us."

"What?"

"You know Bottazzi's getaway cabin in Payson?"

"Sure, I power-washed the whole place."

"And now you're going to burn it down." I took a roll of bills from my pocket. "That will cover your expenses."

Because he was a skunk at heart, he took the money but asked, "Don't you have experts for this kind of shit?"

"Our expertise is having other people do our work, Brad. Because *we* don't exist. I don't exist. But you do exist, and you're going to do this little job for us or you will cease to exist. We'll eliminate you along with Nico."

"If you're going to eliminate him, why burn his cabin down?"

"It sends a nice bright signal to interested parties."

"Who are the interested parties?"

"None of your fucking business."

"I've never burned a place down."

"Just make sure it's empty when you torch it."

"And then that's it? You leave me alone?"

"We'll always be watching you. I'm sorry about that, but that's the way our government works."

A police car rolled by at just that moment. The cop behind the wheel looked our way. I waved and he waved back. It was perfect. "Are you clear about your instructions?" I squeezed his shoulder until his knees buckled under him.

"Yeah, I'm clear," he squeaked.

When I released him, his eyes were the way I wanted them. He asked, "You guys actually work with priests?"

"Since Cain slew Abel, baby." I turned and left him there.

---

Two days later, I again went to Our Lady of Guadalupe and met Father Don. We were sitting in the small white-walled apartment that priests of Our Lady have used since the church was built. "He retracted everything," said Father Don. "He was very contrite and even asked me to forgive him. Do you think he's sincere?"

"He's scared."

"And he won't renew his accusations?"

"No, that's over."

"Is he working in a garage now? He reeked of gasoline."

# 25

"You burned his fucking cabin down?"

"It seemed like a good idea at the time."

"Well, it wasn't."

"He was blackmailing a priest."

"I don't care if he was humping Mother Teresa." Dominic was speaking over the phone from the whorehouse museum, to which a hotel was attached.

"He's not blackmailing the priest anymore."

Female giggling came over the phone, and Dominic said, "Sweetheart, take a break. I have to talk to my cousin." He came back to me. "Did he die in the fire?"

"No. The cabin was empty, I made sure of that."

"So now he'll be coming after you again."

"I'm hoping the loss of his cabin has told him he's fucking with the wrong family."

"He's a bella figura, and you just fried his self-image."

"I was sending a message he couldn't ignore."

"You sound like Primo."

Not only did I sound like Primo, I'd acted like him. And I suddenly realized how much of the old don had rubbed off on me. He'd built a criminal enterprise on rage.

And he passed his rage on to me. Only I didn't have his vision or his powers of calculation.

Dominic said, "Maybe I can get Johnny Squint to negotiate something with Nico. He's retired, but he still does stuff for friends."

"Let's let things ride for a while." I heard more giggling in the background. "Enjoy the desert wildlife."

"I'm meeting a promoter in Vegas tomorrow. He runs your kind of fight, straight brawling, strictly barroom stuff. He's tied in with Bookmaker, Sports Punter, Offshore Bettor. We're talking substantial money."

"I only fight for love."

"You have a brilliant future ahead of you in the ring, Tommy. Don't get yourself killed in the meantime."

He rang off, and I picked up Vittorio's AK-47. I thought I might be needing it now. It was vintage Soviet Union, and the action wasn't smooth. I took off the dust cover and found poorly machined metal. I carried it to Vittorio's workshop in the garage, found his Dremel, and smoothed off the rough spots on the dust cover. The carrier rails for the bolt were also rough. Using polishing compound, I smoothed them out too. It took a long while. It was totally unnecessary. You can bury an AK-47 in sand for a month and it'll still fire. But working on it was therapeutic. I'd stepped over the line with Nico. Now that his cabin was ashes, I couldn't help wondering what I'd had in mind. When Primo burned a place down, it was for the insurance.

I holstered the Beretta and went out. By the time I reached the top of Storm Mountain, dark clouds were moving in. I stayed there looking down into Paloma, and then out to distant mountain ranges. With all the wide-open spaces in Arizona, why was I in a range war with Nico Bottazzi?

As if answering my question, the wind kicked up. The feeling of moisture in the air increased immediately. A storm was coming, but I didn't care. I wanted to get rained on, to put out the fire in my guts. A huge bang of thunder gave me my wish, and the heavens opened. I pulled out my shirt and lowered it over the holster, shielding the Beretta. A torrent of rain had turned the dust of the trail into a slippery slide. My jogging shoes grew heavy with red mud. On both sides of the trail, the cactuses were drinking deeply.

When even my underwear was soaked, I ducked under a shelf of rock in the cliff face. I wanted to be wet, and I was. I relaxed. Clemente and Fortunato would not be hunting me in this kind of weather. They were city boys. They wouldn't want mud on their baby-alligator shoes.

The spirits of the storm were walking, sheets of water undulating in the wind. And then bursting through the sheet was a completely corporal form—a woman, drenched through. I stepped out from under the shelf of rock, pointing to the shelter it provided. She ducked in alongside me.

It was Cheyenne.

Cheyenne as I'd never seen her, hair plastered to her head, water streaming down her face. She was beautiful. The shape of her head, the contours of her face, her eyes, lips, and eyebrows—everything was perfectly proportioned, like a little Venus born from the storm. That nutty pilgrim hairdo of hers had created an illusion of plainness. And the prudish way she dressed completed the picture. But now that her old maid clothes were soaked and clinging to her skin, I saw a fabulous body.

"I'm pretty much drowned," she said, shaking water off herself.

I was dumbfounded. This woman had been in front of me for weeks and I'd seen a different person. I know, women will say that all along I'd known she was a knockout and that I just couldn't face my attraction to her. But they'd be wrong. Cheyenne had projected a puritanical image, and I'd swallowed it, turning all my attention to Sally.

"What are you looking at? Never seen a drowned rat before?"

"I've never seen *you* before."

She had something on her mind more challenging than my altered perception of her. "Dez has disappeared."

I said nothing.

"He's gone," she continued, "and I'm tore up with worry. When did you last see him?"

"After your meeting. The one the NASA guy was at."

I was remembering what Dez had asked me to say. *We had a beer together.* "After the meeting, Dez and I went for a drink. I dropped him off back at the bar where you and Sally were."

"He never showed."

And that was because he'd taken off with his horse lady, and my knowledge of that came under the male code regarding girlfriends and wives. Say nothing, admit nothing, know nothing. But I felt sorry for Cheyenne. When she finally got wind of Dez's new situation, she was going to hurt. She was a proud woman; at her meetings, she presented herself as someone possessing unusual powers of perception. Having her husband take off with a local femme fatale would tarnish that image. Her story was that she'd rescued him from a slimeball existence and he'd made sure everybody knew it. He'd been her champion.

"It's not like him, you know what I mean? Dez is just a puppy dog, but he knows the way home." Raindrops were running off her forehead and clinging to her wide cheekbones. I was still feeling that she'd been born from the rain.

She said, "I just can't figure it out." She turned away from me, as if ashamed that I saw the limits of her intuitive powers. But all I saw was her perfect profile.

She turned back to me. "Should I call the police?"

"I'd wait a little longer."

"But where the hell could he have gone to?"

I tried to gently pave the way for what was coming when he got up the guts to call her. "You know he's still a wild guy."

She clutched at this. "That's true." She was willing to accept a hard fact to relieve her anxiety. Harder facts would soon be following. I figured Dez would call before the week was out.

"So," I continued, "just give him a little space."

"He might have gone off to see his buddies back in Wyoming. I was hoping he was done with those deadbeats."

Her deep-blue eyes were angry now, just for a moment, then went back to that look of hers that reminded me of crystal—hard and cold. And she hissed, "I'll poison their dreams."

How she would go about this was open to question, but I wouldn't want to be on the receiving end. Women can unbalance you with a word that seems to come from hell itself. I'd heard it in barrooms, when an angry woman stopped a drunk in his tracks; she'd spit something out and he'd look as if a snake had bitten him.

Cheyenne peered out from under the shelf of rock. "It's letting up a little. Shall we?"

We stepped back out onto the trail as she continued about Dez. "He's got about as much sense as a sand flea. When he gets an alien drain on him, his judgment falls apart."

In the midst of her confusion and loss, she still maintained her three-card monte game. That's why she was good at it—she never stopped practicing.

But I wasn't interested in the way she shuffled her cards. Following her down the trail, I was remembering Carmelite nuns I had encountered from time to time in Mexico, their bodies always completely hidden by dense folds of black serge. As I looked at Cheyenne's body outlined under her clinging skirt, it seemed as if a nun's form had been revealed. As a tease, it's a hard image to beat.

"He didn't call in at work," she said. "And he never touched our truck."

I could have ended her uncertainty, but their marriage was none of my business. Our shoes were now covered in mud, and the trail was slippery, but she wasn't wasting any time going down. "I thought maybe I'd find him here on the mountain. He comes up after work sometimes." To which she added, as if to herself, "I found Mr. Monk instead."

I made no response to this. Apart from the male code of conduct, there was also the fact that I'd been raised around Grandfather Primo, who'd warned me repeatedly about volunteering information to anyone about anything. *Silence is strategy*, he used to say.

Looking over her shoulder at me, she said, "Dez can't do a whole lot more than write his own name, so I'm not gonna find a note. He didn't say anything to you?"

"We just talked sports."

"What sports has to do with anything on this earth, I'll never know."

"It's an offshoot of men running down their supper."

To this, she made no response, and we continued in silence for a while longer until she admitted, "I know that if anybody can take care of himself, it's Dez. But I worry."

"In my experience, we always worry about the wrong thing."

"Truth is, I love the silly bastard."

Did she? I'd never seen anything like love in her eyes. But how could I know that for sure? She'd already upset my earlier image of her as a plain Jane. Her stunning figure was made more stunning by her not revealing it until now, inadvertently, in a rainstorm. So maybe she did love Dez. If so, there were tears ahead.

We came down out of the mountain by the trail I always took because it was a block from my house. Cheyenne looked up the rain-drenched street. "Jesus, what am I doing here? I parked at the other trailhead. I totally forgot. It shows you the state of mind I'm in."

The wind was still strong. By the time we reached my house, she'd wrapped her arms around herself to keep warm, and her teeth were chattering. I said, "You should come in and get dry first."

"I'm chilled. Maybe I should."

We left our muddy shoes at the front door and went inside. In the entranceway was a glass curio cabinet holding Vittorio's collection of rosaries from around the world. I'd been leaving the display light on inside it. Most of the rosaries were made from gemstones and had been hung to catch the light. The glowing little Christs, dangling from the glittering gems, made me long for the faith that once was mine.

"Some juju in that," said Cheyenne, standing barefoot in front of the cabinet. "Catholics haven't let go of the mystery. That's why nuns and priests usually get a pass from me."

I got out some towels and a thick white bathrobe Vittorio had probably stolen from a hotel. "The bathroom is that way. Toss your clothes outside the door, and I'll put them in the dryer."

"Thank you, kind sir." She padded off to the bathroom.

When I heard the shower taps turn on, I went and gathered her clothes from the hallway and asked myself what I was doing with this woman in my house. "A hot shower will set her right," I said, as if this answered the question.

I got out of my own wet clothes and tossed everything in the dryer. I got into some dry clothes, put the Beretta in my pants pocket, and went to the kitchen. I brewed a pot of coffee and sat watching the storm lash the mountain. We'd escaped it during a lull, but now it was in full force again. The washes would be full, tons of water cascading down the mountain, enough to sweep animals away and occasionally people.

Cheyenne returned, wrapped in Vittorio's robe. Her hair was still plastered down, but she'd washed it and now it was softly shining. The effect was the same—a beautiful woman.

"What are you smiling at?" she asked.

"You. Your plain-Jane act had me fooled."

"I don't have much time for fussing over myself, if that's what you mean. And now that my idiot husband has gone off on a toot somewhere, I have even less."

I thought that if she had fussed over herself a little more instead of trying to work the crowd, her husband might still be around. In any case, my change of perception about her beauty didn't interest her. "Lord, what should I do about Dez?" She dropped down on the couch opposite me.

"How about some coffee?"

"Put a jigger of brandy in it. I need some fire spirit."

Vittorio had collected more than rosaries. His brandy cupboard had Rémy Martin, Courvoisier, Hennessy, Old Admiral, and one made with Irish cream and chocolate. It seemed suitable for the occasion, and I added it to her coffee.

She said, "Just what Mother needed."

"I'm sorry about all this with Dez."

"Not your fault. I discovered a demonic doorway in him a week ago. I should've handled it right then, but I didn't. And now a little piece of hell has come through."

I had to resist saying that actually, a little piece of ass had come through. But that wouldn't be strategy. What *was* my strategic aim?

She blew over the rim of the coffee cup, her lips pursed into a perfect Cupid's bow, which sent another of his arrows into me. She said, "When Dez switched from the dark side to the light, a bunch of evil stuff came at him. Hell reacts big-time when a man tries to save himself."

I wasn't about to challenge her. She had sunk herself so deeply into her con that it was second nature to her. It was what she called on first, no matter the situation. At the moment, maybe it was helping push away her pain.

Meanwhile, here she was in my kitchen, cute as they come, twanging her accent and rocking her bare foot back and forth. She'd painted her toenails blue, which seemed odd, given that she didn't paint anything else.

"Blue is Mary's color," she said, catching the direction of my look. "Secret protection."

"Are you a closet Catholic?"

"Honeybuns, women need all the help they can get. You should read your Saint Augustine about incubi assaulting women in the night. The alien grays are incubi. And Christ knew all about it. That whole virgin birth thing was alien insemination."

"Christ was an alien?"

"He was star seed. From a good alien race."

I was right back in one of her seminars, where she would fork off in any direction. She held out her foot, wiggling her toes, seemingly admiring them. "A little nail polish doesn't hurt anybody. And it cheers me up."

"Nothing wrong with that." I was admiring not her toenails, but the smooth curve of her calf, which peeked out from the opening of Vittorio's robe.

Catching the direction of my glance, she lowered her foot and tucked the robe around her legs. And then, with her Wyoming twang, she said softly, rhythmically, "*Come away, O human child. To the waters and the wild, with a faery, hand in hand, for the world's more full of weeping than you can understand.*"

I'd heard her quote poetry at her meetings. It always moved me, and it moved me now. Was it part of the con to present a poetic side? If it was, she did it well. "Very pretty."

"Yeats knew the truth. The Irish peasants told him the race of the fairies is dying out. They need human DNA to continue. Substitute alien grays for fairies, and you have the real story."

Now that her husband had left her, I had the feeling her UFO story would soon include details on how alien grays destroyed marriage.

She turned toward the high living-room window and stared out at Storm Mountain. I said nothing, just gazed at her lovely profile. I'd been given a lesson in how women disguise themselves. They know where men's eyes go, so they overdrape strategically and the job is done; a man doesn't look again. We thrive on quick decisions, and our views are fixed accordingly.

And suddenly, Cheyenne had her own realization. "Dez has been abducted." She turned back to me. "The grays have been after me, but I'm too tough for them. So they took Dez."

"Cheyenne, that's horseshit and you know it."

"He'll show up in a couple of days, not knowing where the hell he's been. Kind of like a lost weekend."

"He went off with a woman he works with."

I'd broken Primo's rule of silence and strategy, and now I had to continue. "He told me when we went to the bar. And I dropped him off at her place."

"Is she that long drink of water? The bitch who thinks she's the Lone Ranger?"

"I suppose so. I never met her."

"What, exactly, did he tell you?"

"That she'd lined up a job for both of them at a dude ranch. I don't know if he went for her or the horses."

"Did he talk about me?"

"He said he didn't want you to come after him, that he was a slimeball and always would be."

"But he didn't compare me to her?"

"Not that I recall."

"You don't have to protect him."

"I've told you all I know."

"And I'm grateful. You didn't let me make a fool of myself for too long."

"You're not a fool."

"No, I'm the deserted wife."

"That description will never apply to you."

"You're right about that, honeybuns." And she threw open her robe.

# 26

Having been celibate for five years made those first hours in bed with Cheyenne a revelation. Her body was as the rainstorm had promised. And maybe having a husband who'd just left her had something to do with it, but she was anything but the churchgoing lady Dez had described. If he'd been getting what I got during those hours, then he was crazy for leaving her.

We lay together as the rainstorm passed. She said, "Get us some more of that chocolate-flavored gin."

"Brandy."

"Whatever."

"You want it in coffee?"

"I'll take it any way you want to make it," she said, and slipped her hand between my legs.

"Give me a break," I said.

"The whore of Babylon is too much for you."

"She is."

"Still stuck on Sally?"

"Who's Sally?"

I brought back coffee laced with brandy. She sat up in bed, naked, and put it to her lips. "Once again, delicious."

"So are you."

"The son of a bitch dumped me. It's hard to believe."

"It was all about horses."

"You're nice to say so. And you make a good cup of joe."

"Dez was an idiot for leaving you."

"You haven't seen the bitch he ran away with."

This was true. But Cheyenne was the nun and I was the monk, and we'd both gone over the wall. For erotic stimulation, I'll take it every time.

She finished her coffee and set it down on the night table. "What are you staring at?"

"Your breasts, if you must know."

"I can see that. I mean, why?"

"Because you've been hiding them so well."

"The better to torment you, my man."

She stretched back down on the bed, her legs touching mine. I wondered why she hid those great legs under long dresses. Her retreat into dowdy clothing and a haircut designed by the Retired Librarians of America were moves I'd never understand. But men are woefully ignorant of women's reasons for what they do.

She ran a hand over my chest. "I'm going to teach you all about alien DNA harvesting."

"Can we stay off genetic manipulation?"

"It's part of the package." She continued rubbing my chest. "When a monk runs with the witch ladies, he has to be able to talk their language."

"*Fire burn and cauldron bubble.* How's that?"

"That's old stuff. The alien grays are advanced scientists. We desperately need to catch up to them, but we're blinded by prejudice." She reached for the drawer of the night table. "You got any cigarettes in here?"

She lit up one of Vittorio's cigarillos and said, "I'm over Dez."

Her voice was calm, and I believed her. That she could quickly put him behind her seemed part of her restless nature, a nature that made her lovemaking unrestrained and wildly vocal. Had we been in a condo, my neighbors would have thought I was having sex with a bobcat.

And her fingernails had raked my back, which she was examining now. "Sorry about this, it seems I got carried away."

She stroked my wounds gently. "They used to talk about the devil's claws causing marks like these."

"So you're my very own devil." I didn't know how right I was.

# 27

Like every good Cat-lick, on Friday I ate fish. The best fish in Paloma was sold at the holistic supermarket, Natural Born Foods. It had an upscale deli attached to it, and I bought my favorite, garlic-butter salmon. They also sold the best booze in town, and I made my way toward the liquor aisle to get some wine. Sally worked in the store stocking shelves, so a glimpse of her blazing red hair might be a welcome addition to my shopping experience. But what I glimpsed instead was decidedly unwelcome. At the far end of the liquor aisle, reading the label on a bottle of tequila, was Bustamante. There was only one reason for him to be in Paloma. I'd humiliated him in Modelo—him a chosen cartel man, a macho man, a recruiter of the young, a big shot in town.

A little tequila to steady his nerves before whacking me?

The teachings of grandfather Primo: *Suspect the worst and you'll be right most of the time. The rest of the time, who cares?*

A plainclothes security guy was there every day and always had a few items in his cart but never checked out. I'd once gotten a closer look at the raised letters on the clunky ring he wore—*PPD*, for *Phoenix Police Department*. A retired cop. But he wasn't in the liquor aisle, and I reached for the Public Defender tucked under my shirt. Its short barrel made it easy to palm in my hand.

I came up behind Bustamante and spoke to him in Spanish as I pressed the muzzle of the revolver against his back. "Put the bottle down. Slowly."

He didn't turn toward me; he already knew. In his culture, attack was always on the program. He put the tequila back on the shelf in a very natural way. As he leaned forward, I reached inside his shirt, extracted his automatic, and put it in my shopping bag alongside the salmon. Critics of the church say an early pope decreed fish on Friday to save the Italian fishing industry. True or not, fish on Friday had saved my ass today. It had put me where my enemy had not expected me to be.

Bustamante nodded toward the fancy striated bottle he'd put back on the shelf. It had an angel on the label. "That's Gran Centenario. Costs fifty-three bucks. For myself, I buy cheap tequila. It was a gift for you."

I jammed the little revolver into the folds of his Hawaiian shirt. "Walk toward the front of the store." He did as he was told. We were approaching the security cop, and I said softly, "Smile, and talk to me."

"What should I say?"

"You're already saying it."

"I didn't come here for trouble."

"But you found it anyway. Keep walking; keep smiling."

We passed the security guy, and then we were in the parking lot, things going my way until I saw Sally. She must have been on her break, because she ambled over to us, luxurious curves moving gently under her Natural Born Foods T-shirt. She liked big men, and here were two of them to toy with. Maybe it was to compensate for the celibate life Cheyenne had mapped out for her. She asked playfully, "Did I miss lunch? Darn . . ."

She was using her sweet we're-just-buddies style, modified, of course, by her knowledge of just how sexy she was. But unexpectedly, we didn't stop, because I was pushing the revolver hard into Bustamante's back. I'd flattened him in Modelo, but he was a fighter nonetheless and would take advantage of the slightest change in our momentum.

I saw the pale-green license plate of Chihuahua Mexico, *Tierra de Encuentro*, Land of Encounters, and steered him toward it.

Sally kept pace for a few steps, just to save her self-respect, and I was murmuring to Bustamante in Spanish, "I don't give a fuck about her or anybody else, I'll do you right here in the parking lot."

He nodded imperceptibly. From previous experience, he knew I was slightly unhinged. And he'd killed people in broad daylight many times. I called to Sally, "I'll catch you later. I've got to get this guy to the hospital."

"What's wrong? Maybe I can help."

"It's kidney stones. He's in terrible pain."

In Spanish, I ordered Bustamante to open his car. I pushed him past the steering wheel into the passenger seat and got behind the wheel. It was a keyless ignition and started with a touch. "A wrong move and you get lead in your balls."

As I drove out of the parking lot, I saw Sally in the rearview mirror, still watching us. With a cartel assassin alongside me, I couldn't worry about her feelings. Softly, so as not to rile me, he said, "Please, Father Tommy . . ." And here he used the Spanish idiom. "Let me put you into the flow."

"Shut up and pray." I had to make him feel he was as good as dead—a method he was familiar with, for that was how he got his information from terrified citizens of Modelo or from rivals in the business.

I drove through town, then turned onto Thunderbird Road. When we got to my block, I pulled into my drive. In anticipation of a moment like this, I'd been carrying the garage door opener in my pocket. I opened the garage and parked inside.

I got out, circled the car, and motioned him to get out. In my eagerness to get him in the house, I neglected to close the garage door behind us. It would have been so easy, just the touch of a button on the wall. But I was still carrying the Natural Born Foods bag with his weapon in it. I didn't know whether a round was chambered, and I didn't want to mess with it. I stuck it on a utility shelf and steered him into the house with the muzzle of my revolver on the back of his neck. Inscribed on its short barrel were the words *The Judge*. It was so named because judges found it small enough to wear under their robes, and it could be easily gotten to in the event a maniac showed up in their courtroom.

I motioned him to the island in the middle of the kitchen. "Sit."

His eyes were taking in the immediate terrain. It included a statue of the Virgin Mary on the kitchen table. I'd broken it during my first night in Vittorio's house, stumbling around in a layout I wasn't yet familiar with.

This morning, I'd finally gotten around to gluing it back together. Looking at it, Bustamante said in soft mellifluous Spanish, "I swear on the Holy Mother I didn't come here to kill you."

But his eyes continued to shift back and forth—the natural movements of a killing machine, gauging possibilities, weighing chances. "I'm here with a request from the Camel."

He was lying, but that was the cartel way. You never told the truth about anything, because a lie was easier and could always be backed up by another lie. So I listened without trust, wondering what he would come up with.

He smiled to show his embarrassment at having to reveal himself, as if it were a rare gift he was making to me. "Your uncle, the priest, did business with the Camel."

Vittorio had been in Modelo, shoehorning me into the monastery. But how had he met the Camel? Foolish question. The old fox had learned who the players were in town.

Bustamante looked at me, his eyes gleaming with the light of a killer, a gleam that comes from putting people in the ground. "The Camel has lots of money he needs to launder. Your uncle helped him with that. It had to do with real estate."

I was no money-laundering expert, but it would be just like Vittorio to work a deal with a drug lord while he was placing me in a monastery for a life of penance.

Bustamante's eyes were on the Virgin Mary, as if he expected her to back up his story. "Trust was established between them. Every hospitality was shown to your uncle. He stayed in the Camel's own house many times through the years. But in the end, he betrayed that trust." A smile crossed Bustamante's face, childlike guile shaping his features. "The Camel keeps track of everything. He does figures in his head like you wouldn't believe. A man who never went to school."

"Right, he's the seventh wonder of the world."

"He has a lot of business going on, but he finally realized one of his treasures had gone missing. His inescapable conclusion was that your uncle had pinched it. Your uncle, an old man and a man of God, stooped so low as to steal from a friend. Maybe he did it for you, I don't know." The killer's gleam in his eyes remained, but something around his mouth seemed to soften. "I don't like you, but I'm ready to put our fight behind me. I only wish to retrieve that object."

"Which is?"

"But you know that already, Father Tommy."

"All I know is, I'm the one holding the gun."

"A sacred relic. Very old, very valuable. It's—"

I heard the door from the garage open behind me. "It's me, Martini."

In another moment, Sally was beside us, staring at the gun in my hand. "I *knew* something was wrong."

The lapse in my attention was minimal, but for an experienced assassin, it was like a barn door opening, and Bustamante drove through, the Virgin Mary breaking again, this time across my forehead. His next move was one smooth motion, striking the back of my hand and the inside of my wrist simultaneously, the torquing force of the blow driving the gun from my hand. It hit the floor and we dived for it together. He snapped it up and rolled away from me. He was straightening to a firing position, and I saw my death looking at me from the end of the gun barrel.

Then an eight-inch kitchen knife went through the back of his neck and peeked out his throat, just above the Adam's apple. He collapsed at Sally's feet, the hilt of the knife sticking out of his neck like the fin of a fish. And he was flopping like one. She had driven the knife in with both hands, and she was strong. He flopped for a while and then stopped flopping.

"Oh, God," she groaned.

I was remembering one of Primo's teachings, which he'd intoned with the flavor of old Sicily—*a captive may cry out, a dead man never.*

"I wanted . . . to help you," she said with a choking sob.

"He was here to kill me, and you stopped him." I stroked the red hair I'd been longing to touch. It meant nothing now. Her warm body was pressed against me, and it meant nothing, either. I separated from her gently. "Go home. I can handle the rest alone."

She was looking down at him. "He was from the darkness."

"I'll buy that."

"And the darkness took him."

An eight-inch kitchen knife took him, but I could see her point. She asked, "What do we do now?"

"We separate."

She wasn't ready to leave yet, a question hanging heavy on her. "Who is he?"

"A cartel killer. Don't waste any tears."

"Why did he want to kill you?"

There had been a ring of truth in his liar's game, but I'd never know now. I told her what seemed best. "He recruited kids for cartel assassinations. I got in the way."

"Kids?" She looked back down at him as if the word lifted a burden from her. Then she hugged me. "I'll be at Cheyenne's. Call me when you can."

After she left, I dug out one of the throwaway phones I'd purchased.

Dominic answered on the first ring. "What's up?"

"Call me on a safe phone."

I was cleaning up the kitchen when he rang back. I said, "An unexpected visitor showed up."

"Where is he now?"

"On the floor."

"Moving?"

"No."

"Lucky I'm still in Vegas. Bring him to me here. I'll have something arranged by the time you arrive."

"Where will I find you?"

"Parking lot at the Golden Nugget, it's free, no hassle."

"I'll need another hour here. Let's call it six hours altogether, and I'll see you at the Golden Nugget."

We rang off, and I finished cleaning up. Then I put Bustamante in the trunk of his car and drove.

# 28

Outside Bullhead City on I-40, I looked in the rearview mirror and saw a hearse with a crucifix for a hood ornament. The crucifix was growing quickly larger.

I had a dead body in my trunk, and a speeding hearse coming up behind me. As they say in Paloma, was the universe trying to tell me something? The crucifix was illuminated, glowing brightly on the hood of the hearse, which was closing fast on my rear bumper.

The hearse whipped out into the passing lane and drew up alongside me. A middle-aged man in a ponytail was at the wheel, smoking the largest joint I'd ever seen. Doing 110 mph, he blew on by me, his taillights fading quickly, like an apparition in the desert.

After that, I stayed well below the speed limit. A car with Mexican plates wasn't the ideal vehicle for transporting a dead body, but the trip wasn't a long one, and I needed to get rid of both body and vehicle. When a trooper passed me with his misery lights turning, I gave my best imitation of a sober citizen. We do this kind of thing, thinking our characterizations actually mean something to law enforcement.

When the lights of Las Vegas appeared, I had to navigate through heavy traffic, avoiding fender benders, and a midget Elvis in a wig and a white jumpsuit who gyrated in front of my car. A giant marquee showed nearly naked showgirls enlarged to cosmic proportions.

Casino jackpot bells, drums, and pounding bass notes poured from the open doors, so loud it felt as if the jackpots were spilling onto the sidewalks, scattering fool's gold at the tourists' feet. *Come in, come in. Everyone wins!*

I found the Golden Nugget parking lot and saw a concrete truck parked there, its drum turning slowly. I pulled up alongside it, and Dominic indicated that I should follow him.

We drove out of the downtown area, into the suburbs. I didn't watch street signs, just kept my eyes on the slowly rotating mixer drum ahead of me. But in the rearview mirror was a biker on a Harley, a red bandanna around his head. Hanging on back behind him was a guy in a bush hat. They kept pace with me to a building site. Dominic parked the concrete truck next to the open foundation and motioned for me to park beside him and pop the trunk.

Bustamante was curled up there. The red bandanna biker slid his motorcycle into place alongside me. "You need a hand with the stiff?" He had slits shaved in his eyebrows. His arms were covered with flaming skulls, bloody knives, grinning snakes, and naked women.

His partner in the bush hat stroked one end of a drooping mustache and looked into the trunk. The handle was sticking out of Bustamante's neck. "Looks like a kitchen knife."

"It is."

"That works."

Dominic called down to him from his cab. "Just see nobody gets near."

"Not a problem." Bush Hat took a police baton from his saddle bag and snapped his wrist. Telescoping inner shafts shot out. Like the sound of a spring-loaded knife or a pump-action shotgun, the sound of those shafts snapping into place is itself a deterrent. He and his partner walked off to block access to the building site.

Dominic climbed down from the cab and joined me. He nodded toward the bikers. "The Chamber of Commerce provides them."

I nodded at the ready-mix truck. "How'd you swing this?"

"Local Eighteen of the National Association of Mobile Transit Mixers. We help each other."

We lifted the body out of the trunk and carried it into the open foundation, which was laid out in grids six feet square. We dumped Bustamante in the nearest grid. Rigor mortis had begun to set in, so when he hit the ground with a thud, his arms and legs moved like a puppet on tight strings. "Rest in peace and all that shit," Dominic said, then motioned me up into the cab. I said, "Make it fast."

"Relax. Anybody fucks with us, I've got sixty thousand pounds of truck aimed at them." He straightened the wheel. "It's a new design, front dumping." He lined the truck up to the grid where the body lay. "I could drive this through a stone wall and you wouldn't feel a bump." The sound of the drum rumbled behind us. "And it's completely computerized."

He gave a voice command, and a chute extended slowly from the front of the truck, into the foundation. A second command started the mud flowing, the gray mass sliding down the chute. In less than a minute, the body was covered. Dominic got down, opened a tool compartment on the side of the truck, and took out a flathead rake to spread the concrete evenly. "This is premixed. It'll be hard in two hours. In six, you can walk on it."

"In six, I'll be back in Paloma."

"No way, cousin. You're spending the night here in Sin City." He raked a little more. "Look good to you?"

"It's fine. Let's get out of here."

Dominic hosed down the chute and then waved to the bikers. They returned, swaggering as they walked, and it wasn't hard to imagine them robbing a train in the 1800s. "All done?"

Dominic handed them a roll of bills and gave them Bustamante's car keys. "It's yours."

"A pleasure doing business."

"You didn't do much."

"But it's better that way, right?" Bush Hat smiled from underneath the wide brim of his hat. The crown was wrapped with Navajo beading. His buckskin pants had turquoise buckles down the sides. He was the dream of the old West.

Dominic motioned me back up into the truck and put the massive thing in gear.

I asked him, "How much did you have to pay them?"

"Five hundred each and the car. It'll go to a chop shop, and every last thing on it will be taken off. There'll be nothing left but the frame, and that will get melted down. It never existed."

"And when the foreman finds part of his foundation filled?"

"He already knows about it. The elves and fairies did it for him while he was sleeping."

We rumbled out of the building site. The big gray drum behind was like an elephant bearing down on us. He said, "The deceased must have really pissed you off. You shoved that blade right through his neck."

"A Paloma witch did."

"Was she riding a broom?"

"She came in unannounced while I was dealing with the guy. Things got out of hand, and she stabbed him with a Martha Stewart chef's knife."

"The domestic touch. Can she keep her mouth shut?"

"She likes the thrill of having secrets."

"Sounds like a nut job."

"She is."

Driving through Las Vegas at night in a concrete mixer has a surreal quality. But Dominic said there were construction jobs going 24-7, so we fit the picture. Proving the point, cop cars passed us from both directions without a second glance. "They could give a shit about us. There are six hundred gangs in Vegas. Can you believe that? Civilization is breaking down, cousin."

We came to an industrial parking lot surrounded by high fences topped with razor wire. The truck had a remote security chip that opened the gate in front of us, and Dominic took the truck on through and parked it.

"We leave the keys inside, plus a tip." He slipped another roll of bills under the gas pedal. As we climbed down, he said across the seat of the cab, "The number of bodies buried in public buildings would surprise you."

# 29

We ate alongside the facsimile of a canal that wound through the heart of the Venetian hotel. Lining the canal on both sides were facsimiles of Venetian palaces, above international boutiques.

The water in the canal reflected the artificial sky, reiterating the message of serenity and prosperity. Everything was polished, every inch was impeccably clean, and the lanterns along the canal emanated golden light.

A gondola went by us, carrying tourists serenaded by a gondolier in striped shirt and straw hat, singing an aria. Though it was nighttime outside, the curving sky above us was eternal day, its painted clouds illuminated by a hidden sun. Not too bright a day, but one that was subdued to calm the soul, to make you feel that heaven was watching over you. Heaven was. Security cameras were everywhere but deeply disguised. The idea of spying eyes might throw a gambler off his stride.

"So who's the guy we buried?"

"His name was Bustamante. He worked for a Mexican cartel. Vittorio did some business with them."

"What kind of business?"

"He laundered money for them."

"The old devil." Dominic smiled. "You've got to hand it to him."

"And he stole something valuable from the boss. At least according to Bustamante. That was the reason for the visit."

"What did he steal?"

"The witch stabbed him before I could find out."

"What's her story?"

"She follows a cult leader I'm involved with."

"How involved?"

"I visit her in bed."

"A monk on the make."

"I'm not a monk anymore."

"You never were. It was more like witness protection."

The gondolier was singing Puccini. Dominic translated: "He never hurt a living soul."

"Lucky guy."

"Don't get religious while I'm eating."

As the gondolier disappeared under a footbridge over the canal, I heard "*vissi d'amore*," and that much I understood. He lived for love.

"So you're banging a cult leader."

"It's hard not to in Paloma, there are so many of them."

"What's she like?"

"She's smart."

"I'm trying to form a picture here. Smart is not a picture."

"A little brunette bombshell. How's that?"

"I've got a picture." He cut into his chicken cacciatore. "It's serious?"

"Maybe."

"All these cult leaders are rich, right?"

"She's not one of them. She charges five dollars."

"A five-dollar cult leader. This is the best you could do?"

"She has other qualities."

"Such as?"

"She reads my mind."

"So does Bianca. All the fucking time. This is not a quality to get involved with."

After eating, we walked along the Strip. The sidewalks were covered with hooker business cards, handed out to tourists who promptly threw them away. "How was the whorehouse museum?"

"A quality experience."

We passed the midget Elvis impersonator, and Dominic said, "That could be you or me. You ever think about shit like that?"

"I try not to."

"I think about it," said Dominic, and we entered another casino. The dealer at the blackjack table was a gorgeous Chinese girl. As we watched her dealing, Dominic said, "I visited with Carmine Cremona yesterday. I gave him your regards."

"I only met him once, at a wedding."

"He's a good friend of our family. He told me Nico is working with a Chinese gang in Phoenix. The Chinese have a ton of money to launder, and they're investing in real estate."

The dealer's hands were nimble. The cards sailed across the table and dropped neatly in front of the players, like extensions of her grace. Dominic said, "The gang is called Menacing Wind. No matter what happens with Nico, don't get involved with them, because they're way ahead of you. They've been running whorehouses here since the gold rush. Carmine wouldn't touch them with a ten-foot pole."

"I'll bear it in mind."

# 30

Santos Balcázar was a Cuban entrepreneur who also owned motels at the south end of town, and several second-rate casinos just off the Strip. The Contention Fight Club was in one of them. He shook my hand, then looked toward Dominic.

"How many fights has he had?"

"His career has been limited. He killed a guy. Now he's making a comeback."

Santos looked back at me with sudden enthusiasm. "You killed somebody? That's a promotion angle."

Dominic said, "We're keeping it quiet, Santos."

In tones of courtly understanding, Santos Balcázar switched tracks and said, "This will be honored."

I could see he liked the idea of a killer fighting in his cage. He said, "Let's go to the arena."

We went from his office through the main floor of the casino, which was undergoing redecorating. Painters were working, and the slots were silent. We went through a pair of double doors opening into the casino theater. Once, it had put on shows with leggy chorus girls. Now the stage was a boxing cage.

Two men were working out in the cage. "The big one's Sultan Sokoloff," said Santos. "All-Russia Mixed Martial Arts champion last year."

I could see why. He had tremendously long arms. You could dance away from him, but sooner or later he'd nail you with a big right hand and you'd be looking up into the lights.

His black hair was shaved along the sides, in the barbarian look favored by professional martial artists. His high cheekbones hinted at Mongol ancestors. The Golden Horde had hung out in Russia for two hundred years, and they hadn't left the women alone.

Santos said to Dominic, "How about your guy works out a little bit with Sultan? Give me an idea of what he can do."

"Sure," said Dominic, knowing I couldn't refuse him. The concrete had hardened over Bustamante during the night, and a building would be put on top of it. I could let the Russian slap me around for a few minutes.

"Locker room is that way," said Santos. "There's a bunch of new trunks there."

I walked down an aisle with plush theater seats on both sides of me. The gladiators would walk down this aisle to the ring with a crazed crowd cheering them.

The locker room was spotless, new steel lockers shining.

I changed into red-and-white trunks with stars on them and put in a mouthguard. I threw a few practice punches and went back out.

The Russian was alone in the ring. Santos said to him, "This is just a demo. We're not out for blood here. Sultan, you got that?" Sideways to us, he said, "He don't understand much English." But Sultan nodded and I climbed into the ring with him.

We sized each other up with some shadow punching. Then he tried an overhand right that I slipped off my shoulder, but it gave me a taste of his strength. He was a Russian bear all right. He followed with some low kicks I danced away from. If one of them hit me, I'd be limping for a week. We traded some punches, and I ate a few. I was being patient. I didn't want to fuck the guy up—this was his profession, not mine, and he was here in Vegas to make some money. But I could feel something simple-minded going around in his soul, like a dumb ox turning a wheel, grinding grain for the motherland.

In our next clinch, he unloaded a bunch of knee strikes to my hips and thighs. They're meant to wear you down, and I couldn't see the point. He seemed to think he was in a three-round contest for prize money. "Take it easy, pal," I said.

Misinterpreting my reluctance to hammer him, he called me a pussy and gave me an illegal knee shot to the groin. I saw stars. There was no ref—who was going to call it? My grip loosened and he slipped free. I was getting the feeling he hadn't understood Santos's instructions. When our eyes met, I saw dark resolve there. I was big, and he wanted to put my head on his wall. I had to end this before he ruined my day.

I faked to the right and he followed it. He was off balance with his head lowered. I rounded on him with a high kick that caught him along-side the eye. He went down instantly and stayed down.

Santos and Dominic jumped into the ring. Santos knelt beside the groaning Russian. "What's wrong, Sultan?"

I said, "Fracture of the orbital bone." It's a typical barroom injury.

Dominic asked, "Hospital?"

"Ice packs, rest, and he shouldn't blow his nose for a few days."

I climbed out of the ring and walked to the locker room. I was limp-ing from where he'd kicked me. Dominic was alongside me. "You flattened the comrade."

"He didn't follow instructions."

"I saw. But you looked great, Tommy. Who the hell kicks that high?"

"Lots of guys."

"Not guys your size, and not with that kind of velocity."

"He stepped into it."

"Right, you faked him out of his jockstrap."

I took off my trunks, found a towel, and rubbed myself down. In Mexico, I'd practiced that kick every day on bales of hay in the barn.

I got dressed, and Santos met us outside the locker room. At the door to the street, he shook my hand again. "You knocked out a Russian cham-pion. We start here in a month. You're on the program."

"We'll be in touch," said Dominic.

He and I strolled along the Strip. The street had been swept clean of hooker business cards, but many more would be handed out today in a never-ending stream of temptation. The jackpot bells and sirens were sounding as they had through the night. They never stopped.

The Venetian is reached from the street by a bridge over a canal. This one had a real sky above it, and the water sparkled with sunlight. "So," asked Dominic, "do we fight for Santos?"

"I've got to clear up the Nico thing first."

"I'll clear it up for you."

"No, it's mine to do. I'm still looking for answers."

"Your answer's going to be a bullet in the head." He leaned on the edge of the bridge, looking down to the water, where the gondolas were tied up. "This is a great town. Rome falls, and they rebuild it across the street." He nodded toward the towers of Caesar's Palace.

I said, "Vittorio collected casino chips. He had one from every big house. I found them in one of his drawers."

"You can make jewelry out of casino chips. I've seen it. It looks good."

The day was going to be boiling. It would be hot in an Elvis wig and jumpsuit.

Dominic turned around, leaned his elbows on the bridge, and arched his back, which brought his big chest forward. "The family sent Vittorio money his whole life. He was their ticket to heaven. But he didn't do you any favors when he left you that house. He should've left it to Angelina. She would've had Nico whacked the minute he opened his fucking mouth."

# 31

Cheyenne, after removing her clothes, announced to me solemnly, "I have something to tell you."

"You're pregnant?"

"Why the hell would I want to get pregnant? I'm here to save mankind, not add to it."

My next thought was that Dez had come back. But she said, "You've swept that little rat out of my heart. And that's why I want to level with you."

I figured she could only be referring to the con job she was running on her followers in Paloma. I was glad we were about to get more honest with each other, but she had chosen a strange moment to do it, standing before me completely naked.

She paused for dramatic emphasis and said, "Cheyenne is gone."

Since she was very much in evidence, I said, "What do you mean, you're gone?"

"*I'm* not gone; Cheyenne's gone."

She'd just gotten naked, and I wanted to enjoy the view. But apparently, her statement required a response from me, because she added, "It's important for you to understand."

She sat on my bed, fluffing up the pillows behind her. She leaned back against them and drew her knees up against her breasts. There she was, my naked nun, and there I was, at the ready. But first, there was something she wanted me to understand.

"Cheyenne is gone and I've taken her place."

"So who are you?"

"I'm something like an angel." A sure way to dispose of an erection is to tell a man that you're an angel. "I was sent down to do some heavy lifting."

"And where's Cheyenne?"

"She's in a safe place in another dimension. I'm grateful for her sacrifice."

"So what am I supposed to call you?"

"Call me Cheyenne. Anything else would be too confusing."

"I'm already confused."

"Sure you are, hon. Dez reacted the same way."

"You told Dez you were an angel?"

"I had to. He deserved the truth."

I was beginning to understand why Dez had run off with his wrangler.

Cheyenne ran her hand gently across my forehead, as if pulling away webs that clouded my true perception of her. "I'm what they call a walk-in."

"That clears everything up."

"Don't be sarcastic, Martini." She continued running her fingers across my forehead. "We have a tragic love, dear."

"Cheyenne, I'm fine with you never breaking your cover in public. I'll support you at your meetings. You can be a walk-in there. But not here, not in my bed. Okay? In bed, we should be real with each other."

"Hon, I'm as real as it gets. But I'm from another dimension. And it's not fair to withhold that from you. So now you know."

She stretched out and patted the sheet, indicating that I should join her. "We don't have bodies in the angelic dimension. It's kind of a kick for me to be in a body here. No reason why I shouldn't enjoy it."

Then the angel drew me onto her and spent the next half hour in a remarkable display of sexual dexterity, after which she told me walk-ins are prevented from completely surrendering themselves emotionally. "It's because we have to fight to hold on inside a foreign body."

During our copulation, I had detected every aspect of surrender I was familiar with, including cries of *faster, faster* . . .

Now she said, "It matters to me that you believe this, especially while we're making love, because then I can pass special blessings to you."

"Cheyenne, I just got a fabulous blessing from you. In fact, it was the best one so far."

"The problem is, I won't be here all that much longer."

"Where are you going? Area Fifty-One?"

"You can joke all you want, but I meant it when I said we have a tragic love. Walk-ins are fragile. Our connection to the body is tenuous at best. I'm hoping to get a certain amount of work done before I'm called back."

We weren't just two people sweating in bed and enjoying ourselves. An angel had fallen for a mere mortal. She had taken her con job to new heights, and I could see she was enjoying this new tragic aspect. Her voice became heavy with emotion. "I feel a tremendous pull from my own dimension. I think they've decided I've been here long enough. The higher dimension is kind of indifferent about the problem of walk-ins who fall in love."

"So this is it? You're going to keep on with the act? Never a break, no time-out?"

"No, hon, not for one single second." And she smiled, indifferent to my calling her out. The game she was playing didn't permit the slightest deviation from the rule. I was naive enough to think she would care what I thought. Her plan was long-range. But I'm getting ahead of myself. To know Cheyenne, we have to take it slowly.

# 32

Cheyenne's angel impersonation gave me the impulse to look for Dez. I dearly wanted to know what he thought of living with an angel. Maybe I was hoping he'd return to her. I rolled out Vittorio's BMW. It was the X5 in white leather, $71,000 worth of comfort and power, and once again I wondered why he'd bought such a big beast.

I turbocharged my way to the Black Canyon Freeway. The new car designers have decided we need electric steering, which provides no road feedback. Other than that, it was a fun ride to Phoenix, where I changed to Interstate 10, toward El Paso. The Benedictine monks kept me company on the Bang and Olufsen surround-sound system. Twelve speakers and a thousand watts of power lent their enchantment to the experience. I was back in the monastery, so much so that I switched off the audio and just listened to the road. I wanted to give the world a chance.

Eight and a half hours later, I was at the Mexican border. The crossing into Ciudad Juárez was easy, just a stroll across the international bridge. In no time at all, I was on a potholed street with beat-up taxicabs offering overpriced rides. I walked along past shabby little shops until I reached the market. I found a sidewalk chef cooking spiced sausage, which he wrapped in a tortilla with veggies. I ate it with orange juice squeezed by an American expat working at his own little juice stand. "Six people a day are killed here, man," he said, apparently thinking I needed this information. He nodded toward a teenage soldier armed with an assault rifle. "But he'll take care of us, right?"

"He won't?"

"Last night, they found a grenade launcher in a whorehouse down the street." He gave me my change. "The Army loses shit like that all the time." Then he gave me a big smile. "But it's a great place for an entrepreneur. Next year, two orange-juice stands."

Pig meat and pistols—you could smell it in the air. I walked along eating my tortilla and drinking my juice. I was offered drugs, women, and something called an "animal show." I was fairly certain it would not be Spot jumping through a hoop.

I walked through a residential street and exercised my Spanish comprehension on a sign bearing the message, *Mr. neighbor, don't throw garbage here. Throw it to your fucking mother cunt.*

I thought of Paloma's bumper stickers, such as *We are here to awaken from our illusion of separateness.*

. . . and I walked on, comfortable here as I had been in Modelo. My sense of self-preservation suggested I stay in Mexico and forget about Cheyenne.

But at midnight, I turned around and walked back toward the international bridge. How simple my life would have been had I become an expat running a little orange-juice stand in Ciudad Juárez.

Instead, I got a motel room in El Paso. Still thinking about Cheyenne, I watched a YouTube video on the life of a healer who said he was immortal, that death was a government method of control, and that he had software that would make *you* immortal just like him. On the side of the YouTube screen was an update: he'd signed on as guest speaker on a cruise ship and died in his cabin during the second night at sea.

---

Next morning, I continued along Interstate 10 through hilly country that was bleak, dry, and wild. But once, there had been enough grass and water to raise cattle. Dirt roads ran off into rugged terrain where the herds had grazed. This had been a last frontier for cattlemen, and I knew that Dez would like it here. There was room to breathe. With horses to ride and the young woman in the photo to keep him company, he'd be a happy man.

One of the dirt roads off the main drag took me to the Lazy 9. The name was written in wrought iron over a high old gate, the 9 lying flat on its back, hence "lazy." The corral was huge, its fence of mesquite trunks and branches woven together around a frame of iron. I parked next to it and got out. The smell of hay, manure, and horse filled my soul and took me back to the monastery.

I leaned on the fence and patted the white star on the warm head of a stallion. The stallion nuzzled my hand, but he was nobody's pet. Horses keep their self-respect. All that muscle and power—they know what they have to offer. They once pulled the world.

In eleven hours of driving, I'd passed hundreds of small horse ranches. For horse people, it's obvious there is no other way of life, and leaning on the corral fence, I had to agree. A few of the horses pranced around, kicking up dust. The desert sun beat down on us, but the flies were few and the hay was stacked up in an open storage barn nearby, its rich aroma no doubt reassuring to the inhabitants of the corral.

I heard children playing somewhere beyond the corral. I walked around it and saw the ranch office, then adobe casitas in desert garden settings. A few guests were seated under their ramadas. The children were playing in an enclosed area, squealing as they climbed a colorful plastic installation offering chutes, ladders, and monkey bars.

A young woman in a cowboy hat was seated at a nearby picnic table, watching the kids to be sure they weren't murdering each other. Her shirt had the logo of the ranch on it, so I approached her, opening the gate to the play area. She looked up with a smile. "One of them yours?"

"I'm looking for Desmond."

She glanced at a list. "Not here. Some of the other kids are in the game room."

"They call him Dez. He works here as a wrangler."

"I haven't been here that long myself. I don't know all the guys' names. Anyway, they're all out on the trails."

"I'm also looking for a young woman who works as a wrangler. Tall . . ." I couldn't very well say *stacked and beautiful,* which was what I'd seen in the photograph Dez showed me. As I was struggling for a less pointed description, the girl got my drift. "I think you want Miranda. Everybody else does. She's out with guests too. She should be back soon."

I found some shade outside the nearby nature room. It faced the trail the dude riders would be returning on. After a while, I got bored and entered the nature room. It was poorly lit, but one wall had illuminated glass terrariums in it. As I went nearer, I realized that each of them housed a rattlesnake.

"Don't point and don't get too close," said a stern voice from the shadows. "You'll frighten them."

One of the snakes had already risen up in the striking position. I heard its rattle buzzing as a short, matronly woman came alongside me. "It doesn't see the glass. You're a predator and it knows it can't escape."

"Sorry," I said, backing away.

"We have a movie about venom." She pointed to a screen.

"Thanks, but I'm waiting for someone."

I gazed at the rattler in its glass cage, body still coiled in striking position, prepared for some serious killing. I was thinking of Bustamante. And then, for no reason, I was thinking of Cheyenne.

"Their gastric juices are very powerful. They can digest bone." The nature lady spoke this almost lyrically. She had a deep appreciation of rattlesnakes.

What does the eye of the rattlesnake express? Something remote from mankind. And again I thought of Cheyenne.

I was getting a very strange message from this nature room.

"If you're staying long, I really recommend the video."

"I'm not a guest. I'm here to visit one of the staff."

"Which one?"

"Miranda."

"Oh, *her.*"

I resumed my lookout position on the bench outside the door to the nature room.

Then I saw *her*. Tall in the saddle, wearing tight jeans, a white cowboy hat, and a white tank top with the ranch logo. She was leading a string of guests on horseback toward the stables.

I waited until the horses were unsaddled and the guests were on their way to their casitas. She came out of the stable chewing a piece of straw. Her face and shoulders glistened with sweat. "I'll be going out again in an hour. I've got to wash up first."

"I'm not riding, thanks. I'm a friend of Desmond."

The smile left her face. "Did he send you?"

Her long brown hair hung down straight from her white hat. She wore lots of eye makeup. A little glamour in the saddle probably helped with tips from the male guests. A huge silver belt buckle flashed the sun back at me. But there was no warmth in her expression. I sensed something was wrong. I said, "I haven't seen Dez for two weeks."

"That makes two of us."

"He's not here?"

"Nope." The tone of her voice made it clear she was over Dez. A man who doesn't show up for a good-looking woman is quickly history.

"I left him outside your door in Paloma."

"Yeah, we talked half the night. And the other half, well . . ." She managed a smile to indicate the pleasure principle had been served. "I took him back to his place just before sunup. He was going to grab a few things. Always a mistake."

She put her fringed boot up on the corral fence, producing a very lovely curve in her jeans. "Leave home in what you're wearing. Otherwise, you get dragged back."

"Is that what you think happened?"

She lowered her boot and kicked at the sandy soil. "His wife's a world-class bitch with a will of steel. What do you think?"

"I don't know what to think. I expected to find him here."

"Well, you came a long way. They do a nice lunch buffet."

"I might try it after I watch the venom video."

"That's about snakes and spiders. What do you know about horses?"

"I got to know them in Mexico."

"What were you doing in Mexico?"

"I was a monk."

Her eyes showed she was intrigued by the image. Most women will look with sympathy on a man who shuts himself up in a monastery, searching his soul. It's proof, at least, that he has one.

She said, "After lunch, you can join the ride. I've got a mare that will suit you very well."

"Why's that?"

"She has a mind of her own, but she likes a firm rider." Her faint smile suggested I interpret this several ways.

I saw the possibilities. Lunch, ride, take a casita for the night. There's a soft knock at the door, she's standing there in her tight jeans. It seemed that a kind fate was providing an alternative to Cheyenne.

Yes, I should've taken that alternative, just as I should have opened an orange-juice stand in Mexico.

# 33

"He didn't go to the dude ranch in Texas."

"Then where did the little weasel go?" Cheyenne was preparing chili for us in her kitchen. She poked at the stove as if it were an extraterrestrial object she was not completely familiar with.

The apron she wore reinforced the image of her as a housewife, but the chili was almost inedible, its heat level beyond human endurance. The rice was hard and underdone. She didn't seem to notice, eating with the same indifference she applied to her cooking.

After cooling my tongue with ice water, I said, "I don't know where Dez went, but he didn't leave you for another woman."

Her eyes narrowed. "You think I care?"

"I got the impression you did."

"You got it wrong. I gave that man a new life, and he went and got himself slimed again. I'm not shedding any tears."

And I was sitting at the table where Dez used to sit, trying to eat her chili without setting the roof of my mouth on fire. Maybe it was her cooking that drove him away.

She said, "You saw his rodeo queen?"

"I did."

"She seduce you?"

"I resisted her charms."

"And you're right proud of yourself. But she slimed you. You're covered with it."

"I'm sorry I've polluted your immaculate kitchen." I was looking at the storage tins above the stove, on which she'd let a layer of dust and cooking grease slowly form. I felt it had a close resemblance to slime.

After coffee, we wound up where we usually did, in her bedroom. She pressed her bare breasts against my chest, saying softly, "It's hard for someone with my dimensional makeup to be near spiritual toxicity."

This kind of talk no longer drove me up the wall. She had to try out new material, and I was handy. I'd begun to appreciate how seamless her performance was. She said, "I get around your toxicity by tuning you harmonically with my light body."

"And they said it couldn't be done."

We commenced an hour of harmonic tuning. At the end, we were wrapped in each other's arms, soaking with perspiration from the desert sun streaming into her bedroom. She refused to run the air-conditioning, because it interfered with her psychic resonance. She was a complete method actor.

She stood and walked to the shower. From the bed, I reached over to her night table for a book lying there. To my surprise, it was a collection of poetry she'd written, self-published in a small, spiral-bound folio.

To the muffled sound of her singing in the shower, I read her poetry. There was nothing in it about alien grays. It was about romantic love on Bourbon Street in New Orleans, and she'd poured out her feelings. Her lines had a swing, but she'd chosen three-card monte over poetry. Nevertheless, I was certain she'd left her book out for me to see, to show me that her sensitivity could be applied to something other than invaders from outer space. I was wrong, of course. Her game was deeper than that.

When she came out of the shower and saw me reading it, she said disdainfully, "That's just some junk Cheyenne wrote. It all happened before."

"Before what?"

"Before Cheyenne left. Before I came."

I held the book up to her. "It means nothing to you?"

"Just a bunch of foolish girl thoughts."

She was coming toward me, naked from the waist up, towel wrapped around her hips. She let the towel fall to the floor, making sure I got an eyeful of her perfect derriere.

"Close your mouth, Martini. You look downright indecent."

I said, "I like your poems."

"Take them with you. I have no use for them." She sat on the bed and dried her feet. "It's not easy to be me, pretending I'm Cheyenne when in fact I'm a messenger from another world."

She turned her head and looked at me, and I was suddenly clearer about what I always saw in her eyes. They were saying, *How much will you swallow?* It was almost like fair play, giving me a chance to back out of being just another of her shills.

I heard a car driving up. As the car door slammed, Cheyenne said, "I completely forgot. I have an appointment."

"Do you want me to leave?"

"No, you'll be an asset."

"I can't think why."

"A man has been kicking a mousey thing around. You look like you could kick him back."

We dressed quickly and Cheyenne answered the door. "Come on in, hon. Make yourself comfortable. This is Father Martini. He's an ordained priest, and he works closely with me."

The young woman tried to smile at me, failed, and sat down at the kitchen table. Cheyenne said, "We don't have to hear your story, hon. It's all in your energy fields. I see right off the bat you've got alien drains on your womb. Father Thomas and I will get those suckers first."

She scanned the young woman with her hands, and I saw the young woman's face slowly relax. "And you've got an implant in your nervous system. That's typical." She patted the young woman's hand. "But don't you worry your pretty little head. Implants can be dissolved if you know how. Isn't that right, Father? Can we get an amen?"

I had become, at least for the moment, one of Cheyenne's shills. But I felt sorry for the young woman. I nodded my agreement, feeling like one of those hucksters who traveled the old Southwest with elixirs and pills.

Step right up, brothers and sisters, we can heal your joints, your piles, and the rash on your privates.

Cheyenne pretended to work against difficult odds, emitting a few theatrical groans. But when she was done with her bogus healing, the young woman was smiling. The color had come back to her cheeks. She gave me a look of gratitude. "Thank you so much, Father. I felt your spiritual power. Are you an exorcist?"

I told her I wasn't, but she didn't believe me. She thought I was reluctant to trot out my Vatican credentials.

Then she tried to pay Cheyenne, who promptly refused her. "Tell your man if he hits you again, Father Thomas will beat the daylights out of him."

"I'm not going back to him. I decided on that while you were working on me."

At the door, she was still trying to give Cheyenne something in payment, but Cheyenne only laughed. And then the young woman was gone.

"Why did you tell her I was a priest?"

"Because her son of a bitch boyfriend destroyed her trusting heart. Father Thomas renewed that trust."

Her concern for the girl was genuine. I'd seen it with other women she worked on.

But her coffee was on a par with her chili, strong and burnt. Her kitchen table was covered with pages on UFO activity, printed from the internet. A woman claiming to be a walk-in explained that periodically, walk-ins are sent to earth to raise our consciousness. Ordinarily, she's a starship commander from the Intergalactic Council.

They're always commanders. You never get a walk-in who's an intergalactic accountant.

I asked, "Now that Dez's paycheck is no longer coming in, how are you going to get along if you don't start charging for these private sessions?"

"Don't you worry about me."

I should have worried, but not about how she was going to make a living.

# 34

Maybe nightly sex with Cheyenne was responsible for it, but a turf war with Nico no longer made sense to me. I called his office, talked to his beautiful receptionist, and asked for an appointment with the great man. The next day, I was on my way.

The road out of Paloma took me past Eagle Rock. Some locals had climbed it at the summer solstice to await the emergence of a UFO. They believed that the roof of the mountain was hinged and the UFO would fly out.

And then I caught the interstate, doing seventy-five miles an hour through a desert where people had once traveled on foot and hunted with sharp stones. The land looked now as it had then, rugged and dry, its water hidden. Wherever I stopped, I could feel the old Indians. I could also feel the prospectors, those tough customers who had found wealth in these hills, then blew it all on booze, women, and cards and went looking for more.

At a rest stop, I gazed down into the biggest valley I'd ever seen, stretching out below me for miles to the base of a mountain where a few houses stood alone, a dirt road winding up to them. Who was living there, and why? Were they still looking for gold and copper, or just peace of mind?

I would negotiate with Nico and get some peace of mind.

I saw an exit sign to a place called Honeybee. Wouldn't it be nice to live in Honeybee? A bit of quiet buzzing from flower to flower. I was sure there were some pretty flowers down there, desert beauties descended from those women who came out here to make their own fortune when the mines were flourishing.

After a little while, the interstate began to fill up with traffic bound for Phoenix. Into the Valley of the Sun we went, eight lanes of us, the honeybees of the road, swarming together, blending almost miraculously. How do we do it? I often wonder. Manage this breakneck ballet, changing lanes, reading signs, blasting the horn, giving the finger.

The tall buildings of Phoenix rose up before me, giant versions of a pueblo village. I found my exit, left the swarm, and made my way to the Camelback Corridor and the Ritz-Carlton. My reservation was waiting, a deluxe room with a view of the mountains. I wanted to approach Nico with a sense of well-being instead of coming in like a maddened buffalo.

The bathtub was marble, and I soaked in it for a while. Then, wrapped in a thick hotel bathrobe, I sat at the window, watching the mountains. They'd watched over the rush for gold, and now they watched rival gang members fighting to distribute cocaine and heroin. According to Dominic, the Menacing Wind did a brisk business in this, along with slave trafficking and crooked real estate deals.

Sitting in my deluxe window, I called Wendy Wexford. Would she like to join me for dinner?

I heard the bark of a small dog in the background, the eagerness of a terrier in the voice, begging for permission to pounce on a rat.

"What brings you to Phoenix?"

"Just a little business."

Another pause. Then "The priest at Our Lady has been singing your praises, by the way."

"I can't think why."

"He says you saved his church."

"Did he say how?"

"Not really. Only that you'd exerted some influence where it mattered." The terrier was barking again, was told to *shut up*, and then Ms. Wexford told me, more gently than she'd spoken to her terrier, "The effort to save the church has resumed. I'm pretty sure we're going to get landmark status."

"And am I going to get dinner with you?"

"Since you were so helpful to the cause, I suppose it's the least I can do."

"Can I hope for more?"

"Don't push your luck."

# 35

I met her on the candlelit patio of a Japanese restaurant. Her ponytail had given way to shoulder-length blond hair. She came toward me in a beaded white-silk dress, her arms bare. The scoop neckline was low. The night was warm, and she looked very cool.

I'd chosen a banquette because it gave me legroom. She sat down beside me, her own stunning legs on display because the table in front of us was low, coffee table height. She said, "Father Don is like a new man. It seems you did more than give him back his church."

I didn't want to talk about Father Don. But what else could we talk about? I was realizing how bizarre all my exchanges with Cheyenne and Sally were. Wendy Wexford lived in the real world, and the real world required real conversation.

"Cat got your tongue?" Her hand was on the banquette cushion between us, her nails two shades of silver.

"I was thinking how unprepared I am."

"For what?"

"For talking to you."

"I won't hold you to any high standard, I promise." She turned to the waiter and asked me if I wanted to order the wine. I let her order it. Bouncers drink the house wine. The last good wine I'd had was brewed at the monastery and had no name.

The waiter poured. Wendy sampled a pinot grigio and gave him the go-ahead. We touched glasses. I breathed in the faint aroma of some hill in Italy and tasted the grape of my ancestors.

We studied the menu together, but I followed her recommendations and she gave the order to the waiter. When we were alone again, she said, "So tell me about the monastery."

"A lot of very quiet men."

"Sounds good to me. I talk all day long. It can get pretty tedious."

"So can silence. But after a while, it seems normal. I'd go to the village on a shopping trip for the monastery, and the voices in the street grated on me."

"And now?" She gestured toward the crowd starting to fill up the restaurant. "Does *that* bother you?"

"I've had a month in Paloma. I'm getting used to civilization again."

"How do you like it in Paloma?"

"The atmosphere is unique."

"Meaning?"

"A woman buried her computer in the desert because it had a demonic presence in it."

"Every day, I wish I could bury *my* computer." Then she caught me staring at her legs.

I said, "I've only been out of the monastery a short time."

But conversation picked up, and the only interruption was when Nico Bottazzi came into the restaurant and our eyes met. He was with his knock-out Italian receptionist. Because he's an arrogant prick, he left her standing in the patio doorway and sauntered toward us. He greeted Wendy as if they were old friends, and they chatted a bit about the commercial real estate market.

Nico's receptionist was tapping her foot in the doorway. She'd spent hours on her hair, makeup, and clothes to make a grand entrance, and Nico had ruined her momentum.

While chatting with Wendy, Nico cast me a sidelong glance but didn't mention our meeting for tomorrow. He was talking to an attractive woman, and macho posturing did not permit him to acknowledge me. Until tomorrow, I was invisible. He enjoyed ignoring me for a while, then made some gallant closing remarks to Wendy and returned to the other end of the room, where he and his receptionist were shown to their table. But a wall of mirrors allowed me to see them as they ordered, as they ate. And as the evening moved along, I began to see myself and Nico clearly in the mirror of my mind. We were a pair of Italian sausages, stuffed with pride. Along with my supper, I had to digest a hard fact—that five years of prayer and meditation had done little to change me. So I was determined to hold my temper and cut a deal with Nico tomorrow.

Wendy and I ordered dessert—warm oranges in sake cream. As we sipped our green tea, she said, "You're seeing someone in Paloma."

I wondered whether, during my five years in the monastery, all women had learned to read men's minds.

She smiled, but the implication was clear. She would not be going back to my room at the Ritz-Carlton. But we'd had a nice evening, and after handing her ticket to the parking valet outside, she gave me a peck on the cheek and said, "It was fun. Let's do it again."

I saw Clemente and Fortunato across the street, waiting for Nico. I gave them a friendly wave, and Clemente gave me the finger.

"Friends of yours?" asked Wendy.

"We've met a few times."

A Chinese kid went by on a pedicab. A tough job, but it was keeping him in shape. Wendy's car came to the curb and she climbed in, giving me a last look at her beautiful legs. And with a smile, she drove off.

The doors behind me opened, and Nico came out, with his receptionist by his side. Like Wendy, she was lovely to look at, and murder did not reside in her heart. Nico and I were the insane ones. Clemente and Fortunato swaggered up to greet their boss. I turned to him and said, "I'm looking forward to our meeting tomorrow."

"I am too, Tommy. I'm sure we can work everything out, including you burning down my cabin."

The kid on the pedicab had turned around and was on his way back. Because I was facing the street, I saw his hand move from inside his loose shirt. It was a full hand, and I hit the pavement. Two shots rang out, and blood sprayed over me, along with the brain matter of Clemente and Fortunato.

As I pushed their dead bodies off me, I heard the screech of tires and car doors opening. Before I could get to my feet, I was looking at the barrel of a street sweeper from Grandfather Primo's era.

It was a clumsy, outdated weapon, so the guy using it probably liked its ugly look, with the ammo loaded in a cylindrical drum. But it wasn't called a street sweeper for nothing. The drum would advance twelve rounds quickly and blow me into many pieces.

More impressive than this vintage firearm was the young Chinese man pointing it at me. He was a giant, the product of a genetic tree specializing in size extra large. He'd helped nature along with a great many steroid injections and endless rounds of pumping iron.

His shoulders began just under his ears. His lats stuck out like wings, and his biceps were as big as my head. He was made even bigger by the armored vest he was wearing. He waved me to my feet. A second man, unarmed and sporting a dragon tattoo on his bald head, stood beside him, watching with satisfaction. Clearly the boss.

The giant shoved us into the third row of a Chevy Suburban, then got into the second row, keeping the street sweeper pointed at us. The Chevy Suburban, with room for nine passengers, is a favorite of families, and we had just become a tight-knit family.

The bald man climbed into the front seat beside the driver. I could now see the back of his head; the dragon tattoo circled his neck, its nostrils shooting jets of flame up onto his bare skull.

Nico's terrified receptionist let out a cry as the door locks of the Suburban came down with a resounding snap. Nico, sitting beside her, remained calm.

The driver pulled away from the curb. The bald man beside him turned around and asked Nico, "How was your meal?"

"We'll work this out, Rong."

Nico's receptionist hissed to Nico in a low, trembling voice, "I told you . . ."

The implication was that she had warned him something like this would happen if he kept dissing a Chinese gang lord.

"Shut up," he snapped without looking at her, his eyes still on Rong. "I overstepped the mark. Apologies. Okay? I'll make it right."

"You'll make it right for Rong?" The gang lord laughed at his joke.

"Definitely. I'll make it better than right."

"But you liked your meal?"

"I did."

The gang lord nodded and turned away from us. His driver was moving quickly along Camelback, then turning into a side street where another ride was waiting. The Suburban must have been stolen, because it was abandoned without ceremony and we were put into a Hummer.

The Hummer is a very comfortable vehicle. Once again our little family had lots of room. But Nico and his receptionist didn't seem to appreciate the comfort of the seating. She was no longer speaking English, her asides to Nico now in Italian interspersed with sobs, which he continued to ignore. He was trying to deal with the gang lord.

But the gang lord said nothing, only stared out the front window of the Hummer. He obviously had no concerns about having just killed Nico's bodyguards. He'd left bodies on the streets before.

Chinese music was playing on the sound system. Lots of cymbal crashing and wooden flutes along with oddly tuned string instruments. It had the quality of a much older civilization in harmony with nature, until it changed to Asian hip-hop and I realized that the nature part was the introduction.

The driver tapped his fingers to the hip-hop beat.

"You can have the property," said Nico. "It's yours free and clear."

The answer was Chinese hip-hop.

We were threading our way through the grid of Phoenix, where the new wealth of the West is being won by health-care practitioners. Every corner has its dental implanter, its sleep clinic, and health centers with contorted names such as Lifewell or Integrative Specialized Synergy.

I had the feeling Nico was going to need some health care soon. For myself, I didn't know.

Nico continued to seek resolution. "It's the building permits that kill progress here. It takes you a year to get a single piece of paper. Am I right?"

He got no response, so he continued his critical analysis of business ventures in Phoenix. "If you dig up native plants, you have to replant them exactly the way you found them, facing the same direction, with the same degree of shade. The hoops you go through over a cactus, it's nuts. But I finally have hooks into the people who control building permits. I've paid plenty, but it's money well spent. You can take advantage of that. We can get around regulations. We can do things others can't. Come in with me, Rong."

He was talking as if to another reasonable businessman.

We turned off the six-lane thoroughfare and continued until we reached the outskirts of the city.

We were now away from any residential neighborhood. Buildings were spaced far apart. I saw a body shop, several storage facilities, a recycling plant.

We continued until we had empty terrain on both sides of us. I saw a single building ahead, with three large industrial chimneys, and then I saw a sign that said *Tian Cremation Center.*

We drove behind the building and parked.

The giant nudged my ribs with the street sweeper, and we got out of the Hummer.

"What is this, Rong?" asked Nico.

"A family business," said Rong.

Rong went to the door and punched in the entry code on a number pad. The door swung open. Rong gestured for us to enter. I was assisted by a poke in the back from the street sweeper, and we proceeded into the building.

We were in the receiving area, where the loved one arrives, carried in by the cremation handlers. Stacked up were empty cardboard boxes marked HUMAN REMAINS.

Nico's receptionist screamed. I'd heard a scream like that in the monastery garden, when a rabbit was captured by a fox. It was a scream of recognition. Rong nodded to his driver, who pushed her ahead of us.

Rong switched on some hallway lights, and Nico's receptionist continued to scream, stumbling on her high heels as she was pushed forward.

A pair of wheeled stretchers were parked along the wall of the hallway. Rong placed two of the boxes on one of them. "Go forward, please," he said to Nico and me. He followed, wheeling the stretcher. Everyone's familiarity with the procedure suggested they did it regularly.

The giant still had his street sweeper in my back. The wheels of the rolling stretcher echoed in the hallway.

Nico called ahead to Rong. "We need to have a proper negotiation. There's a great deal of money at stake." I noticed that his Italian accent had grown more noticeable.

We proceeded into a large room whose center was a three-doored furnace. Several rakes and other scraping tools leaned against a wall. Rong rolled the wheeled stretcher in front of the furnace. The doors were open.

Nico's receptionist stared at the furnace dumbly, then started to pray. The cardboard boxes marked HUMAN REMAINS stayed on top of the stretcher.

Rong said to Nico, "I offered you a good deal. Do you remember what you said?"

"Whatever I said was a mistake. Okay? I admit that."

"You said go fuck yourself."

Rong flipped a switch, and the furnace chambers filled with flame. The flames were driven by some sort of fan that produced a roaring dance of fire.

Nico said, "I spoke wrongly. It was stupid and offensive."

"Then you hung up the phone."

"I acted like an asshole."

"But you enjoyed your meal tonight?"

"I did."

Rong's hand moved with one quick thrust of the knife he'd been holding out of sight. It went straight into Nico's chest. Nico stared down at it. He was still staring as Rong twisted it in deeper.

Nico's expression softened. He looked like a cherub on the Sistine ceiling. As he started to sink downward, the giant stepped in front of me and put the street sweeper's muzzle against my stomach. "Don't move."

Rong caught Nico, and he and his driver placed him in the cardboard box on the stretcher. He lay there with the knife sticking out of his chest. Rong put two fingers to Nico's throat, feeling for a pulse. Then he looked at me.

"I wouldn't want to burn him alive."

He pulled his knife out of Nico's chest and looked at the bloody blade with satisfaction. Then he wiped it clean on Nico's shirt. He was still smiling. He'd enjoyed sticking his knife into Nico. He'd done it expertly, and death had been nearly instant. I thought he must have gotten the aorta. Living in prison teaches you how to inflict a fatal stab wound, and I assumed that prison had been part of Rong's training.

He removed Nico's Rolex, wallet, and rings. Then he and the driver shoved the cardboard box with Nico's body inside it into the furnace.

The flames danced up around the cardboard box, devouring it.

Rong flipped another switch, and the door of the furnace chamber lowered with a clanking sound, sealing Nico's body inside.

His receptionist let out a wailing sob and collapsed on the floor, hair falling into her eyes. Rong ignored her and looked at a clock on the wall. It was an old-fashioned wall clock with a white face and large, dark numbers.

"He'll be cooking for three hours." Rong looked at me. "Unfortunately, sir, you left the restaurant at a bad time."

"What about the girl?"

"We will sell her. Turn around, please, hands to the back of the head."

They'd seen too many reality police shows. Or maybe the police had said to them one time, *hands behind your head*. But cops know the proper choreography of the move. These guys didn't. I turned as directed, and the barrel of the street sweeper came to the back of my head.

Twisting from the waist, I uncoiled. Oversize muscles and his Kevlar vest slowed the giant's reaction time. My right hand was pushing the barrel of his gun aside as he fired it.

One blast only warms a gun barrel, so I was able to hold on. Still gripping the barrel, I pulled him forward and kicked him in the groin. Then I came around with everything I had, driving my elbow into his temple. When it landed, I knew it was Christmas. Steroids don't bulk up your head, and lifting weights doesn't armor it with muscle. It's just tight skin and bone. I'd jarred his brain, and he was unconscious standing up, and I had the street sweeper.

Using him as a shield, I swung toward the driver, who was firing away, but all I felt was the jerking of the giant's body as the bullets hit his Kevlar vest.

I blasted the driver with the sweeper and swung on Rong, who put his hands in the air. He said, "A hundred grand to you, right now. We have to drive to get it, but it's cool. The money's clean, small bills, wrapped."

I let go of the giant, who fell to the floor between us. Nico's receptionist crawled away, puking.

Rong said, "Why am I cutting corners? Half a million cash. And if you want, you can join my organization. I see you're familiar with this line of work."

With gang lords, it's all about image. I'd damaged his severely, demonstrating his stupidity and, at this moment, his cowardice. He would want to eradicate the memory of that.

Nevertheless, I could let him live, the way he was going to let Nico's receptionist live because she was beautiful.

But he wasn't beautiful, and I shot him.

Life is too complicated for Chinese philosophy.

And I was under pressure. The giant was coming back to consciousness and reaching for the driver's gun on the floor. I kicked him in the head, aiming for the goalposts. My left leg puts you in the hospital, my right leg puts you in the cemetery.

And we were in the cemetery already. Okay, crematorium, close enough. And the giant was dead, his head flopped to the side. I'd broken his neck with my kick.

My adrenaline was pumping wildly. I had to calm down, had to think straight. There were three bodies on the floor.

I wanted to clear out immediately. I closed my eyes and took counsel with Grandfather Primo.

*Even a dead body can talk, Tommy. And there are people who know how to listen.*

# 36

I turned to the receptionist. She was trying to get up, one high-heeled shoe off and one on. She kicked the other one off and managed to stand. Her face was streaked with mascara, and her hair still hung in her eyes. When she brushed it back, I saw the terror on her face as if the muscles were frozen that way. I said, "It's over, but we have to stay here a while."

She nodded, wiping her mouth with the back of her hand. She was trying to compose herself, but her hand was shaking as she drew it away.

I went to the front of the crematorium and got three more cardboard boxes marked HUMAN REMAINS. My pulse was still thumping, so I whistled a happy tune as I came back to the furnace room. I laid the boxes down and said to her, "I can handle this myself."

She said, "I'll help." Then she held out her hand. "I am Renata." She was no longer the aloof receptionist. Her hair and makeup were shot, and her bare feet reminded me of a country girl I'd once seen picking wildflowers in the hills of Sicily.

I removed Nico's Rolex from Rong's wrist, along with the rest of his gold bling, and gave it to Renata. She put the Rolex on her wrist, where it hung like an oversize bracelet. Her dress had slit pockets, purely for the look, but she loaded them up with the bling.

I removed the cash from everybody's wallets, along with their phones. I left the credit and identity cards; eighteen hundred degrees Fahrenheit would take care of them. From the driver's pocket, I took the keys to the Hummer. From Rong's pocket, I took his knife. My pulse was back to normal.

Renata was looking at Rong. "He said he was going to sell me." A question furrowed her brow. "To who?"

"A Saudi prince?"

I removed the Kevlar vest from the giant. You can hit Kevlar with a fire-bomb and it won't burn. Then I threw the switches that opened the furnace doors. The doors lifted slowly, and the fire roared into view.

Inside the flames, Nico was cooking like a turkey, his skin waxy and blistered, with fluids bubbling out of him. Renata drew back, her hands covering her mouth. "Oh my God . . ."

I put Rong in a cardboard box and shoved him in with Nico. They could share hell together. I'd undoubtedly be joining them at some future date.

I had two more bodies to handle, and the heat from the three furnaces was cooking me. I looked around and found gloves and a fireproof apron. I lifted the giant into a cardboard box. He was a load and a half, but I managed to push him into the second furnace chamber.

The driver was last, and I put him in the third furnace chamber. I hit the switches again and lowered the doors. They clanged shut with the sound of hell closing over, and I knew that the Martini family curse had caught up to me again.

I looked at the wall clock. Three hours to go.

"We can't leave until we're sure they're completely burned."

"I understand." She'd combed her hair, but it still had a wild look. She'd straightened her dress. But her shoes were in her hand. If she had to run, she wouldn't be doing it in high heels.

The street sweeper had blown pieces of Rong onto the floor. I got a broom, and she held the pan resolutely. I reopened the furnace door, she threw Rong's remains into the flames, and I closed the door again.

"We've got to get the blood off the floor." There was a sink and mop nearby. I used to mop the monastery hallway. I had good mopping skills. So did she. She got on her hands and knees and scrubbed. More than ever, she looked like a Sicilian girl from the hills.

After carefully cleaning up the floor, we cleaned prints off the street sweeper and the driver's automatic. Rong had been carrying only his knife, and it was in my pocket. I'd be keeping it.

We explored the building. There was no waiting room for bereaved relatives, no display of fancy urns for the remains of the beloved. That part of the business was handled at a more upscale location. This place was strictly for burning bodies.

Renata said, "I don't want to get involved with the police. I want to leave for Italy tonight. You're in Nico's appointment book, but we have a remote computer account. I can remove all trace of you with my laptop. I'll do it at my apartment before I leave."

She was a very competent receptionist.

We had three hours to kill. She found a Chinese newspaper and looked at the pictures.

I found a copy of *People* magazine and forced myself to read it from cover to cover, retaining nothing.

I also found a manual for one of the pieces of machinery in the crematorium, and I retained everything.

When the hands of the clock came to the appointed hour, we returned to the furnace room and I opened the chamber doors. Just bones. The skulls were in pieces but discernible. I took the nearby rake and raked the bones, breaking them into smaller pieces.

"We have to reduce them a little more."

I closed the doors for another half hour. When I reopened them, all that remained were small fragments. I shut off the furnaces.

At the front of each chamber was a wide horizontal slot. I raked the bone fragments into the slots. The slots emptied into rectangular cans. I filled three cans and carried them to the piece of machinery I'd studied up on while we waited. It was a round canister called a cremulator.

I poured the fragments in and switched it on. It was like a large high-speed blender.

After twenty minutes of blending, I lifted the lid. A bit of gray dust billowed out.

I emptied the dust into a garbage bag. Renata put her high-heeled shoes back on, and we rechecked the furnace room, making sure everything was the way it had been when we first entered. We did the same thing in the office. The place was as we'd found it, when our companions were alive and well. Now they were ashes in a garbage bag. I carried the bag and the Kevlar vest.

Renata carried a second garbage bag, containing weapons. I wasn't worried about prints left behind. Tian Cremation Center would not be looking for fingerprints or anything else. All they did was dispose of bodies. When they learned of the disappearance of their relative Rong, they would have no reason to think he'd been turned to ashes in their establishment. I switched out the lights, and we left the crematorium.

We put the two garbage bags and the Kevlar vest into the Hummer, and I drove away with Renata beside me.

She said, "All other nights of my life will be like nothing compared to this."

I didn't drive back toward the city but went farther along the deserted road until I'd left all buildings behind and there was just desert on both sides.

We climbed out, and I emptied the garbage bag containing the ashes. A breeze was blowing, and Renata stepped aside to keep the ashes out of her hair.

The breeze scattered the ashes over sand, cactus, and tumbleweed. Above us, Orion the Hunter was out, his bow of stars bent, his arrow aimed. Above him were the seven sisters he'd saved. Well, I had saved one of them, with a street sweeper, not an arrow, but results are what count.

As the ashes blew away, I chanted some of the *Liturgia Defunctorum*, because Nico and the Menacing Wind were certainly defunct.

"Very good," said Renata. "Complete."

Maybe she would contact Bishop Bottazzi regarding further blessings for Nico, but I doubted it.

I used the Hummer's jack handle to dig a hole in the sand and buried the weapons and the Kevlar vest. We got back into the Hummer and traced our way back through the city. Bars close at two, and the streets were pretty much empty except for 7-Elevens, and we passed a twenty-four-hour fitness place with a few lone lifters pumping iron in the window. A windowless adult store flashed that it was open. For those needing a doughnut in a hurry, Dunkin' Donuts was open. As we drove, Renata called the airport and managed to get an Alitalia flight to Rome, leaving in five hours. When we were a few blocks away from her apartment, I parked on a side street. "Use this," said Renata, taking a small hand sanitizer from her purse. I wiped down the interior of the Hummer, and we left it and walked the rest of the way.

Of her apartment, I remember pale wood furniture covered in white leather. It was all new and tasteful, I'm sure. There was a nice view of the city lights.

She sat at a desk in the window and opened a laptop computer. "I'm connecting to Nico's database." Her voice was calm, but she hadn't regained the look of the chic receptionist. Her hair was still a little wild, and she'd kicked off her high heels. She wouldn't be traveling to Italy in them.

While she worked the laptop, I looked at Italian fashion magazines. Then I took out the knife that had ended Nico's life. The hilt was polished pearl with little red dragons painted on it. The button lock was a ruby. I touched it, and the blade came out smoothly. The blade had a wave pattern, delicately inscribed. Knives like this go for thousands of dollars. Those ancient people who had lived around here would have thought the blade now carried a piece of Nico's soul, extracted when the knife came out of his heart.

Renata snapped the laptop shut. "You're out of Nico's life. There's no trace of you anywhere in his corporate records." She stood. The lights of Phoenix were behind her. And beyond the lights, the mountains in darkness. "Can you help me pack?"

We got everything she wanted into one large suitcase and a carry-on. She couldn't fit all her clothes in, and she left some expensive perfume behind. "Perhaps you have a girlfriend who would like it."

I put the perfume in my pocket, where it nestled beside Rong's knife. She took a last look around at the kitchen appliances, a vacuum cleaner, several carpets, and the furniture. I said, "Give me the keys. I'll get rid of what's left."

"Is there need of that?"

"The landlord will charge you for moving it away."

"Nico's corporation pays the rent. I'm not even on the mailbox. We leave it."

She called for a taxi, and we went down to the parking lot. The taxi driver was a woman, ex-military from the Air Force Base in Tucson. Renata told her we were pressed for time, but she told us not to worry, she knew the fastest turns, and she did.

As we walked through the airport, I asked Renata if Vittorio had really skimmed two million dollars from Nico. She said that had always been Nico's story. "Your uncle was a charmer. I liked him. So did Nico, until the money trouble. He said to me, *there's something wrong with that priest.* But of course, there was also something wrong with Nico."

I walked her to the ticket counter and waited while they issued her boarding pass. That was as far as I could go with her. As we said our goodbyes near the security gate, she took my head in both her hands and put her lips to mine. Her mouth opened, and the whole wild evening was transmuted into a kiss. I wanted to get on the plane with her. As our lips parted, she said, "You're burned into my heart."

I got a taxi back to the Ritz-Carlton. The lobby was deserted. I had cremation dust in my nose, but the Ritz-Carlton sprays its elevators with a pleasant scent. I rode the elevator to my floor and walked down the silent carpeted corridor. When I entered my room, I saw that the maid had turned down the bed, and a chocolate lay on the pillow. The fiction of a safe, sanitized world was complete. On the far side of town, three chimneys were cooling down, the dissipating heat all that remained of three gangsters and a bella figura.

# 37

"The alien grays turn us into robots, controlling our thoughts and emotions."

As I listened to this crap, I thought, *what a man will do for love.* But after events at the crematorium in Phoenix, it was a relief to get back to Cheyenne's crazy lectures.

"Grays are like that ocean parasite that moves into a crab and takes over its brain . . ." Had she taken over *my* brain, or just my body? As she addressed her audience, she walked through the room.

"It's frightening to see that crab walking along and you know somebody else is controlling it from within. You don't want to be like that crab."

And crazy as they were, Cheyenne's lectures were harmless, or so I thought until we went out to her favorite bar afterward and a man approached our table. He wore wire-rimmed glasses and khaki shirt and pants of the hiking variety, an outfit often seen around Paloma. There was a grim expression on his face as he stared at Cheyenne.

"Oliver, you need help," she said, calmly. "But I can't give it to you."

"Help from you is like drinking poison." He leaned his hands on the table and put his face close to hers. "You killed her. You know it and I know it."

Sally tried to intervene. "Oliver, we all feel terrible—"

"You don't feel anything."

The man from NASA stuck his oar in. "This isn't the time, Oliver."

"Fuck you, Marvin. There's never a time." He turned his attention back to Cheyenne. "You told my wife she had no soul. And she believed you. She believed she had no reason to live."

"Your wife was sick, Oliver."

"You're the one who's sick. A sick, twisted, power-tripping freak." Tears were forming in his eyes as he struggled between anger and despair. I was trying to gauge the level of his anger. I didn't want to frog-march him into the street.

He solved things by turning away and leaving the bar.

"Oliver's wife committed suicide," said Sally.

To which Cheyenne added, "She threw herself in front of the Verde Canyon train, and Oliver blames me. Grief takes people in different ways."

The NASA guy changed the subject, asking Cheyenne how the grays managed sexual intercourse and reproduction with humans, "being as they have a completely different genetic makeup from us."

I had the feeling Marvin was thinking of sexual intercourse with Cheyenne or Sally, or both. I left the table and went outside. A figure stepped out of the shadows behind me. I had him by the throat before he could do whatever it was he had in mind.

It was the grieving widower. After he finished coughing and massaging his throat, he croaked out, "You're wound up awful tight, my friend."

"Sorry, I was expecting somebody else."

"Well, I'm not him."

"Let me buy you a beer."

"Thanks, but I'm not going back in there."

"We'll go somewhere else."

"I've got nothing good to say about Cheyenne, so we'd better leave it at that." He walked away, and I watched the broken rhythm of his steps. It was as if he couldn't remember where he was going or why.

I wish I had followed him. We might have found something else to talk about. Instead, I went back into the bar and rejoined Cheyenne, Sally, and the NASA guy. As I listened to their bizarre conversation about aliens and Area 51, I thought of Wendy Wexford, a sophisticated, stylish businesswoman whose company I'd greatly enjoyed. She was elegant. She was smart. Her worldliness brought her a very good living. Cheyenne was out of this world and money meant nothing to her. But she had what Wendy didn't—the glow of enchantment called charisma.

"Martini is thinking again," said Cheyenne.

# 38

In a phone call to his parents, Dez had mentioned my name. So they came to see me, Thurston and Maybelle, two shy people with quiet country manners. They said they lived beside a great mountain range, in the high country of Wyoming. "Plenty of elk, lots of water," added Thurston.

Maybelle handed me a postcard dated a month ago. The large looping script said, *Moving out.* "He never was one for writing. But he always called me on my birthday. Which has come and gone."

"And he's not answering his phone," said Thurston.

I told them about my trip to the dude ranch. Maybelle said, "We got in touch with them too. They never heard of our Dez."

Thurston was looking through the living room window at Storm Mountain. "We've got red rocks in Wyoming, same as here. Ever seen the Killpecker Dunes?"

"I can't say I have."

"Biggest in the country. You don't want to get lost there." He was trying to talk about a missing son but having trouble. "Wild horses roam it. They got the longest manes you ever seen."

"Desmond never should've married *her*," said Maybelle. She'd used Cheyenne's name only once. It hadn't come easily and now wouldn't come at all.

"People think nothing could grow there," said Thurston, "but there's lovegrass and scurfpea. The sand holds the snowmelt." He let out a long, slow breath. He didn't want to drive this conversation. He hated where it was going.

"We knew he wouldn't last with *her*," said Maybelle. "So that weren't no surprise. Not hearing, that's what's got us worried."

Thurston asked, "You mind if I light up?"

"Go ahead."

He rolled a ragged cigarette, which flamed and crackled when he lit it. Then he started coughing with satisfaction. He seemed more comfortable coughing than talking.

"*She* was as hard a woman as you'll find," said Maybelle. "Desmond needed something softer."

"He's out there looking for one," said Thurston, with sudden commitment. It was an idea he liked.

# 39

I was contemplating Storm Mountain through the living room window when a sidecar motorcycle pulled up in front of the house. Their weather-beaten faces, their manner as they climbed off the motorcycle, told me the riders spent most of their time outdoors. They looked at the mountain first, not the house. They stood that way for a while, then gave it up for what they'd come for. As they turned toward the house, I opened the door with the Beretta on my hip and walked out to where the motorcycle was parked. They noted my firearm and introduced themselves as Stumpy and Turk, friends of Dez from Wyoming. But first we talked sidecar motorcycles. "They're trickier to drive than you think," said Turk.

Stumpy nodded. "You got uneven weight in a sidecar, which plays with your steering and braking."

After a discussion of sidecar driving, I invited them into the house.

Stumpy said, "I got a bunch of phone calls from Dez when he was jumping ship on the bitch."

The bitch was Cheyenne. I didn't defend her. I wanted to hear them out. Stumpy continued. "Dez and me always talked on the phone, but we talked a lot more around the time he planned to leave. He needed encouragement. I said hell yes, that woman's poison, call me when you're a free man. Only he never did. And that ain't like Dez."

Turk said, "There's something wrong."

Stumpy said, "Turk's got a sixth sense. Find you a pronghorn in the dark."

"And darkness is all I get from Dez," said Turk. "I could always feel him out there fooling. Now it's flat. No activity. No Dez."

Stumpy looked at me as if he were sighting a pronghorn down the barrel of his rifle, one eye closed. "What do you think?"

"This is a peaceful town," I said. I'd killed two people here, so I was in a position to know.

"The bitch says she don't know nothing," said Turk.

I thought I should clear the air. "I'm seeing her now."

"How long you been with her?" asked Stumpy.

"Since Dez went away."

"She don't let the grass grow under her feet, does she."

# 40

Cheyenne's house was one of the modest bungalows of Paloma, and more run-down than the others. It had one and a half stories with a wide upper dormer and a narrow cellar. An abandoned car came with the property. The driveway was unpaved, which I liked, and the house was adjacent to a vacant lot, which I also liked. Beyond the vacant lot was a street of double-wide trailers. No one in the dilapidated neighborhood had a view of the mountains. It was where the red rocks came to an end and drab rolling hills took over. It's why it had escaped developers. And I had begun to spend more time there, as if that salve she'd rubbed on me *had* made me her slave.

But it was simpler than that. Despite her being a con artist, I was wildly attracted to her. She was never boring. She sang to me, quoted poetry and philosophy, and told me hair-raising stories about her father who suffered from alcoholic delirium and saw snakes and dead people coming after him. "He thought I was in league with them and tried to kill me on several occasions. I finally set him straight with a shotgun."

"May I ask how?"

"I put both barrels to his head and told him I was Belle Starr. There was a statue of her in our town, holding a shotgun. From that point on, whenever he got the DTs he called me Belle and begged me to marry him."

Cheyenne and I were sitting in her messy kitchen. Dishes were in the sink, grease was on the stove, and red dust was on the floor, but I was completely comfortable because this shabby house echoed my childhood. Grandfather Primo had lived his whole life in a rundown house to hide his wealth and power from the FBI. He let the yard fill with rusting auto parts to give the look of a family barely getting by.

The front door opened, and Sally entered in one of her tight cowgirl outfits. Cheyenne mixed drinks for us even though it was ten in the morning. The example of her father didn't stop her from liking her own daily nip. She liked her nightcap too. As the gin spread through my veins, the ladies discussed the electric company putting smart meters on all the houses to better monitor power consumption. They thought smart meters were part of a plot to spy on us. Cheyenne mixed another drink and now they discussed chemtrails. "The government is making everybody in Paloma sick," said Cheyenne, "because the high level of intelligence here threatens them."

Sally said, "You can always tell government chemtrails by how long they last. Normal jet exhaust disappears quickly."

"It's because heavy chemicals stay in the air," said Cheyenne authoritatively. "Barium, aluminum salts, polymer fibers, and silicon carbide. That's what they're dumping on us."

I said, "It's condensed water vapor."

They looked at me, smiling as they might while looking at a zoo exhibit. I continued. "Hot exhaust mixes with cool air. It makes microscopic ice crystals. If there's already moisture in the air, the vapor can last for hours." The motel scientist had informed me on this subject when I'd mentioned chemtrails.

They ignored me and went on about government conspiracies, so I got up and went out into the yard, which, like Primo's, was filled with junk. I put my arms around the trunk of a large cottonwood tree and tried to lift it out of the ground. A great Punjabi wrestler trained this way every day and said, *After a tree, what is a man?* He was still fighting at seventy-two but couldn't find anyone in India willing to wrestle against him. Bouts there can go for hours. You die of heat stroke first.

I wrestled the tree for a while, then let go before I died of a heat stroke myself. I stepped around cactus and dried coyote turds and went over to Cheyenne's work shed, where she had dried herbs hanging. There were many kinds. Along with herbs, there were dried toads and lizards, and dead beetles in plastic boxes. Any of these items could wind up in my tea.

Her notebooks were in a pile, filled with herbal prescriptions I'd rather not see. But the work shed was the only space she'd organized properly. Stuff hung neatly, and there was a row of plastic cabinets of the kind used for storing nails and screws. Hers were filled with dried leaves and berries, all the drawers carefully labeled.

I watched a car drive up and a client emerge—another young damsel in distress. They were all young damsels in distress. I'd had enough of damsels for one day, so I drove back to my house. As I pulled in the driveway, I knew something was wrong. The blinds were down. I hadn't left them that way. When I got to the front door, I saw that it had been forced open, probably with a crowbar.

The curio cabinet in the hall had been smashed open. Vittorio's collection of rosaries was gone. But I knew this hadn't been just a robbery. They'd been searching for something. The couches had been upended and split open. The paintings had been pulled off the wall. Drawers were scattered around, and Vittorio's unpriestly king-size mattress had been sliced.

Angelina wouldn't have spoiled the house this way. She'd be afraid Vittorio would haunt her. And Nico and Bustamante were dead. So who had done this, and why?

In the laundry room, I pulled up the loose board and found the AK-47. They'd missed that, but I took it out in case they came back. I carried it with me into Vittorio's office.

The drawers of his desk were on the floor, and the desk was tipped over on top of them. Its old veneer and worn wooden legs were familiar to me. The desk had been Grandfather Primo's. Vittorio must have liked it. It had memories for him, as it did for me. And now as I lifted the desk back into place, one of my memories popped up, of me as a little kid watching Primo sitting behind it. There had been something odd about the way he was twisted, his left arm extended deep into the desk. Sensing my presence, he'd swung around with a look that froze me. He said I was never to come into his office without knocking. And that I mustn't tell anyone what I'd just seen. Scared shitless, I swore I never would. But I hadn't really seen anything.

Or had I? I sat down at the desk, trying to remember that day in child-hood. I twisted my body the way Primo's had been twisted, putting my left arm as far into the desk's cavity as it would go. I felt a slight indentation at my fingertip, pushed it, and a spring-loaded drawer opened. A set of keys was nestled inside it. A tag was attached to the keys:

*He who follows Me, walks not in darkness.*

Numbers were Primo's language, not poetic Scripture. Vittorio had written the words. And another childhood memory came to me, of Vitto-rio's sleight-of-hand card tricks, after which he'd say, *Never let yourself be distracted, Tommy. That's only for suckers.*

His letters were scattered around the floor. I gathered them up, but I didn't expect to learn anything more from them, so I just put them in a drawer.

Apart from his desk and a simple wooden crucifix, the rest of his office was given over to bookshelves. I started scanning the spines of the books. I paused at the *Imitation of Christ* by Thomas à Kempis, in raised gold lettering.

When I went into the monastery, he'd given me a copy, saying that of all the books a priest might read, this was the most important. This edition had the original Latin on one page and the English translation facing it. I opened it to the first page and saw *He who follows Me, walks not in darkness.*

Sixteen letters on the page were pinpricked, and putting them together, I had *Reliance Self Storage.*

# 41

A young employee wearing a Reliance cap looked at the number on the keys and checked them against a database in his phone. "ID, please."

I showed him some ID, and he opened the security gate and instructed me to park in front of a large cinder-block building. Through its windows, I could see pallets stacked up to the ceiling. A forklift was working on the floor, moving a pallet around. The young Reliance guy led me to a row of five-by-five storage units. Each of the units had a corrugated steel door. He pointed me toward one of the units and then left me alone to make my discoveries.

I turned the lock and opened the garage door. A light came on automatically, and I saw a single cardboard box. On top of it was a large cruciform shape encased in bubble wrap. I cut through the bubble wrap and liberated a cross of yellowing ivory.

The tiny faces of Christ and his apostles were carved on it in incredible detail, their cheeks smooth and lifelike, eyes expressive, hands gesturing gracefully. Their figures were embedded in the arms of the cross, horizontally and vertically. Ivory lends itself to detailed carving, but I'd never seen anything to compare with it. It came from a time when the world's greatest artists were imbued with faith. And Vittorio had stolen it from the Camel.

I set the cross down. The box it had been sitting on was sealed with packing tape. I cut through the tape and opened the box. It was filled with hundred-dollar bills. At a guess, about two million dollars' worth. There was a note on top of them.

*Dear Tommy, you're here, which means you solved my little puzzle. I always liked playing games with you because you were a good audience. And now you're no longer in the dark about me. I never should have been a priest. Primo said there had to be one in the family, it pulled the heat away from him. As a result I probably conned more people than he did. What a laugh. I scammed Bishop Bottazzi and his smart-ass brother, whose attitude I didn't like. It's his dough in this box. He thinks he's in our league but he's dreaming, so I'm confident you'll win that one.*

*The other laugh is that even while I was skimming the faithful, I was falling under the spell of Christ. Not all priests are exemplary men, but they're still priests. I know drunks, spongers, and skirt-chasers who carry an indelible mark of faith. I carry it and I'm a crook. The Lord moves in mysterious ways.*

*Vittorio*

# 42

My house was still a mess from being tossed, and I set about returning it to the way it had been before my intruders rearranged the furniture.

Cheyenne arrived when I was straightening up the kitchen, and she dug in to help me. She wasn't much of a housekeeper, but putting my house back in order inspired her, "because it sends a message to any slimy entities that entered during the break-in."

She then pronounced my house slimed from top to bottom. "Forced entry always attracts low-level spirits. They piggyback in on the perpetrator and hang around your house for months if you don't get rid of them."

It was her usual bit of method acting, but I was glad of her help. She moved furniture and burned sage, which she always carried with her. Our last job was taping the slit in the king-size mattress and wrestling it back onto the bed. Then we wrestled on it a while ourselves.

Later, she insisted we light up a couple of Vittorio's Cuban cigars, "because low-level spirits hate tobacco." So we puffed our cigars and admired the beautiful ivory cross, which I had set up in the bedroom. "There's a lot of juju in that cross. You should stash it at my place until you track down the people who messed with your space."

I was going to mess with *their* space if I could find them, but I thought her suggestion was a good one. "Coming with me?" she asked. With the cross in her arms, she looked even more like a nun than usual.

I said, "I've got to repair the door frame."

It took me the rest of the day to do it, painting and replacing the jamb and casing, then installing a new dead-bolt latch. I used deep screws on the dead-bolt latch so the bastards would have to try harder next time. Like every macho idiot, after finishing the job I felt the need for female admiration, so I drove over to Cheyenne's. Her truck wasn't there, but I hung around in the backyard. She'd started a raised-bed garden and abandoned it. Weeds were growing up out of the cinder blocks that framed it. I moved my gaze to her bird feeder. She had a visiting pair of cardinals, some cactus wrens, and a couple of woodpeckers. But then I saw some action I didn't like—a pack rat on a daylight mission under the foundation of her house. Looking for nesting material and anything else of interest, especially objects that shine, pack rat bling. I'd taken apart a pack rat nest at the monastery, and it had been filled with neat rows of mesquite beans along with broken glass rosary beads. Maybe he'd been saying his prayers, but it didn't stop me from busting up his nest. The nests attract rattlesnakes, who eat the pack rat and then move in permanently, not the sort of resident you want around your hearth and home.

I checked the pack rat's entryway, which turned out to be a two-inch crack in the foundation. Concrete would patch the crack, but I had to check the cellar first to see if there was any damage down below.

Arizona cellars are moist only in monsoon season. Otherwise, the air is dry and warm. I felt as if I were entering Pharaoh's tomb. It was a fair description. A boot heel was protruding from the concrete floor. I stared at it, wanting it to be something tossed into the cellar, old footwear left behind. But there was no mistaking what I was looking at.

The boot was attached to a human foot, and the rest of the body was buried underneath it.

For an insane moment, I thought Bustamante was haunting me, surfacing out of the concrete grave I'd put him in. But Bustamante hadn't been wearing cowboy boots.

My feelings continued playing with me, telling me Cheyenne hadn't been the first occupant of this house. Some other owner had done this.

As a teenager, I'd lugged cement for union masons. Their work was smooth as glass. The concrete on this floor had been laid by hands unfamiliar with the task. The color didn't match the walls, which had a faint yellow tinge of dust and age. And the mud on the floor hadn't been properly mixed, hadn't compressed as it should, and had cracked easily.

The air in the cellar held a faint smell of curing concrete, something most people probably wouldn't notice. But carrying mud every summer, handing it off to masons, watching them work, returning to jobs at various stages—that knowledge surfaced now, affirming what my instincts told me, that this floor was new. As a little kid, I'd been spooked by cellars. I knew that the devil lived down there, lying in wait to grab me. That feeling came back now; the walls seemed to breathe with a low, dry voice, whispering *get out and don't come back.*

But why the hell had his foot come through? She must have done a piss-poor job of burying him just after death, and when rigor mortis set in, his leg stiffened out. And she hadn't been down here since.

I heard her truck pull up, then listened to the sound of her footsteps overhead, and then her voice. "Martini, honey, where are you?"

She figured it out and came down the stairs. I pointed to the boot heel. "So this is what happened to Dez."

"Oh shit," she said softly, staring down at it in dismay.

Outside, there was a rumble of distant summer thunder. I felt as if it were in me, a storm in my mind now, where I was trying to reconcile myself to the thought that Cheyenne was a murderer.

Recovering herself, she said, "He was possessed." Feeling that this was inadequate, she added, "He was *perfectly* possessed."

"And now he's perfectly dead."

"He was completely under the control of the dark force." She let out a sigh. "Poor Dez. I tried to save him. But it was too late."

I wanted her to say that he had attacked her and she'd been fighting for her life, that she did the only thing she could do.

Instead, she said, "I don't expect you to understand. It's spiritually over your head."

Her hand was on her hip, her stance a lazy one, sloppily sensual, her bedroom look. She said, "I let you into my heart, Martini." As if this gift of intimacy would make up for my lack of spiritual discernment regarding her killing her husband.

"How did you do it?"

With thumb and index finger, she mimed firing a gun. I'd seen Dez's Colt revolver, the one with the three-inch barrel he'd said would be easy for Cheyenne to use.

I heard Sally's footsteps overhead. I watched her face as she came down the stairs. She let out a little gasp, then looked at Cheyenne. "How did his foot come through?"

Cheyenne shrugged and said, "I guess we won't be getting a job as bricklayers."

So they'd done it together.

Sally came across the cellar floor and put her arms around me. "Don't judge her too harshly."

I was remembering Grandfather Primo's cellar, and Angelina pointing to the drain in the floor, which she thought was there *to take away the blood, Tommy.* Maybe it had all been in her imagination. Or maybe not. But no imagination was needed here. They'd dug a hole in the dirt floor, dumped in his body, and then poured the whole floor. "You used too much water. Were you getting tired? Did you want to make it easier to pour? That's why it cracked."

She was looking at me defiantly, false bravado in her eyes.

I said, "Bodies move after death. Did you know that? Gases bloat the internal organs. Sometimes there's strange twitching in the muscles."

"You seem to know a lot about it."

"One of my uncles owned a funeral home. I worked for him one summer."

Sally said, "You'll help us, won't you?"

Did Sally detect gallantry in me? Maybe she thought I'd want to protect the Messenger who was here to rescue mankind. But the truth was, I would help them because that's the code of my family. If shit happens to people you're close to, you take care of it. No questions, no complaints, just get it over with. What was already over was my love for Cheyenne.

# 43

I found a handsaw in Cheyenne's workshop. As I carried it in through the kitchen door, she said, "I like a man who's handy around the house."

So her con at the moment was a show of calm indifference, which every con artist needs in order to swindle the world. I suppose she'd long ago made the discovery that icy nerve is how to back a hand.

I carried the saw down the cellar steps into Dez's tomb. The cellar light shone on his boot as I knelt beside it. He'd hammered tiny nails into the heel, in the shape of an eye, presumably a charm against making a misstep. He couldn't have been wearing it on the day he met Cheyenne.

I studied the angle the cut required. It would be like going through a small stump, flat to the ground. But this wasn't ground, it was concrete, and the teeth of the saw would be immediately dulled if I hit it.

"Dez, I can't leave you half buried . . ." I started with the saw. "And to dig all of you up, I'd need a jackhammer."

I sawed through the leather of his boot. As I broke the skin, there was a strong smell of decay, but the teeth of the saw continued biting through the ankle bone. It was a sound you hear in a butcher shop. I talked to him as I worked the saw back and forth. "You're not alone. She fooled me too." The teeth of the saw chewed through the last bit of bone and sinew. "She thinks she's Belle Starr, queen of the West." The final cut was through the other side of the boot. It had been a nice boot, with swirls of decorative stitching in leather that was soft as butter, and it came off with his foot inside it. "You died with your boots on, and today doesn't change that." I held up boot and foot. "I'll bury this in the desert."

But when I carried boot and foot upstairs, Cheyenne had other plans. "That smell will draw coyotes and they'll dig the damn thing up. So we're going to take the flesh off."

That afternoon, like the witches in Macbeth, she and Sally boiled Dez's foot in what Cheyenne identified as "sal soda. I cleaned animal bones with it when I was a kid."

I slept over that night, reluctant to leave the two madwomen alone. Cheyenne tried to lure me into her bed. I said I'd sleep on the foldout couch in the living room.

Sally slept in the guest room, and I heard her taking turns with Cheyenne at the stove while the foot cooked and the moon passed slowly overhead. The smell was bad, but the witches didn't seem to mind. When I asked Sally about it, she said she had Vicks up her nose, and gave me some. I returned to the couch and mentholated dreams.

By sunrise, Cheyenne was pouring off a gelatinous blob into a jar. Sally came out of the guest room wearing nothing but her long-tailed denim shirt. Her thighs were ample and nicely proportioned to the rest of her. That I could take note of this at such a time gave me invaluable instruction about myself.

Cheyenne was in a ratty bathrobe, tied tightly at the waist. Her feet were bare as she padded around the kitchen, casually frying breakfast for us. We ate with a pot of human bones on the stove, and the rest of Dez in the basement below. Vittorio's cross was still on the table, Christ and his disciples looking on as we ate.

"Now we need to boil the bones in bleach for a few hours," said Cheyenne, dipping her fried bread in the yolk of her egg. "That should finish the job."

I returned to the cellar and mixed up a small batch of concrete to patch the floor. I worked the mud around Dez's leg, covering flesh and bone and the ragged edge of his jeans as I chanted, *Requiem æternam dona eis*, eternal rest grant him. Then I smoothed the patch out with a trowel.

I stayed in the cellar, sitting with my back against the wall, thinking about Dez. Had he ever suspected Cheyenne's true character? Maybe at the last moment, when he was looking down her gun barrel, he realized who he'd been in love with.

I heard footsteps and saw boots coming down the stairs. Sally's were much fancier than Dez's, with multicolored flowers carved into the leather. Thousand-dollar boots, I'm sure. Her denim shirt was now tucked into her jeans behind a big turquoise belt buckle. She looked at the patched floor and then at me. "You can't sit here forever."

"Don't worry, I'm going."

I pushed myself off the floor, stepped across Dez's concrete tomb, and climbed the stairs. The smell of boiling bleach filled the air. Cheyenne was still in her bathrobe, reading one of her online newsletters, garish illustrations of demonic entities bordering the text. "Going out, hon?"

This was an evil-minded woman born under some malefic sign. I had to get away from her. I got in my SUV and headed out of town. At first, I wasn't sure where I was going, but I wound up at the little copper mining town where Vittorio was buried. I drove out to the old cemetery and stood at his grave. Carved on his tombstone was a quote from Saint Augustine: *Such Is Man.*

I took Vittorio's message to be, *We're meant for the grave, so don't get too worked up about anything.*

Underneath was his name. Vittorio Martini. Nothing else. No indication that he was a priest.

From there I drove to another place of the dead, a sinkhole around which an ancient village had been constructed. The sinkhole held water year-round and for this reason had been the home of a tribe of desert dwellers. The hole was deep and protected by a guardrail. A pair of ducks were paddling along in the water below. The water filled the crater from edge to edge, forming a pond the size of a football field. Beneath the rocky overhang, I could see the stonework of the old dwellings, and I worked my way down to the ancient rooms. They were cool inside, and the ceilings were layered with soot from fires that had burned a thousand years ago.

I was alone in what had once been a home. No records had been left, no papyrus, no skins, no sacred rattles. But I was sure the ancient rooms had heard it all, including rumors of approaching enemies. In the desert, water is gold, and people have been killing each other over it since time began, for good reasons, bad reasons, and no reason at all. The people who lived here had just disappeared one day, no one knew why.

I knew I should disappear the same way. I climbed back up to the rim. A man was standing there, looking down into the well as if he, too, wanted to vanish. It was Oliver, whose wife had thrown herself in front of a train. He recognized me and nodded. I saw his eyes were filled with tears. I wondered if he was planning on throwing himself into the well. I said, "I'm sorry about your wife."

"What the hell for? You didn't kill her."

"I'm sorry for the way she died."

He looked back down into the well. "I'm saying goodbye to the places she loved. And then I'm leaving. Paloma is eating me alive."

"Where are you headed for?"

"Somewhere flat. Away from those fucking red rocks." His gesture took in Eagle Rock and Storm Mountain in the distance. Then he returned his gaze toward the well, with tears still on his cheeks. "I suppose Cheyenne filled you in regarding my wife."

"She gave me her version."

"Whatever she said, it was hot air. Cheyenne's got plenty of that." He didn't seem to notice his tears. I had the feeling he cried every day.

"Did your wife ever get any real medical help?"

"Whenever I suggested it, she went ballistic." He turned to look at me. "Cheyenne was the only answer. Cheyenne understood dimensions. Cheyenne had the truth, that my wife was suffering from an alien abduction in childhood and that's why she was unstable." He closed his hands around the protective rail that faced the well. I saw his knuckles go white.

"Cheyenne's followers saw that my wife was getting worse. They put questions to Cheyenne about it. She couldn't stomach this, so she began saying that her cure wasn't working because my wife enjoyed being a victim, that she liked all the attention she was getting. My wife's deterioration continued to embarrass Cheyenne, so she came up with another explanation, saying that my wife was hopeless because aliens had completely taken over her soul." He looked back into the sinkhole as if trying to penetrate its murky depths. Still gazing downward, he said, "Cheyenne knows how to bring out the morbid side of people. My wife started telling me I should move out of our house, that she was toxic, that she'd only infect me with alien programming. Of course I couldn't leave her, I loved her. She grew more desperate and finally, to save me, she threw herself in front of a train."

I just listened. He didn't seem to expect an answer.

At last, he said, "Paloma has a load of phonies, but Cheyenne tops the list."

"Why do you put her at the top?"

"Because she's incredibly good at it."

We returned to the parking lot. He drove off to somewhere flat, and I drove back to Cheyenne's house.

She held up a clean toe bone. "Pure and white. Almost like your cross."

# 44

I laid Dez's bones on the workbench in Cheyenne's herbal shed. I covered them with a cloth and hit them with a sledgehammer. They popped and I hit them again. As I hammered, I was back inside the family curse, disposing of a body. As I hammered, I noticed that the cabinet at the far end of the wall had a padlock on it.

One of my skills learned from Grandfather Primo was lock picking. My cousins and I did it with him as kids, thought of it as a game. But he'd considered it a handy thing to know, and he was right. I took a paper clip from a stack of Cheyenne's herbal recipes, broke it in half, and formed a torque wrench and pick. Her lock was a cheap one, and the keyway was easy to manipulate. The lock popped, and I swung the cabinet door open. It contained jars of roots floating in clear liquid. The last jar contained a human penis.

There was no time for hanging around with my mouth open in wonder at the degree of Cheyenne's madness. This thing was further proof of a homicide, and I had to get rid of it. I took the jar out of the cabinet, fastened the lock, and stowed the jar in my SUV. Then I went back into the house, carrying the bones I'd hammered into small pieces.

"You've been slimed, hon," said Cheyenne. "You're white as a sheet."

"It must be the heat." I handed her the fragments, and she put them in her meat grinder.

"Dust to dust," she said, and switched it on. White powder poured from the spout.

"Going to keep it in a cherished urn?"

"Very funny." She poured Dez's dust into a plastic shopping bag from Natural Born Foods and applied a twist tie. She handed the bag to me. "On your next hike. Spread it around."

I carried the shopping bag to my SUV and climbed in. Some people have a compass on the dashboard, the needle shifting gently as the direction changes. I had Dez's dick in a jar, shifting gently when we went over a speed bump.

Did she bite it off? I wasn't going to look for teeth marks. But why had she done it? Was it to make sure that Dez wouldn't be fucking cowgirls even after he was dead? Or did she have some other hocus-pocus reason, like the ancient people who mutilated the body of an enemy to keep him from haunting them? Whatever her reason, it was crazy.

Until recently, I hadn't seen her true craziness, just the gleam in her eyes and the con in her heart. Was there a drop of madness in me that I'd failed to read her clearly? Maybe the rage in my guts was that drop of madness. I'd stayed in the monastery five years trying to dissolve it.

I drove to the Eagle Canyon trailhead and took the trail toward Blind Pass. A retirement-age couple came my way, greeting me with the warmth of people enjoying their golden years in peaceful Paloma. And I had a bag of bone dust in one hand, and a dick in a jar under my shirt.

I followed the trail until I came to a natural amphitheater of rock, resembling the stage set for a gigantic musical, a sheer red wall with a natural overhang. I left the trail and headed downhill, through desert grass and cactus. The dry earth moved easily beneath my boots, and I was soon in front of a huge red rock stage, whose only actor was a crow perched on a stony overhang.

The crow lifted off and went sailing past me, wings whispering against the thin desert air. In seconds, it was gone but still calling faintly from behind an outcropping of rock.

I said a Benedictine prayer for the dead and scattered Dez's dust. Spreading dead men's dust was getting to be a habit I'd have to break. Then

I dug a hole in the sand. I opened the dick jar and poured off the formaldehyde. Then I dumped Dez's organ in the hole. Somehow, I wasn't moved to recite a prayer over a severed dick. I covered it with sand, then put the largest rock I could find on top of it so the coyotes wouldn't dig it up.

That was when someone came riding through the sky on what appeared to be a lawnmower. The wheels spun negligently in the air, free of the ground. The rider was harnessed into some kind of seat attached to a growling motor. And billowing out over his head was the huge sail that kept him in flight.

He saw me and waved. I waved back. He dipped his sail and angled down toward me, so that I could see his gloves and helmet and the wild grin on his face. At the last second, he pulled up and floated on by me, the motor spitting and snarling.

He gained altitude again and headed out over the next mountain, the wind taking him straight up. I watched as he got smaller, crested the mountain, and vanished like the crow, leaving only the fading sound of his motor. Since Paloma is a town that believes in heavenly signs, I could no doubt find someone to tell me this was a sign that I should vanish beyond the mountains, leaving no tracks behind. And they would have been right.

# 45

When I was a kid, Primo had taken me to visit a relative who was doing time. *Always remember this place*, he'd said. As I drove back toward Cheyenne's place, I was remembering it. I had to break with her before I wound up in jail myself.

I found the cross in Cheyenne's living room, on a table covered with a white silk shawl. It was framed by large candles. The smoothly worked ivory had an almost supernatural glow, giving the little figures an uncanny appearance of life as the flickering flames animated tiny hands and feet. Cheyenne and Sally were standing in front of it in pious devotion. But when Cheyenne turned toward me, devotions were over.

"What did you do with my jar?"

"I got rid of it."

Cheyenne gave Sally a withering look. "Did you tell him about the jar?"

"You know I'd never betray you." Sally burst into tears and ran out of the house.

Cheyenne watched Sally's Jeep pull away. Then with a dramatic sigh, she said, "The Messenger is always betrayed. That's the rule. But I understand Sally. Before I leave, I've got to help her fulfill herself. She has the makings of a great healer."

"She has the makings of a jailbird, and if you leave evidence of a homicide lying around, she might become one."

Cheyenne's eyes were madly bright. She slipped her hand inside my shirt. "There's a lot that's appealing about this earth. Even the frailties of human beings are endearing. I'll stay as long as I can."

"For which the world is grateful."

She pressed herself against me. "Martini, I've seen holy Christians, Indian shamans, Tibetan monks, and all of them had nasty stuff clinging to them. I can overlook it when I have to." She slipped her other hand behind my back. "I need your strength. Messengers depend on people like you."

She grabbed my hand and shoved it between her legs, closing her thighs as she whispered, "We're caught between the heavenly powers."

I picked her up and carried her from the living room to the bedroom. Her face was close to mine, her eyelids half closed. I tossed her on the bed, where she bounced. Then I headed back toward the door.

"*Bastard*," she hissed after me.

I closed the bedroom door, took the cross, and started toward the front door. And then I saw a car stopping in front of the house. Two men got out of the car, police written all over them. I hurried to her bedroom. "The cops are here. Get your story straight."

The doorbell rang; then, getting no answer, the cops rang it again. After a few minutes, Cheyenne came out of the bedroom.

In a few seconds, she'd managed to make herself look harried, worried, and disoriented. She was a born actress. She moved past me in her ratty bathrobe and slippers and opened the door to two detectives from the Yavapai County Sheriff's office. One of them was round and taciturn, the other trim and friendly. After identifying himself, the taciturn one asked if Desmond was at home.

"He left me," she said, "that's all I know."

"We're here because his parents got in touch with us. They're concerned about him."

"So am I. I've got bills to pay and he's not around to help."

The friendly one said, "Ma'am, he's made no contact with his parents at all. They say it's not like him."

"He's a cowboy," said Cheyenne. "They don't write and they don't make good husbands."

"You have no idea where he might've gone?"

"Not a clue. You gentlemen mind if I throw some clothes on? I'm here in my altogether."

The taciturn cop nodded his bald head. "Go right ahead, ma'am."

She was breaking their rhythm with her costume change. As I'd anticipated, she was cool and resourceful under fire. As she left the kitchen, the cops looked at me. The taciturn one asked, "I take it you're a friend?" He made it sound vaguely criminal.

"A neighbor."

"And do you know Mr. Booth?"

Mr. Booth was sleeping under the concrete in the cellar, and maybe because I was now a Paloma resident, I felt Mr. Booth giving off vibrations and wondered if the detectives could feel them too. "Yes, I know him. He's a nice guy."

He looked around the kitchen, probably noting its sloppiness, but that's no crime. "How long have you known Mr. Booth?"

"Maybe a month. We had a couple of beers together."

"Is he a hunter? Does he go out into the desert alone?"

"I don't know. We talked about baseball, that's about it."

"Diamondback fan?"

"Aren't we all?"

The detective shook his head unhappily. "It's been a disappointing season."

"Time to rebuild, I guess."

The friendly detective said, "We understand Mrs. Booth is a healer. Is that right?"

Knowing that you could be busted for practicing medicine without a license, I answered, "She gives talks on UFOs."

The detective continued, using his smile to make every question sound innocent, just the opposite of his colleague, Detective Taciturn. "You've been to her seminars?"

I nodded.

"I'm interested in UFOs myself," said Detective Friendly.

Somehow, I doubted this.

He added, "NASA said we're definitely going to discover life on other planets."

Just as long as they didn't discover Dez in the basement.

Cheyenne returned in her pilgrim lady outfit, black skirt to the floor, flat shoes, and a white shirt buttoned to the collar. She looked as if she should be holding a Bible in her hand. "Sorry to keep you," she said.

"That's all right," said Detective Taciturn. "We're sorry to bother you at this difficult time, but you understand we're only trying to help."

"I understand."

"Excuse the question, but could you tell me why you didn't call the police when your husband first went missing?"

"Because it's not the first time he's taken off somewhere. He'll come back with his tail between his legs."

"Had you been quarreling?"

"We never quarrel. He's just a big kid really. Like they say in the song, I love him just the same."

"So you're not concerned."

"I'll tell you what's concerning me." She sat down heavily in the kitchen chair. "We've got a mortgage payment coming up and he's gone. I'm running scared."

Detective Taciturn checked his notes. "The truck outside is registered in your name. So how did he get wherever it is he's gotten to?"

"He's got pals with trucks. They'll drive a thousand miles to a rodeo."

"Any idea where that rodeo might be?"

"I don't follow the rodeo circuit."

"Does he have a computer? We could see if he's checked out any rodeos or emailed anyone."

She reached under the morning's newspaper and brought out a laptop. "The computer's mine. Dez never went near it. He doesn't type all that well. You can look at it if you want."

She opened it to a home page filled with flying saucers. They declined the offer but asked a few more questions. She continued to come across as the abandoned wife running scared about money. She certainly didn't have any money; her seminars made very little, and unless she got a real job—which I doubted—she'd stay broke. So her story sounded real to me.

The detectives thanked her and left their embossed police department calling cards. When they were gone, she picked up one of the cards and looked at me. "Now I know who to contact."

"About what?"

"About you killing Dez and burying him in the cellar."

# 46

Ignoring the sign I'd gotten to leave town, I stuck around. I'd run once before, to the monastery, and wasted five years. So instead of leaving, I bought an iPad and started doing some online research on the Cross of the Apostles.

I found information about a sixteenth-century Spanish conquistador named Captain Hector Buendía. His name meant "Good Day," but it was not a good day for the Aztecs he put to work mining gold for him. When they resisted, he hanged them, burned them, or threw them to his hungry dogs. He was a very important man, and a painter had depicted him in shining armor, standing with his horse.

In the painting, Captain Buendía was holding up a perfect match for my ivory cross.

The cross had not brought Captain Good Day good luck. His horse fell on him in battle, and the cross vanished, probably taken as plunder.

I gazed at this exquisite work of art on my kitchen table, marveling at how it had survived the centuries, through many adventures, I'm sure, finally to land in the hands of a shady priest. Now the cross was in my hands. I felt history in the room with me, and the spirit of men long gone, those who had owned the cross before me, and the sculptor who made it. There had been a workshop somewhere, possibly in a monastery, where this masterpiece was created. I certainly wasn't worthy of it, but then, who was? Similar crosses, of which there were only a precious few, were valued around a half million. Maybe Vittorio had taken it for other than religious reasons.

My research was interrupted by a high-pitched ring coming from the driveway-alert device I'd installed along with a house alarm system. Vittorio's Beretta was tucked neatly into my belt in back. I was wearing it as I looked through the window and realized I didn't need it.

My visitor was a scholarly-looking man in horn-rimmed glasses and a felt fedora in the style of Indiana Jones. I'd seen him at one of Cheyenne's meetings describing how the pyramids were built by extraterrestrials.

He touched two fingers to the wide brim of his fedora. "Hope you don't mind me calling unexpectedly, but Cheyenne said it would be okay. I'm Julian Talbot. I'm ghostwriting her book."

"I didn't know there was one."

"It was my idea. She's completely on board with the project."

It was 103 degrees outside, and I asked him if he wanted a beer.

He did, and we sat in the kitchen, where Bustamante and I had faced each other down.

He said, "I've ghosted a number of spiritual books, and I think Cheyenne is an undiscovered gem."

Julian Talbot was obviously not a follower, just a professional writer looking to make a buck. I wasn't so sure Cheyenne would pay off for him, but I wasn't about to offer my view on her potential in the marketplace of zany ideas.

We drank our beer, and he expanded on his plan. "I'd have to get her to go easy on the UFO angle, which is somewhat passé now."

"I wouldn't count on that."

"Yes, she's dug in on that point, but she's a natural in front of an audience and would do very well on a book tour. Once that's rolling, I'll get her on the speaker circuit. There's an agency that's good at representing speakers like Cheyenne. Although I must say, she's pretty unique."

Since the other speakers probably hadn't murdered their husband and buried him in the cellar, I felt this was an accurate description. As Julian continued with his vision of Cheyenne's future, the fact of Dez under two feet of concrete remained in my mind. I was sure Cheyenne wasn't giving it a thought.

He said, "I'm going to start filming her meetings so we can push her brand on YouTube and sell DVDs of her teaching. You only get the full impact when you see her."

Her full impact came with a Colt revolver in her hand. "Yes, you definitely need to see her in action."

"I'm gathering vignettes from people Cheyenne has touched with her healing power. She told me you just got out of a monastery. I think a Catholic monk who's been helped by the Messenger would add some really outstanding flavor."

"I'll take a vow of silence regarding Cheyenne."

"May I ask why?"

"She's a phony."

"There is that."

"You know she's a phony and you still want to help her write her book?"

"Truth is not necessary for success in this field. It's more a matter of sincerity." He put the cold edge of the beer can to his forehead. "I have a good track record with books like hers. I'm calling it *New Mystery Teaching*. What do you think?"

"Perfect."

He finished his beer. "Mind if I smoke?"

"Help yourself."

He lit a cigarette and I brought two more beers. Julian reminded me of Johnny Squint, who could make murderers sound like Boy Scout leaders. Blowing a neat little smoke ring, he said, "She's part of the amateur crowd in Paloma. They have no concept of the real publishing world, or the real world at all. They live in a bubble of mutual admiration or burning jealousy, but always at a very local level. Cheyenne is naive in many ways, but she'll catch up quickly."

His eyes drifted toward the cross. "That's quite a crucifix. Cheyenne mentioned she'd loaned it to you."

"It's mine. I inherited from my uncle. He was a priest here in Paloma."

"I see." He took this in stride. He had no illusions about Cheyenne. Except one, which he now described. "When I first saw her, I thought she was a homely little thing." He blew another smoke ring. "Strange, isn't it?

I mean, the way she presents herself. I really had no idea she was a knock-out. Something wrong with me, right? Not to see it straightaway?"

"I made the same mistake."

"She said her husband recently left her. Any idea why?"

"None at all."

"I'm not being nosy. I just don't want anything to disturb her work on the book. A domestic squabble could upset her creativity."

"I think you can count on her husband not returning."

"I can understand her being too much for him. She's got all the charisma and he was just background."

He was actually underground, though not deep enough for my peace of mind.

Julian took the last drag on his cigarette. "I don't want her to suddenly shut down out of grief."

"Not a chance."

"She tells her story very well. She just needs editing."

"That's where you come in."

"I'll do what I can. But in the end, it's all about her."

"With Cheyenne, it's always about her. Nobody else enters her mind for a second."

"You'd be surprised how well that works in the self-help field."

# 47

I was working in the garden when my cell phone rang. Dominic's voice came across the miles. "I'm back in Vegas."

"Have you developed a gambling habit?"

"I've been hanging out with Santos at the Contention Fight Club. He hasn't forgotten that you decked his Russian champion. The guy couldn't see straight for a month."

"He called me a pussy."

"I'll have somebody in the first row calling you a pussy."

"It won't be the same."

"Right, never listen to the crowd. But you're working out?"

I'd filled a feed sack with sawdust and hung it from a tree in the yard. I walked toward it now. "I practice my kicks."

"So when do you think you'll be ready?"

"When I get my head straightened out."

"What're you, conflicted or something?"

"Dominic, have you been exposing yourself to therapy?"

"Naw, just exposing myself. Listen, Tommy, if it's women you're talking about, you can't straighten out your head. It's not possible. What you do is pretend to listen to them while you think about bowling."

"This is priceless advice."

"Hey, I'm here for you."

We talked some more about Vegas. He'd be there for a week and why didn't I come and see him? I told him I'd think about it. After we hung up, I walked to the feed sack hanging from the tree and drove my foot into it. The sack split and sawdust ran out, and I concluded I hadn't lost any kicking velocity. Then a shower of termites followed the sawdust. They'd already set up house inside the bag, eating the sawdust and some of the bag. So a conclusion on my kicking power would have to be postponed.

I dug a hole to plant some desert lavender. It was supposed to attract hummingbirds. As I watered it, a bird showed up, but she was big, round, and soft and her wings weren't humming. Sally's eyes were bloodshot; the pale skin under them showed dark circles. At a guess, I'd say she'd been up all night crying.

It was boiling in the backyard, so I showed her into the kitchen and we sat down at the table. She toyed with a little bouquet of dried flowers lying there, as if she were speaking to the dead blossoms. It was difficult for her to start whatever it was she'd come for. I waited. She shredded some of the blossoms. Then, realizing she was wrecking the bouquet she pushed it away and just stared at the table.

"Sally, what's the problem?"

"Now that Julian has come, Cheyenne won't need me."

It all came out then. She talked about how she'd been traveling aimlessly around the Southwest until karma led her to Cheyenne, what their early work had been like, how it was slowly revealed to Cheyenne that she was the Messenger.

"Because she's the Messenger, she needs constant emotional support. Nobody is up to that demand, not even you. I'm the only one. Now Julian is offering the same commitment. His reasons are crass, but the Messenger doesn't see that."

Despite her being an accessory to Dez's murder, I felt bad for Sally. A big woman in pain seems to hurt more. She said, "Even though she's a true Messenger, things got messed up when Dez became possessed and started dominating her sexually. Messengers are innocent about sex."

I didn't tell her that Cheyenne could have given lessons in a Nevada brothel.

"When you came along, being a monk and all, Cheyenne said the universe was intervening and that the situation with Dez was going to change."

"With a little help from a handgun."

She ignored this. "You should go back to her. It's too late for me, but you can still help the Messenger."

"The Messenger put Dez's dick in a jar."

"I don't want to talk about that."

"Just tell me if he was alive or dead when she did it."

"I hated what Cheyenne did with his—genitals. But I saw the necessity. We could feel the evil in the air. It was horrible."

"Genitals? Plural? She's got his balls in a jar?"

"I can't talk about it. It's too upsetting."

The tears were running down her cheeks, and I said, "This is stuff that could send you to prison. I got rid of the dick. You get rid of the balls."

"We have to keep them a while longer."

It's like they were living on the banks of the Amazon. Or maybe Paloma is a tributary of the Amazon.

"She had to do what she did. Dez was possessed by evil."

"Sorry, Sally, it's much simpler. He fell for another woman, and the Messenger couldn't stand the fact that her number one disciple dumped her." She got up from the table. She was crying again, with the bouquet of dried flowers back in her hand. Some of the blossoms were rust colored, matching her red hair. I thought of old-time paintings where voluptuous females were shown naked, holding flowers and looking confused, as if wondering how they'd shed their clothing and what they were doing in the painting at all. Those big naked ladies always seemed vulnerable, and so did Sally, which is why I embraced her when she asked me.

After she left, I felt somehow lighter. I reached around to my belt in back. The Beretta was gone.

# 48

Maybe I was becoming telepathic. Or maybe it was my survival mechanism kicking in, but I felt Cheyenne's eyes boring into the back of my head. I looked in the rearview mirror of my SUV, and there she was in her half-ton truck bearing down on me. I knew she was still angry with me for tossing her onto her bed "like a sack of grits, you bastard." Was she crazy enough to ram my bumper? I thought it was wiser not to test this idea, so I acknowledged her with a wave of my hand and she eased up on the gas.

With a safe distance between us, I turned onto Thunderbird Road and drove into my driveway. She parked behind me and we met on the sidewalk.

Vittorio's Virgin Mary statue in the yard watched our meeting. Cheyenne's gaze of tenderness rivaled Mother Mary's. It was not her usual look.

"I want us to get back together."

"Forget it."

"We had something rare, Martini."

She'd come straight from the shower, her hair still wet the way it was when we first met. She was trying to call up that moment again, when we came down from the mountain drenched to the skin and I'd realized she was beautiful. She was still beautiful, but I wasn't having any of it, not now, not ever.

She stepped closer. She was wearing a white silk shirt whose lacy folds hung over the top of her cutoff denim jeans. She'd dumped her Bible school look, and I approved but only in the abstract. Cheyenne's transformations no longer fascinated me.

"I drove you away," she said, "but you're my one true love."

I was startled by the tears welling up in her dark-blue eyes. I'd never seen her cry. She took another step toward me. "What can I do to make it right?"

She couldn't bring the dead back to life. She couldn't put the bullet back in the Colt revolver. "Just forget about me and make your way as best you can."

"I can't forget you. You've got a piece of my heart." The tears streamed down her cheeks. "Give me a chance."

I didn't trust her tears and I didn't trust her, but I couldn't leave her sobbing in my driveway. I said, "Let's go in the house."

As we walked toward the door, she pressed her breast against my arm and said, "I want to get naked with you." She *was* going to be naked very soon, but not in the way she expected.

Her playfulness distracted me as we came through the front door and I missed something crucial in the entrance hall. My alarm system wasn't beeping its ten-second warning: *turn me off or I'll start screaming.*

It had been overridden by a skilled hand, which was now holding a gun to the back of my head. His English was good. "One move, señor, and your brains fly out." He removed the Judge .45 from my pocket. Another hand appeared alongside my neck. The fingernails weren't human. They were the large claws of some noble bird, probably an eagle. They were mounted on the end of a short piece of wood held by a wrinkled little Mexican Indian. He waved the claws like a wand, much too close to my eyes.

A third figure pressed a gun into the middle of Cheyenne's back and said, also in good English, "Be nice, *chiquita*."

"Now," said the man behind me, "the living room."

He moved the muzzle of his gun to the base of my skull and wedged it into the convenient indentation found in the occipital bone.

When we reached the living room, I turned slowly, careful not to make the sort of abrupt move that would get me killed. But as I looked at the intruder's face, a shiver went up my spine. He was the guy I'd chased up Storm Mountain.

Here he was again, alive. But I'd seen his body with an agave sword sticking out through his neck. He'd been very dead. So this had to be his brother. The brother's eyes were darting around. He was jumpy. I could see all three intruders were coked up.

"Where you want it? Here? Here? How about here?" He was swinging his arm up and down, pointing his pistol wildly at my head, my stomach, my knees.

On the living-room coffee table was a walkie-talkie. It had disarmed my security system. The one flaw in wireless systems is that you can blind the receiver electronically by sending a stronger signal on the same frequency. A walkie-talkie can do that, but you need experience to bring it off. And when the guy holding Cheyenne turned toward me, I knew where his experience came from. He was the Camel's security specialist, and I'd knocked him down in Modelo when he and Bustamante tried to recruit a boy to be an assassin for the Camel. When he saw my look of recognition, he said, "That's right, I don't forget."

He turned to Cheyenne and shoved his hand under the back of her loose-hanging shirt. "I go to feel a nice ass and what do I find tucked in your jeans?"

He held up my Beretta, twisting the barrel of the gun back and forth in front of her face. "You would have blasted me, right?"

The question was, would she have blasted *me* with it if I didn't take her back into my life?

The little guy holding the eagle claw came over and stuck the claw between her legs. Then he stroked the curved talons over her crotch. "What you got here? What else you hiding?"

A familiar rage twisted like a snake in my guts. They'd broken into my house and were feeling up my girlfriend. Well, ex-girlfriend, but it came to the same thing.

He inserted the claw into the waistband of her jeans and tugged. "I want to see your chili pepper." He withdrew the claw and pointed at the polished tips. "Poisoned. I make it myself from the *machineel.*" He used a Spanish word I'd heard from the herbalist in my monastery, who'd warned me about the *little apple of death.* The whole tree is poisonous. You can die from being tied against the bark.

The little sorcerer waved it near Cheyenne's face, his voice full of pride. "I add the blood-letter, the crying flower, the put-to-sleep. So take off all your clothes or I give you a scratch."

I could see her eyes. There was no fear, only contempt changing to repugnance, as if her tormentor were sculpted from shit. She unzipped her jeans but did it slowly, stalling for time, looking at me, figuring our chances. I knew she'd be hell in a fight, if we got that far.

The gremlin continued waving the claw at her. "Come on, hurry it up."

The security specialist was enjoying this. He said to Cheyenne, "He's a crazy *brujo*. You better do what he says."

The guy holding the pistol on me said, over his shoulder, "I told you not to bring that lunatic."

"He's for laughs," said the security specialist. He poked his gun into Cheyenne's belly. "How come you're not laughing?"

She kicked off her jeans and started slowly unbuttoning her shirt, her eyes still looking to me for some kind of move, but I didn't see it yet, not with all three of them in one room. The little sorcerer was cackling happily. "We all going to fuck you, lady, how about that?"

"Whatever you say." Her voice was calm. She wasn't going to give them the fun of seeing her fear, if she had any. I couldn't tell, for her movements were unhurried, deliberate, as if she, not they, were in control of the moment. She slowly slipped out of her shirt and dropped it on the floor. She was naked except for her bra and panties.

The sorcerer hooked the claw of the eagle under a strap of her brassiere. "Come on, show me your *tetas*."

"I'm going to drink your blood," she said quietly, and the little sorcerer gave a nervous laugh, as if he could detect a venom in her equal to the concoction in his claw. She was a killer, with a killer's soul, and he had just caught a glimpse of it.

She undid her bra and dropped it on the floor. The little sorcerer, regaining confidence, nodded his appreciation. "Nice and round. Natural." He hooked the claw under the waistband of her panties. "Now drop your *chonies*."

She coolly pulled her panties down and give them a little kick toward him, indifferent to him, his eagle claw, and anything else he had in mind. She was boiling mad and had courage. Whatever was racing through her mind, she wasn't going to give these macho pricks the satisfaction of seeing her afraid of them.

Still tracing my body with his gun, my shooter said, "Your fucking uncle offend my employer." He waved the gun in my face. "He insult the wrong guy. Know what I mean?"

His tone of voice was that of a man planning to leave only dead bodies behind. "Come on, where's the cross?"

It was back in the storage unit at Reliance. I said, "It's in the house. I'll take you to it."

"Move." His eyes glittered with anticipation as we walked from the living room. The odds had just improved in my favor. We were one against one. But if I blew it, he'd revenge his brother slowly, probably shoot out my kneecaps first, and move on from there until I bled out. I felt he had that kind of nature. I opened the laundry room door. Standing in the doorway, I said, "One of the floorboards isn't nailed down. That's where the cross is. I'll get it for you."

I lifted the floorboard.

"Shove the board forward, out of the way." He was concerned I'd use it as a weapon. I had a better one. An old priest planning for his future and mine had kept an assault rifle around, but looking at it, I realized I'd get a bullet in the back of the head before I could lift, turn, and fire. So instead I brought out the wallet I'd taken from his brother. Still kneeling, I held up the driver's license.

GOBIERNO DEL DISTRITO FEDERAL

LICENSIA PARA CONDUCIR

Beneath the driver's name was a face he'd known since childhood, and it might have been the head of Medusa, because it froze him for a precious second, during which I yanked his feet out from under him.

As he went down, I was coming up, going after his gun. I caught his outstretched arm between mine, and his elbow broke with a sharp little pop.

The gun flew from his hand, bounced on the washing machine, and fell behind it. I didn't have time to retrieve it, so I hit him in the throat. Cartilage crunched and the stuff in his neck bunched up, leaving no space for breath. He grabbed his throat, but he was choking to death and nothing would stop it.

I got the AK-47 from its hiding place. I could hear the security specialist coming along the hallway cautiously. I yanked the washing machine from the wall and got behind it. It wasn't Kevlar, but it was better than nothing. Any exchange of gunfire with him was going to be tricky, and I needed something more. For some reason, I found myself thinking of Rong. I'd turned him into dust, but apparently, he was still with me. And then I realized why. The jeweled eyes of his dragon knife were looking at me. The night before, after emptying the pockets of my dirty jeans, I'd stuck his beautiful knife on the laundry shelf.

I had it in my hand as the specialist came through the doorway. I sliced through the hoses of the washing machine and twisted them in his direction. Jets of hot and cold water struck him in the face, and he fired blindly toward the washing machine. The bullets tore through the metal of the washer, and I was expecting to get one in the chest, but owing to my bachelor habits, the machine was filled with two weeks' worth of dirty clothes, the operative thought always *I'll wash them tomorrow*. Balled-up jeans, shirts, underwear, and socks absorbed the impact of his rounds, and none of them got through to me. I rose up and gave him one burst of the AK-47. It produced what gun instructors call rapid collapse. With lead in his heart and lungs, he went down fast.

Carrying the AK-47, I ran to the living room to deal with the gremlin. He was holding a lump on the side of his head. I saw the paperweight Cheyenne had hit him with, a rearing bronze mustang now on the floor, so in a sense he'd been kicked by a horse.

And Cheyenne had the eagle claw. She went after him with it, and the little bastard hopped straight sideways, like a spinning grasshopper. And then he hopped again, out of the living room into the entranceway.

It must've been the cocaine that put so much spring in his step, and he would have been out the door on the next hop, but Cheyenne threw herself at him, raking the claw across the back of his head. It was razor sharp and some of his scalp came off, followed by a gush of blood.

The spring instantly went out of his step. He hadn't been bluffing about the poison. As it flowed through his bloodstream, he began twitching around like a puppet.

Cheyenne, completely bare assed, raked him across the face, removing three strips of skin from his cheek, along with part of his nostril. The words *naked fury* fit her perfectly. The gremlin collapsed, but his body kept bouncing up and down in spasm as his own poisonous concoction spread through his system. His face puckered as if sucked inward by a terrible force, deep creases forming around his nose and mouth.

Cheyenne stood over him, watching him die. She was like something from Greek mythology, a naked Amazon at the kill. Her breasts heaved up and down as she caught her breath.

Then she knelt beside him and put her face near his. "Your magic wasn't strong enough."

She grabbed his chin in her hand, forcing his dying eyes to gaze on hers. "My magic was stronger."

His eyes lost their focus, becoming dark, expressionless beads. He was staring into eternity, taking Cheyenne's face with him.

She stood and turned toward me. "You and I are an unbeatable team."

The control panel for the alarm system was on the wall beside us. I disarmed it so it wouldn't go off when I started cleaning up. I didn't want a security company notifying the police I'd had intruders. I shut off the water to the washing machine while Cheyenne got herself dressed.

"What do we do now, Martini?"

"I'll take care of it." I was collecting the weapons, including the little Beretta she'd brought with her today. "Were you going to shoot me with this?"

"I don't kill all my men, Martini, just some of them," she said with a smile.

# 49

My intruders had parked their car somewhere in town and walked to my place, so I had no concerns about disposing of their vehicle. I only had to dispose of them. Dominic answered on the first ring. "What's up? You coming to Sin City?"

"Yes, and I need Local Eighteen of the Cement Masons union."

"We're filling in another foundation?"

"And it's three times the size of the last job."

"So we use a little more mud."

As we ended the call, I remembered the time when we were kids and he explained to me that my father was never coming back. After which he gave me not just half his toys, but the best half. *I like these better*, he said of the junky ones he kept for himself.

I wrapped the dead men in carpets from the guest rooms. As I loaded their bodies into the back of the SUV, I was glad it had so much cargo space. The thought crossed my mind that this was why Vittorio had bought such a big vehicle.

Two hundred and seventy-six miles later, my GPS guided me to the front entrance of Rocket Repair, where I saw a familiar red bandanna. Then a bush hat. The two Las Vegas bikers, once again in Dominic's employ, waved me into a cavernous motorcycle maintenance shop.

I parked and stepped out into the smell of gasoline and WD-40, the quintessential masculine essence. Several motorcycles were up on hydraulic lifts. Large red rolling toolboxes were placed around the shop, and other tools were held by magnetic bars on the wall.

I opened the hatch of my SUV, revealing three rolled carpets with feet sticking out of them. "You're a busy motherfucker, brother," said Red Bandanna as we shifted the rolled carpets and their occupants into a panel truck.

"You keeping the carpets?" asked Bush Hat.

"No."

"They look like wool."

"They are."

"They shed?"

"I hadn't noticed."

"Wool rugs shed. That's the thing about them. For about six months, you get balls of fuzz all around, look like mice."

I carefully removed the sorcerer's wand from the SUV.

"What's that fucking thing?"

"Watch out, the claws are poisoned."

"No shit? I could use something like that."

"It gets buried."

"You don't mind my asking, what'd these guys do to piss you off?"

"They felt up my girlfriend."

"The old story." Bush Hat and Bandanna climbed into the front seat of the panel truck. Bandanna asked me, "You okay riding with the stiffs?"

"I've been riding with them for hours."

"Right, a few more won't hurt. So climb in."

I got into the back of the panel truck and sat on the stiffs.

Dominic was waiting for us at a building site about seven miles from the Strip. The glow of Lady Luck could still be seen against the clouds. Dominic climbed down from the cab of the concrete truck, and the four of us carried the bodies into the open foundation. Then Bandanna and Bush Hat positioned the van to block anybody coming our way. I asked Dominic, "What's this place going to be?"

"An eco-friendly supermarket."

I couldn't see houses anywhere near. "Who's going to shop here?"

"You build an eco-friendly supermarket, and people who love expensive carrots will come."

There were other construction sites nearby, so I assumed that the developers knew what they were doing. Dominic climbed back into the cab of the truck. He started the mud out of the chute, and I watched it pile up around the bodies. I had put the claw-tipped wand on the sorcerer's chest. The points of the claw were the last thing to be covered. Dominic got down, and we smoothed the concrete. We did it quickly, then hosed down the chute and got back in the truck. Once again the truck's huge drum made me feel as if an elephant were following us.

We rumbled along through the Las Vegas night, and Bandanna and Bush Hat followed in the panel truck. Dominic said construction was still going on around the clock. Old casinos were being knocked down and new ones put up, along with resorts, retail complexes, offices. "The mud is flowing, cousin."

"How much are we paying the bikers?"

"A thousand each. They're worth it."

"I'm not complaining."

"On a job like this, you don't want flakes. These guys are good."

I saw their headlights in the side mirror outside my door. Irrationally, I felt that their headlights were protecting us.

Dominic said, "They do jobs for Carmine Cremona."

"What kind of business does Carmine do here?"

"Up until now, it's been titty bars with slots. They're a place to do some loan-sharking, some auto fraud insurance, small shit like that. But like I told you, he's getting into construction. It's a good time for wops in Vegas because law enforcement has their hands full with the Russians, who are truly brutal human beings. And then you got the street gangs looking to take everything over. So we *paisanos* are under the radar at the moment."

Dominic drove the mixer truck back to the industrial parking lot. And again he left a large roll of bills under the gas pedal. He slammed the door and said, "The Brotherhood of Cement Masons doesn't let you down."

"What does the driver think you do with his truck?"

"He doesn't ask. As long as the mud goes where it's supposed to go, he doesn't care."

The bikers were waiting for us outside the industrial gate. Dominic and I got in the back of their van, and I breathed easily for the first time in twenty-four hours. The bodies and I had parted company.

"Okay back there?" Bandanna asked as we rolled.

"Perfect," said Dominic.

"That's a nice cement truck you drive. With the tri-axles and all."

"It does the job."

We rode back to the motorcycle repair shop and pulled straight in. Dominic handed an envelope to each of the bikers. "It's all there."

"We trust you, brother. How about a beer?"

I wanted to get out of there, but Dominic said, "Sure, let's look at bikes."

So we looked at bikes being customized and heard about replacement engines, high-speed transmissions, stretch gas tanks, and other refinements. One particular bike came in for special praise. "You get no challengers when you're riding this," said Bandanna. "Somebody pulls up alongside you, they look, they listen, they turn their head in shame."

The bodies of my attackers were hardening into support for eco-friendly shopping, and we were talking motorcycles. After our beers, we left with invitations to return anytime. "Always happy to be of service," said Bush Hat as I backed out of Rocket Repair.

"The Venetian," said Dominic, and I drove there.

# 50

We ate at Mario Batali's Italian Steakhouse. "Hormone and antibiotic free," said Dominic, reading from the menu. "I like hormones in my steak, but what the hell." We ordered filet mignon that had been aged sixty days and cost eighty bucks.

White-shirted waiters in black ties brought us Chardonnay and arugula salad with trumpet mushrooms peeking up through the leaves. Not far from us, a huge sculptured bull stood watch over the dining room. When queried, our waiter answered proudly, "He is Bodacious, the most dangerous rodeo bull who ever lived." The waiter swelled his chest, standing in for Bodacious. "Broke every bone in the face of the best rider in the world. Nobody stayed on him for even eight seconds."

"And we're eating him tonight?"

The waiter smiled. "Signore, he was retired with honor, to entertain the ladies in his pasture ever after."

"That's the kind of retirement package I want," said Dominic.

When our steaks came, the waiter carved them beside our table, flourishing his knife with another show of pride, and I ate with the appetite of a man who has buried his enemies. I told Dominic what I knew about the Camel.

"Why do they call him the Camel?"

"He's got caravans of dope crossing Mexico. But I used to see him around Modelo, and he's very round shouldered. It looks like a little hump."

"You know how it is with guys who have a little hump, they're touchy."

"You think he'll send anyone else?"

"If his hump is itching."

For dessert we had something called blood orange semifreddo. It was mostly cold sweet cream with sugar and fruit, and it came over chocolate ladyfingers. As Dominic licked chocolate from his own fingers, he said, "Paloma is the wrong town for you. Dead bodies keep showing up."

When dessert was finished, I summoned our waiter and settled the bill. We walked back to the Venetian and climbed the bridge over the blue water of the artificial canal that framed the casino entrance. Gondolas tied to the pier were bobbing gently. A gondolier in straw hat and striped shirt was having a furtive smoke, cupping the weed in his hand. "You can get married in a gondola here," said Dominic.

Two middle-aged women were being serenaded by a portly gondolier singing as if he wanted to marry them both. I recognized it as *Nessun Dorma*, a song that Primo had loved, conducting it with one finger as he sat in his recliner like a respectable middle-aged opera lover.

The gondolier hit the last high note as he pulled into the pier. The women appeared very satisfied with his performance, one of them hugging him as the gondola wobbled. "You have to be a trained singer to audition for the job," said Dominic. "And the Venetian makes you speak with an Italian accent. I've got no problem with that."

We finished climbing the bridge over the canal and entered the hotel. The golden vaulted ceiling glowed with reflected light, reminding those who walked beneath it that wealth was here, that you were in the opulence of old Venice, with love and fortune at hand. "Let's play some blackjack," said Dominic.

"You go ahead, I'm going to walk around for a while." I found my way to the interior Grand Canal, where the voices of the gondoliers echoed against the eternally placid noontime sky painted on the high ceiling. The polished tiles echoed the click of women in high heels shopping the Canal. I wound my way along until I found an exit back to the street. I was still shaking off the past twenty-four hours, and the crowds along the Strip helped. The Camel couldn't find me here.

I passed the costumed cartoon characters offering their images for hire. You could be photographed with a flabby-assed Spiderman, or Batman with a chiseled plastic chest. A tired Mickey Mouse was sitting with his back to a casino wall, his head resting beside him on the sidewalk. Jimi Hendrix and SpongeBob were available, but the one who stopped me in my tracks was the most beautiful woman I'd ever seen. She was standing outside a casino, wearing a feathered rhinestone headdress harking back to the old days in Vegas, when all the showgirls wore fantastic crowns. A balding middle-aged tourist was posing with this showgirl as his wife, perhaps not altogether happy about the opportunity, was photographing them. Money exchanged hands, and the tourists walked on. I stayed where I was, staring at her.

It was hard to believe that such an incredible beauty could only find work posing for photographs on the street. Her skin was like ivory, her features were perfect in every way, and her eyes were like the peacock feathers in her headdress—iridescently beautiful and big. She wore a fringed and sequined bikini. A long feather boa traveled from her waist to her ankle.

"Want a photo?" she asked me, with a battery-powered smile she flashed for everyone. Our eyes met for a second, and I could read the resignation and determination there. She was out here making a living, not a great one, but it wasn't being made on her back. And who knows, maybe some high roller from Hollywood would discover her.

I had no right to look at her for nothing, so I handed her a fifty. "I just want you to know, I've never seen anyone as beautiful as you."

"Thanks," she said, flashing me a fifty-buck smile and then turning toward a couple of young guys gawking at her.

And that was that. Men found her stunning, which she already knew. I moved behind the young guys and looked at her for a while longer, letting our encounter sink into me. Kind fate had placed her in my path. Cheyenne and Sally had dazzled me, but so would many women, now and always, because female beauty is a gift to man from whatever god, fiend, or blind force has created the world. Vegas is a microcosm of that world, and chance is king. Chance, here or elsewhere, would put beauty in my path again.

# 51

I couldn't turn Dominic down. He wanted me to fight again in Vegas, and so, against my better judgment, I was in the ring against Janos Zombor, the Balkan Devil. He was another of Santos's fighters from Eastern Europe, the product of a culture raised on Russian oppression, the KGB, and people ratting on their neighbors. There was no give to the Balkan Devil anywhere, he was mean to the bone and ripped with muscle. His black hair was short and stood up as if electrified. Like me, he'd been introduced as undefeated, but he had the fights to prove it, all of them won by submission. Which meant he was a floor fighter with an arsenal of choke holds. I'd stuffed a Chinese warlord in an oven, but the Balkan Devil had been working in a gym day in and day out against sparring partners as strong and mean as he was.

The referee called us together. "No eye gouging, no biting, no throat strikes, no fishhooks to the mouth. Any questions?"

The Balkan Devil and I glared at each other, trying to psych each other out. He snarled at me, "Take dick in mouth."

"Take an English lesson."

I went back to my corner, where Dominic was crouching, stripped to his shirtsleeves, holding my mouth guard. "Knock the shit out of him quick, those are your instructions."

The Balkan Devil was bouncing up and down in his corner. I had at least twenty-five pounds on him, but his chest was like Batman's, only it wasn't made of plastic. I had to get to him quickly or he'd wear me down with speed and agility. Fighters as big as I am don't do well on the long haul.

The bell rang and we touched bare knuckles. The illusion is that boxing gloves are kinder, but they aren't. You can take a hundred punches to the head during one night in a regular boxing ring and wind up with brain damage. Looking in the Balkan Devil's eyes, I saw no brain damage. He was just a bloodthirsty Soviet Bloc bouncer who'd had his share of beatings and take-downs and learned from every one of them. He shot a few kicks at me just to see how well I moved. I avoided them easily because he was still feeling me out. For my part, I just wanted to land one on his chin and get things over with.

Deftly ducking my jabs, he announced through his mouth guard, "I fuck all your mothers." His body was jumping with adrenaline. I was pleased to see this because it burns energy. I was feeling optimistic until he caught my thigh with a kick, his shinbone hitting me like a crowbar, and now I had a taste of his power and I didn't like it. He kept at it, landing one for every six he tried.

I let him burn energy, but my legs were hurting and he'd just gotten started on me. Sparring every day builds a kind of Kevlar in the skin; the only sparring done in a monastery is with the soul. So I had no Kevlar. I wondered what I was doing in the ring with him. He was better trained, hungrier, and meaner.

He caught me again on the leg. I was feeling like Muhammad Ali felt in the dumbest fight he ever had, against a Japanese wrestler who kicked him in the leg so many times he had blood clots that bothered him for years.

Using my weight advantage, I backed the Balkan Devil against the ropes, only to find he was comfortable there, blocking punches with his forearms, which felt like rawhide wrapped around iron. Peering at me between his fists, he lisped through his mouth guard, "On your knees, bith." And then he connected with a series of powerful jabs to my midsection. The crowd was enjoying the hammering he was giving me, and the Balkan Devil was enjoying it too. The cage was his natural habitat.

He slipped out from under one of my punches and went back to the center of the cage. He knew he wasn't going to knock me out, my upper body was too strong for that. He had to weaken my legs. If I got wobbly, he'd be able to take me down. He'd be hell on the mat, where his conditioning would overtake me. When you grapple daily with opponents as he did, everything the other guy does is familiar, so you don't panic, your stress level is less; you hold on patiently waiting for the mistake you know will come. And he was built like an armadillo; he could take a lot of punishment.

"Bodacious!" shouted Dominic from my corner. He meant I had to go crazy, like a bull with a cowboy on his back. But I was using jabs instead, zingers that were quick and to the point, without giving the Balkan Devil a chance to counterpunch or slip in for a takedown.

"What the fuck are you doing?" shouted Dominic when we got near my corner again. "Run the fucker over!"

It wouldn't work, but Dominic didn't know that. The Balkan Devil was too fast to be dumped by a mad rush. I had to agitate him with jabs, get him off balance, so I could get in a really good shot to his nose or chin. Hitting him anywhere else on the skull could fracture bones in my fingers and wrists. I'd learned this in barrooms. It's like hitting a brick wall. Mother Nature gave us hard heads for a reason. She also gave us brains, and if I'd used mine I wouldn't be in this ring.

Jabbing aggressively, I backed him against the cage again and we tied each other up with locked arms; I was looking over his shoulder at the front row and saw *her*. She wasn't wearing her feathered headdress, but I couldn't mistake that face. Her eyes locked on mine in surprise; she'd just realized I was the big son of a bitch who'd given her fifty bucks for a smile. She gave me another one now for nothing.

I couldn't let a Hungarian dickhead show me up in front of the Great Beauty. He missed with a wild hook, and I caught him with an elbow strike to the face. His eyes went glassy, but his body fought automatically until his head cleared. We were both covered with sweat now, and he slipped away like an eel, back to the center of the ring.

I could feel her eyes on me, straight from the front row. She was with a guy, of course; a woman like that doesn't go unescorted at night. But whoever he was, he wasn't the center of attention at this moment; he wasn't fighting and I was.

The Balkan Devil landed another kick. It numbed something in my leg, and I lost balance as I backed up. He smiled. The fight was going the way he'd planned, and he plunged at my legs with his hands, to get behind my knees with his arms and tumble me backward and down. But he made a mistake and plunged too soon. Logging with the monastery's two-thousand-pound Belgian draft horse had strengthened my legs and back more than wrestling matches ever could, and wrestling matches were all the Balkan Devil knew about. Yes, I was hurting, but my legs weren't going to buckle just because he grabbed them. I drove my hips back and brought my arms down, stopping his momentum and causing his head to twist just enough for me to get my forearm against his nose and eyes. This is not a pleasant feeling, and it allowed me to crank his head. I cranked until I had his body sideways.

He was struggling to maintain his stance, but I'd gotten both my arms around his neck and kept cranking him sideways until I had him in a guillotine lock. I spread my legs and bent my knees for stability. He tried to slip his hand in to break my grip, but he had no room. I rocked back, arching for more purchase. Now my weight advantage meant something. I rocked back again, tightening the cinch on his neck. I had the boniest part of my forearm against his Adam's apple. I've had it done to me; it puts you into panic mode.

The crowd was waiting for fireworks. Only the other fighters in the audience knew what was happening, that his oxygen was cut off. When he shifted his weight to get away, it increased the pressure on his throat. I squeezed tighter, and it felt like I was separating his head from his body.

He flapped his hand at the referee, signaling surrender, but the ref was under instructions not to end the fight unless somebody was about to die. So I just kept choking the Balkan Devil until he passed out. Then I dropped him like a sack of shit. He landed on the canvas facedown and unconscious. I threw my hands in the air and went to the side of the cage where the Great Beauty was sitting. If it were a bullfight, I'd have given her his ear. As it was, I just gave her a smile.

Dominic was in the ring, embracing me. "Bodacious, man! You get to fuck all the cows!"

The announcement of my victory was made as the Balkan Devil was helped to his feet. As is customary, we embraced to show that our fight had been high-minded and clean. "I fuck your mother," he snarled in my ear. On this note of sportsmanship, we parted. I climbed through the ropes looking for the Great Beauty, but Vegas mob guys were congratulating me. Carmine Cremona was among them, the old gangster's eyes as warm as such eyes ever get, like those of a king cobra, but he embraced me, kissed me on both cheeks, and rasped, "I like the way you choked that Sputnik. We got a lot of them here. They're a pain in my ass. Want to work for me?"

Dominic said, "I got him under contract, Carmine."

Cremona smiled, tapping Dominic gently on the cheek. These were the voices and faces of my childhood, memorable for their expressions of cunning and intimidation. Photographs were taken, pledges of loyalty were made, and then Dominic and I worked our way through the crowd to the dressing room.

It was in the basement of the old casino, and in the floor were traces of the wiring that had powered a hundred slot machines. "You squeezed him like a pimple," said Dominic.

I slumped down onto a chair, feeling it creak under my weight. My adrenaline was still pumping, and I wouldn't feel real pain for hours. Tomorrow, I'd be limping around Vegas.

We could hear the crowd cheering for the next bout. Some other lunatics were walking up the aisle toward the cage. You had to be nuts to do this for a living.

There was a knock on the door, and a large man entered, diamond stickpin in his tie, and fields of diamonds on his fingers. "I'm Bob Elfwine from Wrestling Universe. I liked your fight. Your look is clean and your size is impressive." After a few comments to me on my fighting style, he started talking business to Dominic. "Why should your guy get the crap knocked out of him in a cage for a small purse? If he signs with Wrestling Universe, he avoids serious injury and makes a handsome salary."

"Scripted wrestling? You're kidding."

"Scripted wrestling is where it's at, my friend. Nobody sets out to kill the other guy, which is what's going on upstairs right now." He looked at me. "You know it and I know it."

I certainly knew it. The Balkan Devil would have torn the heart out of my chest and eaten it if he could.

"You can make serious money with Wrestling Universe, and your face remains in one piece."

# 52

I promised Dominic I would think about Wrestling Universe and Bob Elfwine's offer. Staring into my gas-fueled fireplace in Paloma, I thought about it for a minute and a half. I had a house, two million in cash, and a million in the stock market. I didn't need to wrestle large men for a living.

I looked from the gas flames to the ancient cross that now rested on the mantelpiece of my fireplace. The carved ivory figures of the apostles were miniatures of the men I had known in the monastery, men committed to the cross, fused with it for life. Did I have that fusion in my soul? If I did, why was I thinking of Cheyenne?

I should have put her into the Siberia of my soul, banished to those frozen wastes from which I never want anyone to return, but images of her were going through my head as I looked into the fireplace, which just goes to show how weak is the mind of man when it comes to pretty women. I tried to tell myself I was done with her, completely and finally. Our bout against the cartel hitmen, in this room, had not endeared her to me. She'd fought like a tiger and won, but her fury had been a reminder of what she could do to anyone who crossed her.

I turned away from the fireplace and looked toward my entrance hall, where the little Mexican medicine man had died looking into Cheyenne's blazing eyes and realized too late that he'd gone up against a warrior a cut above himself. She was a cut above me too. She was driven by demons greater than my own, and I wanted no part of them any longer.

My best course would be to sell up in Paloma and take residence in Hawaii. Polynesian girls could sing to me while I soaked in a volcanic hot tub. But I'd run away once and I didn't want to do it again. I liked Paloma's red rocks and its laid-back lifestyle. I was growing protective of Vittorio's house. I'd installed a better security system. I had an AK-47 under the floorboards. So I lit one of Vittorio's cigars and spoke to his memory. "I'll give a hundred grand to the little mission church from which you had yourself buried. And I'll give another hundred grand to Our Lady of Guadalupe so developers can't touch it. That should be enough to get you out of purgatory."

Vittorio had been a man meant for the mob but wound up in the unlikely profession of priest. He'd remained a crook, but I'd found many grateful letters from his congregation, who had marveled at the way he got things done, especially when it came to building contractors dragging their feet. *Those friends of yours, Father, who talked to the contractor really got things moving.* I could easily imagine who those friends were.

There was a letter from a single mother who had needed a car and one showed up, probably with the VIN numbers switched and a clean title to match. A boy without a graduation suit found several on a rack outside his house. His mother wrote, *The driver of the truck left without waiting for us to thank him.*

One Christmas, Vittorio performed his own version of Christ's miracle of the loaves and fishes, but with Vittorio it was the miracle of the loaves and turkeys. A truck full of them appeared, and everyone in Vittorio's flock got one. That driver didn't wait around either.

Vittorio's flock never questioned these little miracles he produced. They loved him. Whether he loved them back is hard to say; loyalty, yes, he gave them that, but love doesn't come easy to the Martinis. But he would be missed. I missed him, sitting here in his living room and imagining his cold, solemn way of doing things.

At which point my newly installed security lights lit up the front yard. At the same time, my motion sensor camera came on and I was getting a clear picture of Julian Talbot coming up my walkway. He was Cheyenne's lapdog, but better him than some pistolero from the Camel looking to spill my blood on the red rocks of Paloma.

I opened the door and he greeted me with an apology. "Sorry to show up unannounced."

"Always welcome," I said, and showed him in. From the entranceway, we stepped down into the living room. I saw him looking at the adobe fireplace and its dancing flames.

I said, "Nights are cold in Paloma."

"I've got the remedy for that." He took a flask out of his boot. It was actually a very small bottle, apparently shaped for stowing in a boot. "Care to join me? Texas bourbon from the Garrison Brothers. As it says in the ads, bold, proud, and authentic."

I put out shot glasses and we sat by the fire, warmed inwardly and outwardly as he explained the reason for his visit. "I wanted to talk about Cheyenne."

"How's the book going?"

"Not very well."

I waited. He sipped his bourbon, then, stroking his neatly shaped goatee, continued. "These days, the trend in self-help is how to make oneself lovable. Cheyenne's message is as dark as the back of my closet."

I thought of the darkness in her cellar. I said, "She cons people into playing her imaginary games. It gives her a buzz. A very peculiar one." It was as close as I could come to telling him he was dealing with a thrill killer. She'd killed Dez while she was high on the thrill of doing it. If Talbot got close to her and they had a falling out, could he wind up in her basement alongside Dez? Primo's voice was in my ear. *After the first kill, everyone else is just target practice.*

He said, "She knows how to work an audience, and there's something electric in her. But the UFO thing peaked years ago." He gazed thoughtfully into the fireplace. "I didn't realize how strong were her feelings about little gray beings who harvest organs while we sleep."

"Did you explain there's more money to be made in love and joy?"

"She said she didn't care about what she calls the succulent side of spirituality." He sighed into his authentic bourbon. "She thinks the FBI is after her."

"That's a new one."

"The self-help ladies in Paloma are mostly sketches, if you know what I mean. Cheyenne is three-dimensional." He ruminated about this, and so did I. On the coffee table between us was the bronze mustang she'd used to brain the little Mexican shaman. He'd had a three-dimensional view of her coming at him with his own poisoned eagle claw.

Talbot stood with a sigh. "I suppose I'll have to find somebody else for my book. Unless you think I can bring Cheyenne around."

"The more you push, the more she'll resist. That's how she is."

"I appreciate your input."

"And I appreciate your bourbon."

He inserted the bottle back in his boot. "Handy, isn't it, the way it fits?"

"I'd prefer a snub-nose thirty-eight Special."

He pulled open his jacket and revealed a shoulder holster with a hefty-looking automatic. "I like a longer barrel." This exchange about deadly weapons brought his mind back to Cheyenne. "She has a gift, you know."

"I know."

"She's put it to strange use." He buttoned up his jacket. "This idea of hers, that she's a walk-in. Maybe something could be made of that."

Her hooks were still in him. I would have liked him to make Cheyenne rich and famous; it would provide cover for her and take her mind off me. Earlier in the evening, I had consigned a love note she'd sent me to the flames in my fireplace. *I still love you, Martini, and I know you love me. We've been through a lot together.* By which she meant, among several things, my disposing of her husband's foot. And his boot. I glanced at Talbot's expensive handmade boots. I wouldn't want to saw one of them off, foot enclosed. "Do yourself a favor."

"And get out of Dodge? You're right, of course."

We walked to the front door. I switched off the security lights and stepped outside with him. Storm Mountain loomed before us, massively heavy in the darkness. He gazed up toward its shadowy peak. "You ever feed feral cats? They're paranoid. So is she, it helps her presentation."

He became silent again, as if the mountain could provide him with a game plan for Cheyenne. He didn't want to quit. He said, "When I suggested she forget the alien entities, she said I had a predatory personality. Then she suspended her crystal pendulum over the top of my head. Where, she said, I had an alien implant, which was controlling me. She ever try that one on you?"

"Frequently."

*We've been through a lot together,* said the note. You see, I'd made a little mistake after we fought the Mexican hitmen. She'd been naked, covered with the sweat of fear and exertion, and she slipped into my arms. I was charged with adrenaline, and we sank down onto the heavy carpet and made love like a pair of feral cats.

I said, "Julian, any man who gets involved with Cheyenne on any basis at all is out of his mind."

# 53

I'd grown up in a family where murder was accepted as a way of doing business and we'd square it in heaven later. But you couldn't square the FBI. They were the evil shadow in Primo's life. You mentioned them in a hush. So Cheyenne talking about the FBI made me uneasy. She shouldn't be talking about law enforcement of any kind. She had a body in her cellar, I'd helped her cover it up, and her shooting her mouth off about the FBI could get us both arrested. Paloma is a small town, and the cops who'd interviewed her might get ideas. So I went to one of her meetings to check her out for myself. She was at the center of a semicircle of chairs, giving her usual talk about surreptitious incisions performed on sleeping women by little gray beings. Followed by a microscopic implant in the womb, powered by alien science. Nothing about the FBI. The room she'd scrounged up was the office space of a now-defunct travel agency. On the walls were leftover posters of exotic destinations. Internet fares to anywhere had killed the agency, but Cheyenne was the travel agent tonight and the trip was through dark cosmic space.

She was back to her pilgrim look, long skirt and shapeless blouse. But I'd seen her naked, seen her perfectly proportioned body. And the little demon of desire whispered that if I slept with her again, I could talk to her about this FBI thing and thereby put it to rest. It was a crazy suggestion, but as I watched her parading around in her modest outfit, I thought of the women the wiseguys brought to family celebrations when I was a kid—gorgeous women with the glint of steel in their eyes. They would bathe me in their perfume and muss my hair, pinch my cheek, tell me I was going to make the girls go wild when I grew up. Was this why I liked hard women? If so, Cheyenne was the only one I'd found in Paloma. Fluff bunnies were the rule. The bumper stickers said things like *Practice Positive Expectation, Karma Is My Copilot*, and *Your Story Is Not Who You Really Are*. I certainly hoped so.

She moved confidently in front of her audience, most of them women. She liked drawing them into her dark web, shaking up their world of harmony and light. I stood at the back of the room, with a faded travel poster of Spain behind my head. Vittorio had told me to look for signs, and I should have looked at that poster and said tomorrow I'm on my way to run with the bulls in Pamplona, to enjoy the fireworks and the free-flowing wine. Being chased by a twelve-hundred-pound animal will be fun.

Instead, I stood in the defunct travel agency watching Cheyenne playing angel, like the wiseguys who, after burning some guy's house down earlier in the day, would tell me *be a good boy*, and slip me five or ten bucks. They loved playing the part of role model and I'd listened to them, I'd been an altar boy, an Eagle Scout, and earned my college tuition by carrying mud for Dominic's old man.

"If you see a kid who seems way too smart for his own good," Cheyenne was saying, "he might be demon spawn, a hybrid of human and alien DNA."

Being part of her audience suddenly seemed to be my fate. A wiseguy had said to me, *Once you're in the life, Tommy, you never get out of it. You can go to fuckin' Timbuktu and the life will be there*. I wasn't a made man, but guys like him had made me anyway, putting that fatalistic feeling on me.

So here I was, watching Cheyenne, and maybe she *was* the image of my soul. She looked out at us through the dim light and asked, "Do you know that poem by Auden? *Time watches from the shadows and coughs when you would kiss*."

I didn't know the poem, and I doubt that anyone else in the audience did. But Cheyenne, the self-educated rhinestone cowgirl, knew it. "Auden had it almost right. But it isn't time that watches you, it's a little parasite from space, intent on using you. That's the cough, and it spoils the kiss of one human being to another. The alien entities come between us. That's their agenda. And they're in this room, watching from the shadows."

And I thought maybe it was Dez who was in the shadows, that it was Dez who coughed when she would kiss, and that he would haunt her for the rest of her days.

"I see Brother Thomas is here tonight. Come on up here, Brother Thomas, and let us get a look at you."

The women turned toward me, curious, and Cheyenne gave them my brief bio. "He's a for-sure Catholic monk, and his uncle was our very own Father Vittorio. Some of you probably remember Vittorio from the charity work he did around here. He was a good man and I loved him like he was my own father."

Once again I wondered about her and Vittorio. Had they ever gotten it on? She would have loved seducing a priest. I pushed the thought aside and walked toward the front of the room—two hundred pounds of male pride, but feeling like the bull being chased through the streets of Pamplona. When I reached her, she put her arm through mine. "Brother Thomas is a good man too."

The women in the audience were not quite ready to embrace me as a good man. Maybe they were all practicing intuitives; maybe they could see the violence in my aura. But I was an interesting addition to their evening, and they were waiting to see which way Cheyenne was going to spin me.

There was an empty chair beside her, and she asked me to sit down. It was a folding chair and it creaked under me. A man will do a lot to understand a woman, and of course he'll never succeed. But Sally was in the front row, directly in front of me, and she was a treat for the eyes, soft, round, and lovely. But she was riveted on Cheyenne, sparing only brief glances for me. Cheyenne was the show, Cheyenne telling her audience that I had an old Spanish cross in my possession, that it was steeped in blood. "It's covered with obnoxious entities from the time of the conquistadors, from all that lust for gold those Spanish soldiers had in them."

She hadn't forgotten; she was still pissed that I'd taken it back from her.

"It's a beautiful cross, but greedy hands touched it five centuries ago, defiling it. And so the obnoxious entities piled on, licking up the dark energy."

I didn't know where she was going with this, but I had Sally to look at, at her tight black cowboy shirt with roses embroidered on the collars, the curling ends of her red hair just touching the roses. The rest of her was jammed into skintight jeans.

"We've got crosses for sale in this town, crosses made out of crystal and silver. You can buy them in the boutique shops. But there's no energy in them. It takes a ton of prayer to animate a holy object. The cross of Brother Thomas is loaded with energy; that's why the obnoxious entities like it and have hung on to it for centuries." She explained that some of these entities had migrated into my energy field. "I'd like permission to remove them, Thomas. Is that okay by you?"

And that's where she'd been going with the cross story, to show that even a Catholic monk was in need of her help. She called Sally up to assist, and they began exorcising my obnoxious entities. While they were doing it, Cheyenne put her lips to my ear and whispered, "You're the most exciting man I've ever met."

Men are ready to accept this kind of thing. But it was balanced by a roomful of women staring at me with amusement in their eyes, as if they were aware that Cheyenne was playing with me. A few of them, however, were true followers of Cheyenne and seriously concerned about the slime that clung to me. Until I was purified by Cheyenne's magic, I was a slimeball. But after working on me for about ten minutes, she declared me "Cleared."

She patted my head as if I were a good dog, and told me to drink plenty of water to flush the last remnants of slime out of my energy field. I left my seat at the front of the room and returned to the back, feeling the way I always felt at her meetings, exploited but fascinated by the way she controlled an audience. And then she began talking about the FBI. "They're into mind control and they're interested in anyone who has a gift for it. You telepaths know what I'm talking about."

Several women in the audience nodded knowingly.

"You've all heard drones buzzing around Paloma. One of those suckers practically came into my front yard. I got hit with some kind of ray that attacks the organs." She placed a hand over her stomach. "With a woman, it's the womb they zap."

She went on this way for an hour, with Sally adding comments to brace the story, and I had to admit that the image of FBI agents under the control of alien grays was perfect for paranoid Paloma, where government chemtrails were already falling on residents.

A bright young FBI agent with an alien implant in his head was a colorful addition to Cheyenne's sinister narrative. After the meeting, Sally drove us to their favorite bar, the one that looked out on a mountainous plateau where you could imagine a UFO coming in to instruct a team of FBI black-ops guys. Cheyenne started knocking back the vodka. She was drinking more these days, but her excuse was the same, that she had to burn out the slime picked up from her audience. "The only buzz I get is from you, Martini," she said with a smile, and took my hand. The vodka was making her more raucous and less saintly. She began to resemble the Cheyenne I'd known in bed. And when the meeting was over, that's where we wound up.

"I knew you'd be back," she said as we lay naked together after an hour of thrashing around on Vittorio's unpriestly bed. Her back was against the pillow, and she was running her instep along my calf. "You missed me. I was in your dreams. I was in your tea and in your coffee."

As on previous occasions, the sex had been an eye-opener for your monkish wrestler. Cheyenne knew holds I'd never dreamed of.

She ran her fingertips lightly across my forehead. "I won't be here for long, Martini, but you've made my stay on earth worthwhile."

I wasn't going to call her on the walk-in routine. If it had inspired this last hour in bed, I had no reason to be critical. And maybe it did charge her up to imagine she would soon be recalled to the angelic choir. We lit a couple of cigarettes from Vittorio's bedside table and tapped our ashes in an ashtray with a miniature of the Basilica of Lourdes pressed into the tarnished silver. I resisted the temptation to ask her if she'd ever practiced her wrestling holds on Vittorio.

After we finished our cigarettes, she traced the tip of her finger across my lips. "Had enough before you say your prayers, Brother Thomas?"

"I'm always ready for more."

"Make it quick because I've got work to do at home."

I didn't ask her what kind of work. We rolled around on the bed for another twenty minutes and ended up panting and perspiring all over again. With her arms around my neck, she said wistfully, "There will be other girls after I'm gone, Martini. Just promise you won't forget me."

I promised and we smoked another of Vittorio's cigarettes. It was heading toward two in the morning. With the cigarette between her lips, she swung her legs off the bed. "Let's fix me a nightcap, honey buns, and then I'll be off."

Wearing Vittorio's robe, which was too big for her, she walked off to the liquor cabinet in the den, clearly knowing the way, and I followed her in a shirt and jeans. She brought out a squat bottle with ribbons crossed around its neck. She held it up to the light, examining its amber hue. "Bacardí Paraíso. Did you buy it?"

"It's Vittorio's."

"It's three hundred bucks a bottle." She unscrewed the cap and sniffed appreciatively. "Vittorio always bought the best." She put out two brandy snifters and poured each of us a healthy measure. I took a sip. It was like silk, with the sweet flavor of a piece of fruit harvested in paradise, which, I assume, accounted for the name. And I hoped that Vittorio was sipping it in paradise now, though I had my doubts.

Cheyenne ran the tip of her tongue over her lip, like a cat sipping cream. "Good old Vittorio. That man knew how to live. But you, my gloomy monk, don't belong in his lovely house and you know it. Of course, neither do I. I'm trash and you're trash. Simple as that."

She was gazing straight at me over the edge of her glass, and maybe she was right. Grandfather Primo had kept our yard filled with junk as a disguise, but it reflected something in him, some basic trashy quality that he was comfortable with. And there *was* that mysterious drain in his cellar. Which snapped my thoughts back to Cheyenne's cellar, where Dez was buried. I'd wound up with a woman cut from the same cloth as Primo.

She touched her glass against mine. The sound was of fine, expensive glass, the dark priest's chalice. "Don't look so sad, sweetie. You can't fight karma."

"Don't talk to me in bumper stickers."

"You shall love your crooked neighbor with your crooked heart. That's Auden."

I looked around Vittorio's den, at the photographs showing him with groups of children, groups of nuns, and loving parishioners with their arms around him. His thick, wavy hair matched his chiseled face, which was handsome in a brutal way, and he was smiling but you could see the smile never reached his eyes; they were hard, the eyes of a player.

Cheyenne followed my gaze. "I wish I had hair like him." She drained her glass. "Okay, I'm out of here." She returned to the bedroom and got dressed. I waited in the living room, looking at the Spanish cross above my gas-log fire. The little apostles had the look they always had at night, as if they came alive by firelight. The delicate carving was the work of a vanished master, and a conquistador had died coveting it. And Vittorio had swiped it. It was perfect for his house.

Cheyenne came out, once again dressed in her chastity blouse and skirt. But she'd fluffed up her hair. Her moments of vanity were unpredictable. She blew me a kiss and headed toward the entranceway. When she reached it, she paused. I could see she was replaying the finale of her battle with the medicine man. Then she turned to me. "I got rid of that little skank, but we're still being watched, I hope you know that."

She could hold her liquor like her no-good daddy, but her eyes were glassy from three belts of paradise rum. "FBI," she said, lowering her voice. "I'm on their radar."

I remained silent, but she saw the skepticism in my eyes and said, "It's tragic when lovers aren't perfectly merged."

"Did Vittorio ever talk to you about his family?"

"Not particularly, why?"

"His father, my grandfather, was dodging the FBI his whole life. His phones were tapped and they raided his house whenever they thought they could nail him. I was there, so I know what it's like when the FBI is after somebody. And they aren't after you."

"Masterful Martini." She ran her hands under the collars of my shirt. "I like it when you come on strong."

"A word of advice. Stop talking about the FBI."

"Why were they watching your grandfather?"

"I never asked him."

We were at a standoff. The FBI was now part of her act, and she'd be trying it on me. But I was relieved because I could see that it was just an act. She was no more paranoid than any of the other conspiracy theorists who populated Paloma. The whole town resided in the Middle Ages.

We went outside to the driveway. "I'm a shady lady, sweetheart. Don't fight it."

She climbed into her truck and backed expertly out of my driveway, a woman for whom a truck is second nature. My shady lady.

After arming the security system, I returned to my gas-log fire and put the Benedictine monks of Fontgombault on the stereo system. It was a high-end stereo system, naturally, and the purity of the monks' voices matched the beauty of the Spanish cross that Vittorio had stolen. I sipped his fancy rum and thought of the men killed in this house. Listening to the monks searching with their voices, I knew how troubled the Martini family was. As long as I lived in this house, I'd be part of that screwed-up family, and I thought, fine. Bring it on.

I was drunk on the rum of paradise.

# 54

The little demon of desire kept me in orbit around Cheyenne. There was something deep between us, and it was under two feet of concrete in her cellar. I had stepped into Dez's shoes, with the guilt any man feels when he's with another man's woman. You see, a good Cat-lick boy like me has to contend with the spirit, and I felt Dez's. His was a heavy ghost, shot into the afterlife with a very loud bang. As for Cheyenne, who had put him there, maybe there *was* a fucking implant in her brain. I'm not privy to the workings of those countless planets capable of sustaining life. Maybe, five hundred million years ago, one of these planets came to consciousness and it resulted in sophisticated beings who eventually exploded their planet out of greed and poor ecological practices and the survivors came whistling down out of space just to call on Cheyenne.

I was trying to tell this to Sally, to get her to help me. I said, "I owe it to Dez." I told her I was in touch with his spirit. That got her attention. That was the kind of talk Sally understood. She nodded, as the women in Cheyenne's meeting had nodded, in complete understanding of a volatile spiritual situation in which alien grays had begun to influence certain agents in the FBI.

"She's got to shut up about the FBI. Dez doesn't like it. He thinks it's dangerous."

"Why does he think that?" asked Sally, eyes fastened to mine in a way

I could never elicit from her with a love song. But sing her a dark song and she was *there*, 100 percent, gazing at me, her imagination already swimming in images of Dez droning at us from the hell we'd put him into.

We were sitting in the café of the Natural Born Foods market, where ecologically enlightened diners were insisting that nothing be GMO. UFO was okay. Just not GMO. There was a man in a cowboy hat glazed with dirt from romping in the dust of the Arizona desert. But he was eating a healthful salad. I was having a heart attack sandwich to keep the protein in my muscles, fortifying them for danger ahead. Sally was in a good position to prevent it if I could get her with the program. "Dez wants his body out of the cellar. He wants me to chop it out. And then he wants me to bury it, but Cheyenne won't let me move him."

"He's here at our table," Sally whispered. "You've opened the channel for me." She closed her eyes to communicate with Dez, and I opened mine a little wider to accommodate myself to the sight of her lush loins crammed, as usual, into the tightest blue jeans she could find. Such jeans were plentiful in Paloma, Western gear was in every shop, and she had found a pair with rhinestones along the side pockets. They formed sparkling doorways into her thighs, and I was slipping through them, roaming along the hills and valleys of her body, right down to her rattlesnake boots. The toes were squared off for kicking a horse, and the heels were high for locking into the stirrups. But going further than this with Sally would be madness. Not with sixth-sense Cheyenne around. So I brought my thoughts back to Dez and my eyes back to Sally's, and she opened them right on cue.

"He forgives us, Martini, that's the first thing he wants us to know. He has no wish to carry feelings of vengeance in the Bardo."

Vengeance in the Bardo, it sounded like a Bruce Lee movie. Well, I was in one at the moment. Dez had to leave the cellar because Cheyenne was going to give the game away somehow. Her FBI flirtation was just the beginning. She'd go on and on, creating investigatory bodies that were out to stop her. She was high on the idea, I saw that every time she ran some newly embodied shade of paranoia at her meetings. And I'd been attending the meetings faithfully because I had to keep track of the curve. As a small plus for my putting up with hours of FBI agents with implants in their head, Sally had grown comfortable around me. She could see that I was now in the light. As far as she was concerned, I had embraced the Messenger, not just in bed, but in my Cat-lick soul. I had accepted that Cheyenne and Jesus were working hand in hand to stop the alien grays from destroying mankind. So we had become good friends, that's how she put it. With a woman of her build and disposition, that meant sincere maternal hugs were included in the friendship. I'd been getting quite a number of them, in full sight of Cheyenne, because Cheyenne knew that Sally was celibate. It was part of the work. And Sally's great pneumatic tits would press into my chest with such devastating buoyancy, it took all I had to keep from putting my hands firmly on her ass. Cheyenne was available only on certain nights, and these corresponded to astrological calculations she made on her computer. So an astrology program was in charge of my love life, and apparently it wanted to tease me along gently rather than have me submerged in nightly fun, the result being that I was horny three days a week and today was one of them.

"Dez is not in a good place in the afterlife," continued Sally. "I'm not surprised you picked up on it, because it's very heavy. Can you feel it right now?"

"Definitely."

"That's his emotional field. He's drowning in slime from the life he led on earth."

I didn't suggest that his emotions might come from having been shot in the face by his wife. Sally reached across the table, pushing aside the plate where my roast beef sandwich had been, and squeezed my wrist. "Can you reopen the channel? I just lost it."

"It comes and goes, Sally. But I know what he's driving at."

"About his burial place. It's a terrible dilemma for him."

I was the one with the terrible dilemma—how to get the dead weight of concrete with Dez inside it into Cheyenne's truck without being seen. But first I had to get permission from a woman implanted with stubbornness by inexplicable forces, by alien grays, by Darth Vader, and by the crocodile god of Egypt, and whoever else she was consulting about Dez's tomb. She wanted to have him under her roof, even if he was encased in concrete.

That way, he would not be riding off into cowboy heaven where sexy angels were waiting for him in their half-ton trucks of delight.

I said to Sally, "If I read Dez correctly, he understands Cheyenne's protective feelings about his body."

Sally's grip on my wrist tightened. "But he wants to free her from that responsibility. Isn't that it? Is that how you read it?"

We were speaking the same language, I just had to be careful that my own emotional field didn't include fucking her. Her knees were touching mine. I could so easily have parted them and explored her thighs. But Cheyenne had sworn me to celibacy unless conjugation was with her. "I don't want some slimy bitch draining the angelic substance out of you, Martini, not when I've worked so hard with your energy body."

At the moment, my energy body was quivering beneath the table. I could have lifted it with my hard-on. Sally was the most voluptuous woman in Paloma, maybe in all of Arizona, softness to die for, surrounded by a thin layer of cowgirl fabric, a shirt with turquoise buttons, and jeans with rhinestone pockets. "Sally, I think you can help Cheyenne in this matter with Dez. You're the one she trusts."

"I acknowledge that privilege, but you're her soul mate."

Once Dez was out of the cellar and buried where neither cops nor coyotes would ever get to him, I could sell up in Paloma and go to Pamplona. I had the travel poster in my mind; I'd been seeing it nightly at the meetings. I said, "Dez wants to protect you and Cheyenne. Every time I sense him, that's what I get."

She looked soulfully into my eyes and brought both her hands onto mine. "And he forgives us."

"Of course he does. On the last night of his life, he told me he knew he was a slimeball."

"Did he? Did he really admit that? Because if he did, then it's just what Cheyenne said, that he wanted us to free him from that karma."

Right, and shoot him in the head. That's the atmosphere they lived in, a strange dream world in which they were the heroines, cleaning up the slime. I had to keep this in mind, because if I didn't, Sally would never listen to me. Whatever I did had to be in that atmosphere. With ordinary people, you could say, we've got to get the body out of your cellar before the cops find it. But not with Sally and Cheyenne. "Sally, I believe your influence with Cheyenne is much greater than you think. She's very receptive to your emotional needs."

"That's so true, Cheyenne is the only one who can fulfill my emotional needs." As if realizing she shouldn't look to me for any emotional need, she released my hands and sat back in her chair. The cozy part of our chat was over. I had to start again. "Want some dessert? How about a piece of cheesecake?"

"Nothing for me." She patted her hips.

I bought a huge chocolate-chip cookie and some overpriced coffee and returned to our table.

"Why did you go into the monastery, Martini?" I could see her trying to work her way back to me, to a trust that didn't come easy to her.

"I put a young man in his grave. With this." I held up my fist.

She stared at it with a startled look. "You killed somebody?"

She knew I wasn't conning her. We were speaking as murderer to murderer. I lowered my fist and said, "I'm on the same page as you and Cheyenne."

"How did it happen?"

"In a bar. I was the bouncer. He was a customer. Things got out of hand."

"I'm so sorry, Martini." She leaned toward me again, our bodies not touching, but as the practicing intuitives would say, our emotional fields were once again united.

"I carry that guy's spirit around with me."

"Let him go, Martini."

"I'm trying to help Dez let go. If I can do that, maybe the young man I killed will go with him."

"I'm so grateful you're sharing this with me."

"We'll chop Dez out and put him in a better place. We've got him facedown now, staring at the cellar floor. It's not a happy position."

"I've considered that," she said. Her voice became solemn. "Gazing at the earth is ruinous for a departing soul. They get dragged back."

"And Dez is looking at the drainpipes of life. The man was a cowboy. He belongs out on the wind."

"Where would you put him?"

"I've got a spot in mind."

"I don't want to pit my will against Cheyenne. You know what that's like."

"The way I see it, Sally, because Cheyenne is a walk-in, she's not completely plugged into some hard-core facts. I'm sure you've seen this for yourself. A certain vagueness that comes over her?" Usually after she's had six drinks.

"I'm listening, Martini."

"She sees Dez the way the Egyptians saw their mummies. As sacred objects to be kept around. Don't you feel that, that she doesn't see a body in her cellar? She sees the way a walk-in sees, only vaguely connected to harsh facts." I was winging this anyway I could, but I knew I had Sally's attention, because her knees were once again touching mine.

"Martini, she told me you were her priest here on earth, that you might even be a walk-in yourself. Do you ever have that sort of feeling? That some important part of you is elsewhere? I do. I'm pretty sure I'm a walk-in too." Her voice grew even more solemn. "And that the three of us have special work to do together."

"Beginning with a proper burial for Dez."

"I can accept that."

"So you'll try and bring Cheyenne around?"

"I will."

She stood and said, "I'll see you at Cheyenne's."

I got into my BMW and followed her over. Trees were leafed out in the yard but in modest Arizona fashion, so there wasn't much shade. The windows were open, and I could smell burning rice, Cheyenne's specialty. The door opened and she stood there in an apron. "Y'all look well fed, but there's chili if you want it."

I did not want to ignite my lips, so I passed. Sally held out a small bowl and Cheyenne dumped some of her rocket-fuel beans and tomato sauce into it. "None for you, Martini? You look all peckered out."

"I had a cookie."

"And roast beef," added Sally.

Standing there in her apron, her hair a mess, Cheyenne still gave off heat, probably from the doors of hell she controlled, and I could feel them opening as I said, "I've got to chop Dez out of the cellar. I've got to give him a decent burial."

"What for? It's not going to improve his looks."

"He's looking down," said Sally cautiously. "Into the darkness."

"Martini told you that, I suppose."

"I think Martini sees something, Cheyenne, something that we might have missed."

"Dez isn't moving." Cheyenne resumed stirring her hellfire chili, then spooned some out for herself. She sat down at the table, opposite Sally. "And don't let Martini into your mind. He'll start giving you his Jesuit logic." She shot me a poisonous look—nothing fatal, just a reminder of who I was dealing with. She was in charge of the dead body. She'd made it, it was all hers.

A string of drying red peppers hung from the kitchen ceiling. There were mystical magazines on the table. I could see part of a Buddha, and a woman's leg in a black leotard.

Sally said, "Martini says Dez wants to be buried out in nature."

Cheyenne put down her spoon and looked at me. "You're channeling now? Is this a new calling?"

"He told me he loved nature."

"When was this?"

"In a bar one night."

"And now he talks to you." Cheyenne grew pensive, and the thought crossed my head that she really didn't want Dez in her basement. She knew that it was like a keg of dynamite waiting to go off in her face. But she'd recruited Sally for the burial detail, with the con job that it was part of a necessary ritual. To deconstruct that now might make the Messenger look bad.

"Let's lock hands," she said. "Take a seat, Martini."

I sat between them and they extended their arms. Our hands touched, gripped. Cheyenne closed her eyes, tilted her head back, and said, "Dez, honey, you want us to shift you?"

We waited in silence. Once again Sally's knee touched mine under the table. We sat like that for a long time. A cricket in the wall began chirping. Cheyenne's kitchen clock was ticking. It had an alien gray on its face, the black slanting eyes staring down at us. She opened her own eyes. "All right, Dez says do it."

I stood up. "I'll get started."

"Just a goddamn minute. Where are you going to take him?"

"To the Devil's Well."

"It's deep enough?" Suddenly all practical.

"I read up on it. A huge limestone cave collapsed a million years ago and water rushed in to fill the space. It goes way the fuck down."

"An offering to the water deities." Cheyenne nodded sagely, which was fine by me. She could offer it to whomever she wanted. But Dez was going down. And so was I, into her cellar. She called after me, "You get hungry, hon, just give a shout."

I bent over Dez's tomb. "You're coming out of there, partner." The concrete had cracked some more, forming a jagged web pattern in the floor. If we waited long enough, Dez would crack right out of there and climb onto his horse.

I had stashed a hammer, chisel, and crowbar in the corner. I knelt beside my entombed partner in the madness called loving Cheyenne. "I've taken over where you left off, Dez." I held the chisel to the concrete and began to tap gently. "I'm the one in her bed these days. Don't ask me why."

Properly mixed concrete is hard as hell to break up, but Cheyenne had done such a lousy job, it was breaking without too much difficulty. "I know why she fascinated you, brother. She can be fun." I was speaking softly, but if Cheyenne heard me, she'd assume it was prayer and not a recitation of her high points. "And she's the queen of the snakes in bed. You know what I mean."

I imagined Dez listening from under his concrete suit. "She's still pissed that you cheated on her with that Texas bunny. It's why she's kept you around. To remind herself that nobody leaves her and lives. But I've gotten through to her."

And I'd gotten through to Dez's jeans, the blue fabric showing now.

The cowboy from Montana was taking shape. "She's still got your balls in a bottle somewhere. I've been looking for them, but she's got dozens of hiding places."

The chisel tapped along, a hard, cold sound crumbling the concrete. "She's deep and she's dark, and I suppose that's why I'm hung up on her, but just how dark she is, only you really know." Dez had stared into the barrel of his own gun, the one he'd said was just right for her. Maybe he'd said, in his slow Montana drawl as she pulled the hammer back, "Now, honey, calm down."

I'd reached his waist; one of the metal studs on his belt was peeking through the concrete. Somewhere in the middle was his bronco belt buckle, two horns of a steer in silver. I'd leave that untouched, to help him on his way through the underworld. The pharaohs took all their shit with them, thinking that it mattered, and maybe it does.

The priestess of the damned was rustling around upstairs, her heavy footsteps signaling impatience. The cellar door opened, and Sally started down the stairs, her rattlesnake boots coming slowly into view, followed by the rest of her, skintight jeans stretching around her thighs with each step she took. She was carrying a small rock hammer, the kind used by mineral collectors. "I'd like to help."

I pointed to where Dez's head should be. "Start there and work toward me. We just want to free him from the floor. Don't take too much off the top. I want him heavy."

She knelt, put her lips to the concrete, and said softly, "Dez, I'm awful sorry about what happened."

With her back against the cellar wall, she started chipping. A chunk of concrete fell away under her pick. "Lordy me, there's his hair."

A faint odor of decay was released, and I told her again not to go too deep. My own chisel had just uncovered another piece of denim fabric—his shirt. So now I had a general idea where his arm was, and worked my way along it. I'd felt the wiry strength in him the night we met at the Apache ceremony and he held his hand out to me, saying, "Any friend of Cheyenne is a friend of mine."

Sally finished outlining Dez's head and reached over to touch my hand. "We're between worlds, Martini. We're helping Dez transit the planes."

I was transiting the planes of her rodeo shirt as she bent toward me. As always, she was bursting out of her clothes, three turquoise buttons open at the top of her shirt revealing her cleavage. Cheyenne had forced her to be celibate and she was, but she wanted the attention of men nonetheless, and she certainly had mine. She continued chipping away, experienced with her rock pick. The line she was making in the concrete was neater than mine. As she chipped at the place where Dez's neck was enclosed, she said, "He was loaded with alien implants. Cheyenne said that's why he was so unhappy. It's a mercy that implants dissolve on death."

But the bullet in his skull hadn't dissolved. The legal system would have all it needed to put us in jail for a very long time. I wanted to hurry him out of his concrete bed, but the weight needed to sink him had to remain on his body, so we worked carefully, leaving a layer of concrete on top of him. It would also hold decaying flesh in place.

"He used to beat her," said Sally. "Did you know that? The implants brought on his anger."

I didn't believe this. The Dez I knew was low-keyed and strangely gentle for a man who had wrestled steers for a living. But they had their woo-woo story, and if it made Sally feel better, fine.

"The alien entities implanted him because they wanted to bring Cheyenne down. They've been against her work from the beginning."

She drew my eye, I couldn't help it. It wasn't just the flaming red hair and voluptuous body. I'd been impressed from the start by her independence, her traveling around in a Jeep and trailer, following some kind of star. She could have landed anywhere in the Southwest, but Paloma had drawn her, and Cheyenne had dazzled her with a fairy tale. I felt for Sally, and if we got rid of this body successfully, I'd tell her to get in her Jeep and tow her trailer far away from here, to forget Cheyenne and forget me too.

Cheyenne came down the stairs. "The elves are at work. I hear their little hammers." She was wearing a headband with a small crystal at its center. "Sally, you have to protect yourself." She handed Sally another headband, the center of which was a polished black gemstone. "A whole lot of bad juju is going to come off Dez when we let him out. Get this on you before the negative energy starts releasing."

We had to get Dez the fuck out of there and into the water table of Arizona, but they were playing Vengeance in the Bardo. I chiseled my way down the other side of his body as they continued exchanging esoteric comments about the guy they'd covered in concrete after Cheyenne shot him in the head. In their view, something quite different had happened. They hadn't really killed and buried him, they'd purified him. But I was tuning them out, my thoughts with Dez as he'd been when I knew him, a lean saddle bum who'd given up his love of the open range to marry Cheyenne and drive tourists around in a Jeep, which hadn't been him at all. This thing we were uncovering wasn't him either. It was a second-degree murder sentence, with Sally as accomplice and me as accessory. She and Cheyenne seemed to have lost sight of that at the moment; uppermost for them was to complete his purification, with Apache power words, Christian prayer, and something that sounded like a Tibetan monk having a difficult bowel movement.

I inserted the crowbar a good inch below one of Dez's legs. I wanted to pry him off the hardened pool of concrete he was lying in but keep him in his concrete cocoon. I repeated this along the entire length of his leg, then repeated the process on his other leg. In this way I released his entire body. "Lordy, Lordy," moaned Sally as I got my hands under Dez's shoulders and lifted. He came up like the curse of the mummy's tomb, arms and legs stiff, head frozen in place. His cocoon had cracked in several places, including around the face, and we had to deal with more smell of decay and the sight of a rotting eyeball.

Sally kept moaning, but Cheyenne handed her a bottle of aromatic oil to sprinkle on Dez "and pacify his astral." Whether his astral was pacified is open to discussion, but the oil certainly knocked down the smell of decomposition. Cheyenne had a large pointed crystal in her hand and swept it outward from the body in repeated strokes, muttering some shit, but she avoided looking at his partially uncovered face. When she finally declared the ritual over, I told her to back her truck up to the door off the kitchen.

She didn't agree. "We should wait for the middle of the night."

"No, we want to be just another truck in evening traffic. Sally, there's a tarp in the shed. Put it in the truck and then come back down here."

I kept the body upright and tried not to look at the eyeball, but it kept drawing me back, the blob of goo reflecting a bit of the cellar light and giving an impression of lingering life. I lowered my eyes and saw the toes of his boots pushing out of the concrete. I heard Cheyenne backing up the truck. Then the sound of the tailgate being lowered, and Cheyenne and Sally talking furtively. Then Sally came down the stairs.

I said, "Come here and hold the head while I get his legs."

"Martini, I can't look at his face. I'll get his legs." She squatted, got her hands under his boots, and lifted him upward to the horizontal. I said, "You go up the stairs first. That'll give most of the weight to me."

She walked backward toward the stairs, and we began the slow ascent, Sally muttering "Lordy, Lordy" all the way. At the top of the stairs, another piece of concrete fell off the head, revealing a hideous grin of decaying lips. When we got him into the kitchen, Cheyenne opened the kitchen door, glanced at the face, and said, "He used to be so pretty."

I said, "Hold the door," and Sally and I carried him through it. Cheyenne had put the truck as close to the door as she could. It was a Dodge Ram 1500 with plenty of bed space for a concrete corpse, and we slid him over the tailgate. I threw the tarp over him. From Cheyenne's raised-bed garden project, I took four cinder blocks and put them on the corners of the tarp. "Okay, let's go. I'll drive."

"The hell you will," said Cheyenne, and climbed into the driver's seat. I knew she was already three sheets to the wind; her eyes had that boozy look. But I got into the passenger seat. "Just stay under the speed limit."

"Don't worry," said Sally from the back seat. "We're completely shielded."

This filled me with boundless confidence. If a UFO came by, it would be unable to fuck with us.

The shops of Paloma went by, their candy-colored lights welcoming those who shopped late for spiritual necessities. Cheyenne reached under the seat for a bottle of Jack Daniel's. I said, "Go easy with that."

"I know what I'm doing," she said, deftly unscrewing the cap while steering with her elbows. She took a long swig and handed it to me. I unclenched my teeth, took a hit, and threw the bottle out the window, the way Dominic had thrown out my anger medicine.

Cheyenne started to get angry, then wound up laughing. "Martini, that's alcohol abuse."

But she stayed under the speed limit, didn't cross any white lines, and sang *Ruby, Don't Take Your Love to Town* with Sally. Their voices blended easily, just a pair of sweet country gals with a dead body in their truck.

We were outside Paloma now, heading along the dark desert highway. The edges of our headlights caught cattle fences set back from the road. The days of the big roundups were gone, but out in these open stretches, distant yesterdays seemed close at hand. Cheyenne was a throwback to those days of itinerant preachers and snake oil peddlers, and Sally was a born drifter, both of them out of step with their time.

I listened to them singing, but when they began to talk about government conspiracies and alien grays, I tuned out, letting myself blend into the desert night. At this hour, the animals were stalking, slipping quietly through the darkness with an image of their prey in their heads. Softly, softly they went, while we were barreling along huge and conspicuous. But half-ton trucks are plentiful in the Southwest, and we were just like all the others with a good-looking woman at the wheel and some big dope riding shotgun.

The forty miles went by too slowly for me, but finally we reached our turnoff and headed toward the Devil's Well. It was appropriately named, for the water was undrinkable and nothing could live in it owing to a high arsenic content. The road to it was poorly maintained, and we bounced along over cracked pavement, climbing upward like the TV ads for half-ton trucks, nothing daring to stand in our way. Except the closed gate that led to the well. I climbed down, went to the tailgate, and lowered it. The two ladies came around the truck to join me. "I've got this," I said. "Take the truck back down and drive a quarter mile or so till you come to an old ranch road. It's got a cattle grate. Park where you can't be seen. I'll find you there."

"You've been planning this," said Cheyenne.

"I have."

"Clever Martini."

"I'll help you carry Dez," said Sally. "I'm in direct contact with his spirit now. The channel is open and tremendously strong."

If a park ranger came along, I could fade into the desert. Sally, much as I appreciated her esoteric commentary, would only slow me down. "You go with Cheyenne."

Cheyenne was lighting a cigarette; usually she smoked only after sex. But the hand holding the match was steady. She just needed some smoke to blow into Dez's face. "Goodbye, sweetheart." She blew smoke up and down his body, then ground out the cigarette on the cracked pavement. I picked up the butt and put it in my pocket. We weren't going to leave any traces. Then I slid Dez off the tailgate and lifted him above my head.

He was stiff, a cowboy frozen in stone. The moon had come up and there was enough light for me to find my way along the path. I heard the doors of the truck slamming shut and then the engine coming to life. I kept going, listening with relief to the truck bouncing back down the pock-marked road. I wanted to be nothing more than a shadow cast by the moon.

"It's come to this, old buddy," I said to Dez above my head. "What the love of a woman can do to a man." In his case, it was two women—Cheyenne and the dude ranch gal whose naked picture in her phone gave him an alternate view of life's possibilities. With me, it was Cheyenne and Sally, and I was done with both of them. With this solemn oath, I continued up the path, but the recent nearness of Sally in the cellar remained with me too. "What's a man to do, Dez? What's a man to do . . . ?"

He was heavy over my head now, all that concrete bearing down on me. But I'd been the kid who carried pails of mud up a ladder to Dominic's father, who laid it on wire wrapped around a house. House after house, my summer of mud.

"I carry mud, old buddy, when I carry you."

I heard footsteps behind me and knew that Cheyenne and Sally were following me. They couldn't let me do this alone. But when they came up to me, they were a pair of coyotes, mangy and mean. They gave me the once-over before padding off softly in the moonlight, with that light bouncing gait they have, the pimp roll of the high desert. They weren't going to fuck with me, because they could smell the testosterone coming from my armpits and groin. They've got plenty of it themselves and know how to measure it. I started jogging, enjoying the weight now. I did overhead presses as I ran, moving Dez up and down in his last war dance.

I was running toward my goal line. In high school, when I was a running back, I collided with a safety in midfield and he went down. I ran into the end zone and he lay there under the floodlights, unmoving. Dominic was watching from the sidelines. The guy I had knocked unconscious belonged to a cheerleader. Dominic lied to her and said, "He's dead," and she sighed in her cheerleader costume, and Dominic comforted her.

Up the path, the winding path to the well. There were mountain lions around here, but they kept to themselves, staying mainly in the hills, where they ruled. I could pick up their thought waves, real or imagined; I knew they were out there and aware of me, no matter how far away I was. They knew they could take me, but they were cautious cats. Too much was happening for a cat to feel comfortable: those twin lights of a truck, its intrusive inscrutable sound, the scent of females, it added up to a scene a cat might find interesting, even tasty, but it was no-go. The safer path was higher in the mountain, far from those other twin lights, the human eyes.

When your adrenaline is in overdrive, you pick up all kinds of things, and I could sense that cat and all his ancestors. He must be a big bastard, with a powerful force blowing out of him. I sucked him in, filling up with cat shine and starshine. I could see the mound of the well site ahead, a rough outline in the dark, a fortification for owls.

The path here was reinforced with dried two-by-fours every few steps, to assist the upward-rising tourist. I'm here, Gladys. Get out the camera.

I crested the hill, and the dark shape of the well appeared below, along with iron railings on both sides of the path. I jog-trotted downward, doing my last presses with Dez overhead. When I reached the protective railings guarding the edge of the well, I stopped. Only a bit winded, regulating my breath, slowing it down, just a few more deep inhalations and we're there, Dez and Martini in the moonlight. I walked around the protective railing and trod the narrow edge of the rock ledge carefully, Adrenaline Man taking it more cautiously. The well was directly below me now, a bigger shadow, water that wouldn't support life—not something I wanted to sample.

When the earth had opened here, split rock and soil tumbled down in a sheer drop, leaving no gentle slope to the water. There was no way I could climb to the water's edge with Dez on my back. I was going to have to toss him.

I raised him high above my head, showing him to Mother Moon. "*Lux perpetua luceat eis.*" May eternal light shine upon him.

I tossed him, giving it a little extra so he cleared the vertical wall with room to spare. He arced a little, then corrected course to a perfect vertical drop. I could see the moonlight on the concrete, casting back a faint gray glow, and then he was in the water like a knife, the splash minimal, and he was gone. I listened to the waves touching the shore, listened till they died away.

"*Requiescat in pace.*" Rest in peace.

# 55

I saw the glow of a cigarette in the dark and headed toward it. The truck was parked under a big cottonwood tree, which meant there was lots of water nearby. Probably part of the underground stream that had filled the Devil's Well. "Let's get out of here."

As I said that, a coyote pack let off a volley of yips and barks, frenzied, like maniacal laughter.

"Coyote magic," said Cheyenne.

It was a chilling sound, predators going about their business in the dark, announcing their territory, or protecting a kill. We climbed into the truck, and Cheyenne backed it out toward the road. She weaved slightly, cursing the twisty ranch road, but I no longer cared what she did while driving. If we needed a tow truck, if the police slapped her with a DUI, our connection to Dez's murder was broken and they couldn't touch us for that. He was 120 feet down, and if research was to be believed, the bottom was a false bottom of fine silt bubbling up from an even deeper layer. Dez would go down through the fine silt, ever deeper, ever farther from human reach. "You're safe, Cheyenne," said Sally. "They can't touch you now."

"It doesn't matter," she said. "I'm not long for this world."

"Don't say it, hon. Your mission could change."

"Maybe." Cheyenne looked at me in the rearview mirror. "I definitely want to clean Martini up, get rid of all his drains, that sort of thing."

Dez was sinking down and down, to finally settle far below in the underwater world, where the secret streams run forever.

Sally said to Cheyenne, "I felt the release when Dez went, didn't you?"

"He went out of here like a streak."

"And his happiness flooded over me," said Sally. "I almost peed my pants."

They talked like this for many miles, and I felt the relief in their voices. They'd dodged a murder rap and they knew it. I kept my peace. I was done with both of them. Of course, the last man who broke with Cheyenne got a bullet in the head, so I would have to ease out slowly from her bed.

They started singing again, this time *Blue Eyes Crying in the Rain*, and again I was moved by the sweetness of their voices, how it veiled the cynicism in Cheyenne, and the confusion in Sally. I suggested they start their own girl group and they laughed at me, and pretty soon we were back in Paloma. "We've got to have us a few drinks," said Cheyenne, and drove to her favorite bar, the one looking out on the UFO plateau where, I felt sure, watchers were keeping track of the sky. We sat in the window that faced the plateau, and Cheyenne and Sally drank tequila. I had one of the local beers, and good feeling flowed between us. There might have been a little too much of that, because once again Sally's knee was touching mine.

Cheyenne was checking out another table where the Christ-like, blond-haired guru was transmitting his teaching to three young women. I'd previously heard Cheyenne describing him as having *an alien drain bigger than the one in my kitchen sink*. But tonight her mood was generous. "He's got a few itty-bitty implants that give him that spaced-out look, but basically he's harmless."

"But I feel sorry for those gals sitting with him," said Sally. "Following such a jerk."

"They've got nothing better to do at the moment. And he's cute, we have to give him that."

"He may be cute, but he's weak. I've got no use for weak men." Sally's knee pressed more firmly against my leg. Cheyenne's clairvoyance must have been on vacation, for she didn't pick up on the coziness beneath the table. She was high on tequila and had gotten away with murder. Her eyes were dancing around the room, in love with everyone. I'd once heard a wiseguy say, *when you put someone in the ground your mood improves.* The same can be said for getting someone out of the ground.

Cheyenne was smashed by the time we left the bar, and she didn't protest when I asked her for the keys to the truck. She headed for the passenger side. I got behind the wheel. Sally climbed into the back seat and said to Cheyenne, "Our holy work is done for this day, Messenger. And it feels good."

The Messenger's head was down. She was out. Sally turned toward me. "She sucked up a whole lot of negativity around that well."

What she'd sucked up was a whole lot of tequila. Sally continued, "It costs her a lot to deal with so much darkness."

Cheyenne was deep in darkness now, her breath coming slowly and heavily. Usually she could hold her booze, but tonight she'd met her match. When we got to her house, Sally climbed down and opened the door to the passenger side. She shook Cheyenne gently by the arm. "Messenger, we're home."

Cheyenne opened her eyes and smiled. "My home is in heaven." Then she stepped down and weaved toward her front door. We helped her into the house, guiding her toward the bedroom. She flopped down on the bed and began reprising *Blue Eyes Crying in the Rain.*

Sally looked at me. "I'll get her undressed. Are you staying the night?"

"There are a few more bags of cement in the cellar. I'm going to patch that hole." I grabbed a bottle of beer from the refrigerator and then went to the cellar. They'd done a piss-poor job of creating a new floor, with humps and bumps all over it, but they'd certainly managed to cover Dez. What remained now was the outline of his body, as if a creature of the underworld had surfaced from captivity. I'm sure Cheyenne would have left it that way. I mixed a batch of mud and knelt beside the rough cavity. Eradicating the last trace of Dez in Cheyenne's life brought me slowly down from the adrenaline jag I'd been on, and the smell of newly mixed concrete brought thoughts of my uncle the mud man. His thick, muscular fingers were always gray from the cement nestled permanently in the pores; his natural habitat was a ladder, and he had muscles like iron. After my second year in the monastery, he sent me a letter. *You caught a bad break, Tommy. But it's time to come home. I got a bucket of mud waiting for you. Ha.*

I put humps and bumps in the new layer of concrete to match the rest of the cellar floor, which Cheyenne and Sally had bungled. Then I went outside and patched the pack-rat crack in the foundation. I hosed down the trowel, scraping it clean and then taking it back to the toolshed. When I came out, Sally was waiting for me in the backyard. Coming up to me, she said, "Cheyenne's asleep. I'll be done here soon. Drive to my trailer and wait for me there. I have something for you."

I tried to read her expression, but she was giving nothing away, except what I could see between the open collars of her shirt, down which the moonlight was beaming. I nodded and went to my SUV. Following instructions, I drove to Paloma's only trailer park. It was home mostly to Latino workers who did odd jobs around town. Some had steady work; others would gather each morning at the entrance to the trailer park to wait for whichever contractor might come by looking for extra bodies.

None of the trailers were new, but everybody had a decent amount of space, and the owner provided fifty-amp AC hookups and water. According to Sally, people moved in and out all the time, most of them from Mexico but with a few old American hippies in the mix, smoking grass and writing their memoirs. It was the shadow side of Paloma and she liked it, being a little on the shadowy side herself. The men knew she carried a gun, and they never gave her trouble.

I found her trailer easily; it was a little old aluminum Airstream. Beside the door, wind chimes tinkled. I parked and waited. From a nearby trailer came music from a Mexican radio station, of a tenor crying out for love. Other trailers carried the sounds of soccer games, action movies, and reality shows. There was something homey about it all, a feeling of live and let live. Nobody was going to be too nosy; nobody would complain to the police about anything. As long as you didn't make a nuisance of yourself, you'd be welcome. And when you left, nobody would remark upon your going.

I heard a rooster crowing and wondered what he was doing up so late, then remembered that Sally had told me one of her neighbors raised fighting cocks. And then I saw her Jeep approaching. She parked beside my truck, and I followed her to the door of her trailer. The wind chimes greeted us as we passed through. The inside of the trailer reflected the life of somebody valuing freedom; she had few possessions other than those necessary for cooking and cleaning. She could at any moment hook up her Jeep and drive away with her home rolling along behind her. This free spirit had been caged by Cheyenne.

She opened a tiny closet. I saw her modest wardrobe on hangers. She reached in behind them and brought out Dez's nuts in a jar. "Get rid of them."

They floated in formaldehyde, bobbing gently as I took the jar from her. I was past being appalled by anything connected with him and the two women he'd had the misfortune to meet in this life. She said feelingly, "It might be nice if you put them where you put his penis."

I set the jar on a small table hinged to the trailer wall. It was the middle of the night, and this gorgeous woman was a foot away from me, looking like she was waiting for the next move, and it wasn't me leaving the trailer. My nuts were not in a jar, and in the next moment I had her pressed against me. We turned, bumping the table, and I could see Dez's nuts bobbing vigorously as if signaling me to grab them and go. Instead, I pivoted Sally toward the sofa. She was already undoing her shirt, the little turquoise buttons opening with a succession of snaps. Her shirt came off, followed by her red bra. It was a substantial garment for it had much to contain, and I gazed in wonder at her incredible rack. "Come on, Martini," she said, pulling at my jeans. "If we stop for a second, we'll come to our senses."

So down went my jeans, joining hers on the floor. All that was left were her little red panties, and when they went to the floor, she stopped rushing. But I saw hesitation in her eyes, as if she didn't fully understand how she'd gotten naked for a man once again. It checked me with the thought that I'd taken advantage of her. We stared at each other. The rooster was crowing again, ready to fight or fuck, but Sally and I were at an impasse. In stopping for a moment, we had come to our senses. Dez's nuts were on a nearby table. The shadow of his murder was hanging over her, or maybe it was Cheyenne's crazy teaching, but her need for me was gone. And the vulnerability I saw in her killed my own desire. I didn't need her and I was glad. I bent to retrieve my jeans, and that's when the wind chimes exploded and Cheyenne burst in.

"Motherfuckers, I knew it!" She was holding the Colt Python. "You're getting it in the balls, Martini." She swung toward Sally. "As for you, Judas . . ."

I could tell she was bluffing. She loved drama, and this was the perfect time for an operatic performance, but it didn't include murder. But Sally's hand went under the sofa cushion and came out with the Beretta. It was pointed straight at Cheyenne's heart. Sally had been traveling a long time, high and low, and she could take care of herself. "Messenger, calm down. Things look bad, but nothing happened. We realized it was a bad idea."

"Messenger? You brainless bitch. There is no Messenger."

Sally looked like she'd been hit with a two by four. "What do you mean?"

"It's just some crap I thought up. And you swallowed it like a cow chewing her cud. I used to laugh myself to sleep thinking about you."

Very calmly, without a word, Sally shot Cheyenne. Cheyenne staggered backward, blood spreading on her blouse as she returned fire. Sally's head twisted, and she crumpled to the floor. Cheyenne was slowly sliding down the wall of the trailer. She landed heavily, her legs spreading apart. She was gazing at me with a smile. "I told you I wasn't long for this world."

The sound of the soccer game continued, and the reality show, and a Latino group singing of love's betrayal. I bent over Sally. Her right eye was a gaping hole. Her other eye was open but saw nothing; she was stone dead.

I turned toward Cheyenne. She was struggling for breath, and the veins in her neck were bulging. She had a sucking chest wound. I grabbed my shirt from the floor and pressed it against the wound. I could feel one side of her chest growing larger. Her lungs had been pushed sideways. She was losing blood pressure. The smile seemed stuck on her lips, and I knew that I loved this cold, crazy beauty who had lived life on some strange level of her own. She was looking up at me, not surrendering an inch, her eyes in that medieval dream of absolute certainty of being correct. But correct about what? That was my question as I watched her die. About herself, I suppose, that she had every right to play savior knowing it was bogus. And why? Just for the hell of it, for something to do.

Her head fell sideways, she took one last gasp for breath, and that was it. I had two dead bodies on my hands. I called Dominic.

# 56

Because she was paranoid, Cheyenne used only disposable cell phones. I found one in her jeans and called my cousin. "Where are you?"

"Still in Vegas. Bob Elfwine and I are talking."

"About what?"

"My being part of Wrestling Universe."

"In what capacity?"

"Business development. What's up with you?"

"Call me back on a burner phone."

Twenty minutes later, he called. "So tell me."

"I've got two unfortunates in a trailer."

"How unfortunate?"

"As unfortunate as you can get. And their trailer is very messed up. I'd like to bring them and their trailer to you so we can put them in a place where they'll be happier."

"Stay put. I'll get back to you."

I pulled aside the window curtain and checked outside. Televisions were still going, with soccer crowd noises and the soundtrack of a shoot-'em-up movie; its frequent gunfire exchanges had covered the two shots in Sally's trailer, which just blended in. This is the night everywhere, a violent film filling the quiet mind.

I opened the sofa bed and laid Cheyenne and Sally on it, then covered them with a blanket. I had no inclination to indulge my feelings about them. If I started down that road, I'd be no good for what lay ahead.

Several hours went by, which meant Dominic was having trouble. I began thinking of alternate plans. I'd been lucky at the Devil's Well and couldn't risk it again. I could drive to Death Valley and try burying the bodies there. Or make an acid bath. Or cut them into small pieces, drive to the West Coast, and dump them in the ocean.

Cheyenne's phone rang. "It's gonna cost you twenty-five large because we're running out of space."

"I can get the money, but it will take time and I don't have time."

"I already fixed that. Carmine will front the money for us. How soon can you leave?"

"Twenty minutes."

"Take down this address."

I did and we ended the call. I found Sally's purse and extracted her key ring. I locked the trailer and drove my SUV back to my house. I took all the cash I had but left my weapons. Traveling unarmed seemed better under the circumstances. But I armed the house and took off down the road, jogging in the dark, staying on unlit streets, angling my way back toward the trailer park. The Paloma police patrol at night, but they're usually checking shopping areas and I steered clear of those areas. I had a couple of miles to cover and I did it at my best speed, that of the animated water buffalo, which isn't all that fast, but I got back to the trailer park soon enough. I encountered a man carrying a rooster in the dark, and we exchanged nods, neither of us interested in conversation, and the rooster kept his beak shut.

I backed Sally's Jeep up to the trailer. After some fumbling around, I got the trailer connected to the ball on the Jeep's rear end, along with the equalizer bars that would hold the trailer steady on the road. Finally, I connected the electrical and emergency brake cables. Sally had angled the trailer for easy extraction, and in very little time I was pulling it out of the trailer park and onto the road. The trailer was light and the Jeep had plenty of pep, and soon we were rolling, I, two dead ladies, and Dez's nuts in a jar.

By the time I steered the Jeep and trailer into Vegas, the early morning rush hour had begun. Maneuvering the trailer got me instantly rattled. I went over a couple of curbstones, narrowly escaped several fender benders, and enraged other motorists with my stop-and-go progress, but I was following Sally's aftermarket GPS unit on the dashboard, and the bossy son of a bitch residing in the unit did not always provide me with sufficient time for turning, after which he told me, "*Make a U-turn at the next available intersection.*"

"You prick, get it right the first time!"

But he didn't have time for my insults. He was busy gathering data from nearby base stations, satellites, hobbits, who the fuck knows. He reacquired the signal, crunched his numbers, and gave me the instruction once again, to which he could have added, *you fucking idiot*, but his tone remained superior to that sort of language and I executed the turn in time. It was a narrow side street and I went over another curbstone, but the terrain looked familiar and the address turned out to be Rocket Repair. The door opened and Dominic stepped out. I parked alongside him and got down from the Jeep. He put his arms around me and said, "Everything is set."

Bandanna came out, gave me a big grin, and looked at the vintage trailer. "A 1961 Bambi Airstream. There's a serious market for these. Fix it up and it'll be a real collectible."

Dominic said, "And it comes with two bodies."

"I can work with that." Bandanna knelt and quickly undid the trailer hitch and cables. When they were free, the overhead garage door opened and Bush Hat stepped out. He, too, looked appreciatively at the trailer. "Going to Grandma's house," he said, and the four of us muscled the little trailer into the cavernous repair shop until it stopped alongside a van bearing the logo of Figuration Concrete Casting.

I opened the trailer, and we got in. I pulled back the blanket from the bed, revealing the bodies. Nobody said anything until we'd shifted them into the van. "How'd it happen?" asked Dominic.

"They blew each other away."

"Over you?"

"They had religious differences."

We had to wait until nightfall, so Dominic and I spent the day on the Strip, going from casino to casino, playing a little blackjack, having lunch during which we watched an elderly woman mind-pumping a slot, her hair flying from side to side as she uttered strange cries. "She's moving on a high energy level," said Dominic. My own energy was low, and he didn't ask me any more about Cheyenne and Sally, so we talked about wrestling. "Wrestling Universe has got some big stars now, but they're touchy, jealous, and half nuts, which goes with the territory. But they get out of line. Elfwine needs somebody to keep them in line."

"Which would be you."

"I've turned around on pro wrestling. I like the craziness of it, and I like the crowds. I might do it."

"What about your masonry business?"

"My old man is handling it for the moment. He likes being out of retirement."

"And Bianca?"

"She loves Vegas. She's got a thing for bling. And she figures with me in Wrestling Universe, she'll be meeting alpha males in neon jockstraps. If she don't run off with one of them, we'll be fine."

When suppertime came around, I learned that we would not be dining alongside Bodacious the bull. Mario Batali's Steakhouse had closed, Batali having been accused of sexual misconduct. "A guy has to watch his step around women these days." Dominic gave me a significant look, but we didn't get into it. We went to Cipriani's for salmon filet and veal Milanese. By then it was dark, and we returned to Rocket Repair.

Bush Hat and Bandanna had already pulled out the bloodstained carpets and replaced them with a new vinyl floor. "There's a bit of rust on the frame," said Bandanna, "but we can sandblast it off and slap on metal primer and some industrial enamel." Bush Hat pointed to travel stickers at the back of the trailer. "They're baked on and they'll leave a nasty residue, but they've got to come off. Eyes have seen them, if you know what I mean." Neither of them mentioned the two bodies.

I gave them the keys to the Jeep. It was theirs to keep as part of the deal. Then Dominic and I got into the Figuration Concrete Casting van. With Dominic at the wheel, we pulled away from Rocket Repair. Cheyenne and Sally were in back, along with Dez's nuts in a jar. I'd grown used to traveling with them.

"Carmine sends his regards," said Dominic.

"I owe him. Not just the twenty-five G's."

"He's not looking for anything, he's happy to help. He and Primo were tight."

"Even so."

We left the lights of Lady Luck behind us and motored on to a part of town given over to light manufacturing that served the casinos. Figuration Concrete Casting was one of those businesses, and it was housed in a large one-story building. A garage opener from the console of the van opened an overhead door, and we drove in.

The inside had the appearance of an animal cemetery, large beasts standing around in silence. "Molds," said Dominic as we got out of the van. "Take your pick."

"We're going to put the bodies in a statue?"

"Carmine wants a pair of lions to liven up the doors of his casino." He let this sink in before he continued. "He's used Figuration Casting before."

We chose a pair of the largest lion molds, placed them on dollies, and wheeled them into a curing chamber. "The heads come off for easy pouring," said Dominic, removing them. "Now the hard part, cousin."

We opened the van. Cheyenne and Sally were stretched out there. We picked up Cheyenne. I tried not to look at the chest wound or anything else, just buttons and zippers. This had been a powerful woman with a persuasive voice, but now she was as silent as the menagerie surrounding us. We carried her into the curing chamber and lowered her feetfirst into the lion. It was a big lion, resting on its haunches, and Cheyenne was small; she fit with room to spare. We put Sally in the other lion. It was a tighter fit, but we muscled her into place.

"We'll use high early strength cement. We'll be able to move them in a week."

"That long?"

"They have to be kept moist for seven days. You get fifty percent more strength that way. And we want strength."

We mixed the concrete. A hose ran from the mixer to the ceiling of the curing chamber. We filled both lions up to the neck, which covered the bodies. There was just a bit of hair floating near the surface. I went back to the van and got the jar with Dez's nuts in it.

"What the hell is that?"

"Her husband's nut sack." I pushed the jar into the mix, alongside Cheyenne. Then we clamped the head molds into place and finished by pouring concrete through small holes in the lion heads.

We cleaned up afterward, leaving everything just as we'd found it. "Who's our guy in here?"

"The foreman. Now twenty-five G's richer."

"A *paisano?*"

"And a friend of Carmine's."

"How often has Carmine used his services?"

"I didn't ask. But the Catholic hospital in Carmine's neighborhood has a nice big Saint Joseph in the courtyard."

Dominic called Rocket Repair, and Bandanna picked us up and drove us back to the Luxor. He kept the motor running in the parking lot, and I gave him the agreed-upon payment for the friendly service of Rocket Repair.

"Anytime, my man. That trailer is a nice little rig. Maybe I'll take it to Disneyland." He shook my hand, wished me luck, and drove away.

Dominic and I went into the casino. The bar off the lobby has a ceiling made of dangling colored glass that simulates the Northern Lights. We sat beneath the dazzling display, looking like a pair of polar bears gazing at the Arctic sky. Finally, Dominic said, "You want to tell me about them?"

"The big one stuck a knife in a guy's neck."

"And the little one?"

"She shot her husband in the head and put his nuts in a jar."

"If you ever miss them, you can always visit them when you're in Vegas."

During the week, the foreman at Figuration Concrete Casting kept the statues moist, then applied a sealer that would further protect them and improve their appearance. On day seven, they were transported to the Fortune Rock club. It was a good-size building just off the Strip, and Carmine Cremona watched with satisfaction as a very large crane put the statues down on either side of the massive wooden doors of his club. He patted one on the neck. "These are some good-looking lions."

I had gone back to Paloma during the week and rounded up his money. I handed it to him in a Luxor shopping bag. He handed it to one of his managers, who returned a few minutes later and whispered something to Carmine, who smiled at me. "A five-G sweetener. You're a good boy, Tommy."

It had nothing to do with goodness. It was expected. I'd lived long enough with Primo to know how business was done in his circles. After admiring the lions for a while, we went inside for a drink. "Dominic told me how much they mean to you. They're safe with me. If the club falls through the cracks, I'll put them in my yard."

I doubted this, but he'd find a place for them somewhere, an old cemetery, whatever. These lions would never come back to bite me.

"So," he said, "are you going to fight in Vegas again?"

"He's got other plans," said Dominic.

# 57

The abbot of the San Juan Diego monastery sat at his rough wooden desk. On the desk in front of him was my old Spanish cross. The Camel and I gazed at it from the other side of the desk. The abbot spoke to the Camel. "The cross will stay in the monastery." His huge scarred hands were folded on the desk. In the dim light of his chamber, the scar across his leonine forehead had a pale, almost luminous quality. He was not someone to fuck with and the Camel knew this, but a protest was necessary and we waited for it. He turned toward me. "This son of a whore and his uncle, that other son of a whore, stole it from me."

The abbot nodded toward me. "Brother Thomas practices contrition and repentance here. That being so, he is under my guidance and protection. Your dispute with him is a dispute with me. Is that what you wish?"

The Camel brushed this aside as beneath his dignity. "I have no quarrel with you."

"Nor I with you. Your gift of the cross to the monastery will be acknowledged by a brass plaque below it, bearing your name. The penitent kneeling before it will be kneeling to Christ and you. Is that sufficient?"

The Camel nodded agreement.

The abbot continued. "As regards his uncle, Father Vittorio is dead and his sins are God's concern, not yours." The abbot stood. "Therefore, I think we're done here."

The Camel gave me a look that drug lords use when measuring you for a box, but I had a forty-five automatic under my robe, and the look I gave him conveyed that message. On that basis, we parted company. When he had gone, the abbot waved me back to my seat.

"In the village, they say the Camel sent two men and a sorcerer to kill you, but they never returned."

"Perhaps they lost their way."

"Perhaps." We sat in silence then, which is the habit of the monastery after business is done. Finally, he said, "I'm grateful for the money you've given us. By any standard, it's a fortune."

"It was Vittorio's. He ended up a wealthy man."

"Poverty eluded him." The abbot smiled. "Your uncle was an old fox. And you are his cub."

"I'm afraid so."

Our interview was over. I went to the stables and combed the horses. One of them was high-spirited and irritable, but combing him calmed him down. I breathed in the odor of his rich sweat and prayed for the souls of the dearly departed, and some not so dear. My house in Paloma was gone, the money divided between Our Lady of Guadalupe, in Phoenix, and the little church where Vittorio is buried. Half of the two million Vittorio scammed off Sacred Promise went to the monastery. The rest is in my bank account, gaining interest while I gain interest in heaven, if there is one. I bought perpetual masses for Cheyenne and Sally, and every day I light a candle for each of them. They had little use for formal religion, but it can't hurt, and there are no altars for those in the church of the UFO.

When I finished with the horse, I climbed in the truck and drove to the village for oats and hay. Outside the feed store, I saw the woman whose son I had spoken to regarding the power of horses. She approached me shyly in the way of such women. I asked after her son.

"Because of you, he has remained at the School for Social Improvement."

"And has he improved?"

"He no longer wants to be an assassin."

"Definitely an improvement."

"More than that." She took my hands in hers. Her fingers were rough from picking candelilla plants on the mountain. Then I watched her go and the cartel guys watched me. I could feel their hostility. The hell with them. I bought my hay and oats and drove back to the monastery.

The abbot was carrying the old Spanish cross of the apostles into our chapel. A row of monks was following him. I joined the procession. The chapel was cool, its heavy stone walls doing battle with the fierce desert sun as we did battle with our devils. The smell of frankincense hung in the air. Candles burned on the altar. The abbot placed the old cross on the altar, and we knelt before it. The little figures of ivory danced in the shadows, as I have danced on a cross made of anger and desire. It never lightens. It only gets heavier. I'm in training, but for what?

At the doorway of the chapel is a life-size statue of the Virgin. It is a tradition among the monks to run their hand over her feet as they pass. And outside a house of cards in Las Vegas are two stone lions gazing sightless at the sky. Gamblers run their hands along them for luck.

I linger before the statue of the Holy Mother. The eyes are beautifully rendered, filled with mercy. But all I see are those sightless eyes of the stone lions in Vegas. They'll never stop looking at me, nor I at them.